MY COUSIN SKINNY

MY COUSIN SKINNY

E.J. Copperman

SEVERN HOUSE

First world edition published in Great Britain and the USA in 2023
by Severn House, an imprint of Canongate Books Ltd,
14 High Street, Edinburgh EH1 1TE.

Trade paperback edition first published in Great Britain and the USA in 2024
by Severn House, an imprint of Canongate Books Ltd.

severnhouse.com

British Library Cataloguing-in-Publication Data
A CIP catalogue record for this title is available from the British Library.

ISBN-13: 978-1-4483-0971-9 (cased)
ISBN-13: 978-1-4483-1436-2 (trade paper)
ISBN-13: 978-1-4483-0972-6 (e-book)

Typeset by Palimpsest Book Production Ltd.,
Falkirk, Stirlingshire, Scotland.

Praise for the Jersey Girl Legal mysteries:

"Copperman has [zaniness] on tap for his latest dose of legal mayhem"
Kirkus Reviews on *And Justice for Mall*

"Those seeking pure escapist fare will be delighted"
Publishers Weekly on *And Justice for Mall*

"Fans of bizarre characters and spirited sleuths will appreciate this offbeat, humorous story"
Library Journal on *And Justice for Mall*

"Copperman knows how to entertain"
Publishers Weekly Starred Review of *Witness for the Persecution*

"Terrific . . . This breezy book is a pure pleasure to read"
Publishers Weekly Starred Review of *Judgment at Santa Monica*

"Legal mayhem at its finest"
Kirkus Reviews Starred Review of *Judgment at Santa Monica*

"Readers won't want to miss a minute of the mayhem. In or out of the courtroom, Copperman's right on the money"
Kirkus Reviews on *Inherit the Shoes*

About the author

E.J. Copperman is the nom de plume for Jeff Cohen, writer of intentionally funny murder mysteries. As E.J., he writes the Haunted Guesthouse and Agent to the Paws series, as well as the brand-new Jersey Girl Legal mysteries; as Jeff, he writes the Double Feature and Aaron Tucker series; and he collaborates with himself on the Samuel Hoenig Asperger's mysteries.

A New Jersey native, E.J. worked as a newspaper reporter, teacher, magazine editor and screenwriter, before his first book was published to critical acclaim in 2002. In his spare time, Jeff is an extremely amateur guitar player, a fan of Major League Baseball, a couch potato and a crossword addict.

www.ejcopperman.com

For all Jersey girls, guys and anything in-between.

PART ONE
Love And . . .

ONE

'It's over,' Patrick McNabb said.

He looked unhappy, even distraught, but it was clear his mind was made up and there would be no changing it. I'd known Patrick for more than two years now and we'd spent a lot of time together. I knew his expressions. He had decided.

'Over? How can that be?'

Patrick closed his eyes momentarily. He was causing pain and he hated to do that. But when something is wrong, there is no joy or kindness in prolonging it. This had to be done like, in that cliché of clichés, tearing off a Band-Aid™, quickly and abruptly. Sure, it would sting, but in the long run, it would be less painful, leading to fewer scars and faster healing.

'I did love you,' he said. 'But too much has happened now. Our trust is gone. Face it. We don't love each other anymore. You don't love me, not after what I did to you.'

He turned away. He didn't want to make eye contact. He was lying but he didn't want to show it. This was Patrick being noble. He was still very much in love but thought his infidelity had caused an irreparable tear in the relationship and he was trying to do the right thing, even if it was wrong for him.

I looked over at him in the airline seat next to me and took the earbuds out. I turned away from the image of him on the screen of my iPad on the pull-down tray. 'Who wrote this stuff?' I asked him, pointing at the screen. 'It's terrible.'

Patrick, who had been dozing in his seat but not really sleeping, blinked a couple of times and shook his shoulders. Even in first class, a plane ride is a plane ride, and five and a half hours going east and north will curve your spine and cause brain fog. 'Which one?' he asked.

'*Royale Boulevard*,' I said. 'Season Twelve, Episode Six.'

Patrick smiled at my question. 'It was ten years ago I was on that silly soap opera,' he said. 'Do you think I remember who wrote every episode?'

'Yes.' I know him. 'I do think that.'

Not a second of hesitation. 'Chelsea Carter,' he said. 'Although I believe her real name was Sadie Cheese.'

'Cheese?' That couldn't be right.

'You see why she changed it. Anyway, why are you watching that?' Patrick leaned over to look at the screen on my tablet. 'God, I was young.'

'I wanted to know more about you from before we met,' I said. 'I found it on YouTube.'

'You're watching the wedding episode,' Patrick noted. 'Is it because we're going to a wedding?'

Angie, across the aisle from me, could not resist sticking her nose in. Angie is my best friend since forever, and I have come to love even her foibles, such as having absolutely no respect for anyone's privacy including her own. 'She's nervous about seeing her mom and her sister,' she told Patrick, as though that was her business.

'I am *not* nervous,' I said into the nonexistent wind. (It was a jet airliner. The windows were, thankfully, not open.)

'Of course not,' Angie said. Angie could make 'hello' sound sarcastic. It's a Jersey girl thing.

'I know your mother is difficult,' Patrick said. Patrick, even with an actor's ego, is empathetic – it's pretty much a requisite for his work – and can be a peacemaker or arbitrator when he thinks it's the way to smooth things over. He's not much for confrontation. 'But you hardly ever mention your sister, so I'm not sure what to expect.'

Angie let out a rueful laugh. Angie can laugh sarcastically, too. Truly, it's an art form.

'Delia is perfect,' I said.

Patrick sat and looked at me for a moment. Maybe two moments. 'Is that a problem? You make it sound like it's a problem. Am I misreading your accent?' Patrick is British and I'm from the Nation of New Jersey, but he didn't believe for a second that he wasn't hearing me right.

I shook my head. 'You don't understand, and I don't blame you. Delia is four years older than me. She is, in my mother's view, the most amazing person who has ever lived. She always got better grades than I did, she never got into trouble, she married her college boyfriend, she went to medical school and became one of the leading surgical oncologists in the state, she has two children and an immaculate home, which she does without a nanny or a cleaning person. She is perfect, and she always was. She blazed a trail that I could never hope to follow. And she does it all without actually trying to show me up, except that she always is trying to show me up.'

Patrick looked at me carefully. He was trying to decide if I was being jealous for no reason or if he should play it like every word I'd said was true and accurate. 'I have a sister in the same profession as mine, and a lot of people would say she is more successful,' he said. 'In fact, *I* would say she's more successful. But Cynthia is a dear friend, and I don't envy her.'

Cynthia Powell – yes, *that* Cynthia Powell – is Patrick's half-sister, if we're being technical, and in all the time I'd known Patrick, I'd only see her perhaps four times in person (except when I was defending her in court). She shows up on screens considerably more frequently. The two of them do get along famously, and Cynthia is a lovely person, but their situation is not the same as the one involving my sister and me.

I was about to tell Patrick that, when the pilot, speaking almost understandably through the plane's PA system, informed us that we were about to begin our 'final descent,' which has always sounded a little more ominous than the airlines would like to believe. There would be bags to retrieve (someone would do that for us, because Patrick), a car to find (a limousine, because Patrick) and traffic to brave (something even a TV star can't fix), so the discussion would have to wait.

We fell into the whirlwind of arriving at an airport, even one I'd been to a hundred times before. When I was sentient again, I was sitting in the back of the limousine, Patrick had already made friends with the driver, whose name was Esteban and who was a great fan of Patrick's first American TV series, *Legality*. Angie had caught Esteban's eye but was pretending not to notice. And I was attempting to ignore the tight feeling in my stomach I have whenever I have to spend any time with my mother and my sister together.

'It's not that I don't like them,' I said out of the clear blue sky once we were headed for the Garden State Parkway. (Patrick had wanted to book a hotel in Manhattan because he knows New York, but the wedding was in Westfield, New Jersey, and it just made more sense. Besides, *I* know Westfield, New Jersey.) 'I just always feel intimidated when they're around, especially Delia.'

Angie was nodding because this was not new information for her, but Patrick, once he got over the complete lack of segue that had preceded this outburst, looked either baffled or concerned.

'You don't need to be intimidated,' he said quietly. 'You're a remarkable woman in your own right, and there's no reason your family should make you think otherwise.' Then he turned toward the window, looking at one of the Parkway billboards. 'Judd Hirsch is doing *King Lear* on Broadway,' he said, as if that were a completion of the thought he'd just been expressing.

I decided that Mr Hirsch's current booking was not something I need concern myself about right now. I looked at Angie. 'You know what it's like,' I told her. 'They conspire to make me feel like a sixteen-year-old failure.'

Angie, who was looking at the back of Esteban's head as an evaluation exercise, tilted her head a little to the right. 'I think *conspire* might be a little bit of a stretch, but they do gang up on you. That's a fact.'

Patrick had lost sight of the billboard and was no longer wondering how the star of *Taxi* might do with iambic pentameter. 'I don't doubt that it's difficult for you, love,' he said. 'But you've been away for years now, and you've built up a very successful division in a prestigious law firm in Los Angeles. Surely they're impressed with all you've accomplished.'

Angie stifled a laugh. Patrick didn't catch it.

'This is a cousin of yours, the bride?' he said, hoping to shift the focus from the upcoming family reunion to the reason I'd been roped into it in the first place.

'Yeah.' Angie likes nothing better than to fill in the gaps in any knowledge Patrick might have of my life before Los Angeles. 'Stephanie is Sandy's first cousin, the only daughter of her Aunt Fern, her mother's sister.' Angie should work for Ancestry.com.

'Aunt Fern?' Patrick said.

'Seriously,' I told him, 'we can turn right around and get on a plane for LA in minutes. Esteban?'

Esteban glanced in the rearview mirror, but Patrick waved a hand at him. 'No worries, Esteban,' he said. 'Just keep going and thank you for the water bottles.' The limo didn't have a wet bar and nobody cared. Except a gin and tonic was sounding good all of a sudden. Why had I agreed to this trip? And bringing Patrick? Would he still want to buy a house with me after he'd met my entire family?

'We're not going back to LA,' Angie said in what she imagined was a calming tone. 'We're going home.'

'LA *is* home,' I tried.

'Sit back, relax and enjoy the ride,' said Esteban for no reason whatsoever.

We didn't even stop at our hotel, although Esteban was instructed to bring our luggage there and do the checking-in. Mr McNabb, after all, was a well-known figure and didn't want to cause a ruckus. This had been arranged well in advance, back when I'd thought I would probably renege on my RSVP because this was a stupid idea.

The invitation had arrived only two weeks before, which led me to believe I was on the C list for the wedding, and I was going to decline because I was backed up with work. But the thought of explaining to my mother why I wouldn't be at a family wedding was intimidation enough, and Patrick had been inexplicably eager to see the place where I'd grown up.

Still, I was more convinced than ever that this trip had been a poor decision when Esteban pulled the enormous limousine (which he insisted was a hybrid) up in front of the house where I had spent my childhood, adolescence and young adulthood. It was, in the eye of Patrick McNabb's girlfriend, the most average house in America and frankly in need of some maintenance.

My mother's house, which she was awarded in the divorce from my father, is a split-level, vinyl-sided, one-car-garage special that was probably built in the 1960s. It was an especially bland shade of blue now, something I never would have thought growing up because blue was my color. That was another thing my mother found to be disappointing about me. I didn't even favor the same colors as the other girls. My sister Delia's current home was a pristine white, with actual pillars in the front and a landscape artist who merely assisted the lady of the house with her own designs.

She – my mother – opened the front door when the *USS Enterprise* pulled into the driveway and walked out in a way that Patrick could probably recognize as similar to that of Queen Elizabeth II. My mother has always thought she was regal. My mother was born in Passaic.

'Sandra!' she called. She is the only person on the planet who gets away with calling me by my birth-certificate name, except sometimes Patrick, who pronounces it 'Sondra' and that makes it sort of hot. 'How long is this great big car going to be in the driveway? Delia is on her way.'

And so it began.

TWO

E steban, giving Angie a last longing glance, had driven away, leaving me with no practical means of escape when we had settled into my mother's living room, a space that didn't have clear plastic slipcovers on all the furniture but looked like it probably did when no one was around. I could attest to the fact that it didn't. My mother simply bans dust from her furniture through sheer strength of will.

'It's so nice to meet you, Patrick,' she said with her patented 'warm' smile. 'After all this time.' That was a dig at me for not producing my boyfriend in person before. The idea that my mother might visit me in the City of Angels was simply not to be broached. Because then she might take me up on it.

'A pleasure, Mrs Moss,' Patrick answered. Angie, no doubt annoyed that my mother had chosen to focus first on Patrick and not her, the woman she (Angie) had always considered Mom's 'second daughter' because she doesn't count Delia, was sitting in one of the side chairs with her arms folded. No doubt she thought she was being shoved aside for the TV star. 'Sandy has told me a great deal about you.'

'Really.' My mother's voice had freon in it. 'I'm sure she had quite a lot to say. But now we have a chance to get to know each other on our own, don't we?'

Angie squirmed a little in her seat. She knows what my mother's traps look like.

But Mom went on. 'And don't you call me "Mrs Moss," either,' she told my boyfriend. 'I'm Barbara.'

Patrick nodded, all charm. 'Barbara,' he said. He did not extend a hand to shake. Maybe he was afraid she'd bite it.

Angie, unable to contain herself any longer, cleared her throat. 'Um, Mrs M., did Sandy tell you I'm now the management executive for Patrick's production company?'

'Isn't that lovely, Angela.' Seriously. Maggie Smith on her best day couldn't have been more imperious.

Before Angie could crown my mom with the imitation Ming vase she had on a side table, I decided to jump in. 'So, Mom, did Skinny decide on how many bridesmaids she's going to have?'

It was the first time in years I'd seen my mother look uncomfortable. To be fair, it was the first time in years I'd seen my mother be *anything* except on Zoom, where people are never themselves at all. 'Bridesmaids,' she repeated.

Patrick raised a hand. 'Hold up,' he said. '*Skinny?*'

Angie loves filling in. 'When they were little kids, Sandy always called Stephanie "Skinny." She couldn't pronounce "Stephanie" and someone had once said Steph was skinny.' She laughed and looked at me, then stopped laughing.

Because my life is a sitcom, the door opened at that moment and my sister Delia appeared in the room, dressed impeccably, makeup expertly applied to the point that you didn't think she had any on, but she did, shoes with just enough heel to make her taller than me, a rolling suitcase being dragged behind her.

'Oh my god,' she said as if she'd just heard that the Nazis had taken Paris. 'I'm exhausted.' From walking to the door from the driveway?

Patrick stood up, seemingly because he thought he was supposed to. He waited a few seconds for someone to say something and then stepped forward. 'Hello,' he said. 'I'm—'

'Please,' my older sister said. (And I'm going to keep alluding to the difference in our ages, so get used to it.) 'You don't have to introduce yourself. I'm a huge fan.' She was actually an annoyingly slim fan, but there was no sense in pointing that out. Delia extended her hand as if to be kissed.

Patrick, knowing what was good for him, merely took her hand between his and held it, then let it go. 'A pleasure to meet you . . .'

Now, let's be clear about a few things. First, Patrick knew *exactly* who this model of a modern major surgeon general was, and he knew how I felt about it. I love my sister, but I don't always like her, and she brings out every possible atom of competitiveness in me, which is one of the reasons I don't always like her. Because she always comes out on top.

'This is my sister Delia,' I said, scrambling to my feet before she could reach over and swallow him whole. 'Delia, Patrick McNabb. My *boyfriend*.' Never let it be said that my mother has had no influence on me at all.

Hellos were said all around, and Mom hugged Delia. (She had hugged me when I'd arrived, too, but only with one arm.) Eventually, we all retreated to our various seats around Mom's coffee table, which sadly had no coffee on it at the moment. I don't sleep great on flights.

'I thought Mark and the kids were coming,' I said to Delia. Mark, if you haven't gotten that from context, is her husband the pathologist. Because of course. She's an oncological surgeon. Because even more of course. 'Are they coming later?'

Delia did not look away, which Patrick would tell me later was a sign she wasn't in a badly directed episode of television like the one I'd been watching on the plane. 'No, not this time,' she answered. 'I told Mark I wanted a little me time and, to be honest, my children were not invited. So Mark decided to stay home.'

Wow. Her kids weren't invited? Major snub!

'I'm sure it was just an oversight,' Mom said, with a tone that suggested it should put an end to the topic. I was watching Delia's eyes and decided my mother might be on to something.

Angie blinked a couple of times and recovered. 'So we were talking about the wedding just before you got here,' she said to Delia. 'Do you know if Stephanie decided on bridesmaids?' Because that seemed like the subject that I'd wanted to know about, I guess. I'd seen my mother evading the question and didn't know why, but I was cringing inwardly.

'Oh, sure she did,' Delia said. 'I'm going to be in the wedding party.' She turned, the very picture of innocence. 'Aren't you, Sandy?'

For the record, I did not want to be in Stephanie's wedding party. I figured it would have required trips to dress stores and tailors ahead of time, and I'd have to be standing outdoors (because Stephanie was getting married outdoors no matter what) in some big floppy dress. I wasn't especially close to Stephanie, although we were fine with each other, so I hadn't expected to be asked. But Delia was.

'No,' I said.

'Well.' Patrick pushed his hands together as if he'd meant to applaud just once. Maybe the show wasn't that good. 'It's going to be a long weekend, I think.' He looked over at me. 'Should we get back to the hotel and unpack?'

My mother's face darkened a bit. 'You're staying at a *hotel*?' she said.

THREE

My cousin Stephanie was a lovely woman, truly. Nothing about her was wrong in my view. She was polite without being stuffy, warm without being phony, content without being superior.

There were times I could barely stand her.

Families are funny things. You're forced into interaction with people who share your bloodlines and not necessarily anything else. There wasn't anything wrong with Stephanie, but we had absolutely nothing in common at all. We didn't connect. We had never clashed and we had never gotten close. We couldn't communicate on anything but the most superficial level.

So when, at her wedding rehearsal (at the Woodbridge, NJ Elks Lodge), she rushed over to me and embraced me in a bear hug, it was something of a surprise. I don't know if we'd ever actually touched before.

As with most such situations (people showing me unexpected affection, which had been happening somewhat more frequently since I'd moved to LA), I attributed this demonstration to the fact that I happened to be standing next to Patrick McNabb when Stephanie caught sight of me. That tends to elevate my social status in some people's eyes.

'Sandy!' As if she'd been waiting all week for me to show up. 'I'm so glad to see you!'

She finally let me out of her suffocating grasp, and I took in some oxygen, which had been my habit for some years now. 'Nice to see you too, Steph,' I said. I generally don't call her 'Skinny' to her face anymore because I'm no longer six. 'Congratulations.' I was doing my best to keep the exclamation points out of my tone of voice. I think it's underhanded to mislead people with implied punctuation.

'On what?' It really seemed to confuse Stephanie for a moment. 'Oh, the wedding.' Yeah. The reason I'd flown thousands of miles and put my job on hold for four days. But hey, it was just her getting married to some guy I'd barely even heard mentioned by anyone in my family. Why make a fuss, or even remember you're the bride?

'Yes. You must be excited.' That was Patrick. I hadn't introduced him. I'd gotten out of the habit because pretty much everyone knows my boyfriend, or thinks they do. Have I mentioned he's a television actor?

Stephanie's emotional level dropped down to definite shyness. 'Mr McNabb,' she said. 'When Delia told me you were coming to my wedding, I was absolutely thrilled.'

When *Delia* told her? Hadn't I filled out the RSVP card? No. Seriously. Hadn't I?

'I wouldn't have missed it,' Patrick said. His smile was the one he uses during what he calls 'press tours' – when he's promoting a new movie or project. 'I go wherever Sandy goes.' Patrick nodded in my direction to remind Stephanie that I was the one she'd (eventually) invited to her nuptials. Now I was starting to wonder if she would have done so had I not been bringing an A-list celebrity as my plus-one.

'Of course you do,' Stephanie said. 'So am I going to be invited to *your* wedding anytime soon?' OK, so maybe there were a couple of things about Stephanie I would definitely change.

'You'll have to talk to Sandy about that,' Patrick said, giving me a sly look. 'I'm not allowed to ask her anymore.' We actually had to have a talk about that because when we first got together, Patrick asked me to marry him about once a week. I had put the brakes on that practice because we met when Patrick was on trial for murdering his wife and I was his defense attorney, and then because I thought Patrick was being hasty and impulsive with his proposals, but only because he was. He hadn't asked The Question for about four months now, and that was working just fine in my opinion. Why Stephanie had felt it necessary to raise the subject was a mystery, or at least an irritation.

'Not allowed?' Stephanie seemed genuinely puzzled.

'When do we get to meet the groom?' I asked. There are ways to change the subject, and most of the successful ones involve shifting the focus to the other person in the conversation.

'Michael?' Stephanie said. I thought it boded badly for the marriage if she had to ask me the name of her fiancé. Her head swiveled back and forth a bit. 'He's around here some-where.' She walked away, presumably in search of the man she was marrying the next day.

This might be the spot to clarify the whole bridesmaid thing. I was *not* disappointed to have been left out of Stephanie's wedding party, and I mean that wholeheartedly. What had thrown me was that Delia *had* been asked. I wasn't aware the two of them were especially close. It was one of those things that, if I were in therapy, I would undoubtedly chalk up to my inferiority complex in regard to my sister. That would lead to my feelings that I'd been nothing but a disappointment to my mother all my life. And this is why I was not in therapy.

'Are you OK?' Patrick whispered in my ear.

I nodded. 'Let's find Angie.' Angie knew the cast of characters in the building and would be able to help me in ways Patrick could not, like being snarky. It's probably Angie's most valuable asset.

We found her at a table to one side of the Elks hall where the 'rehearsal event' (that's what it said in the invitation) was being held. The ceremony itself would be in a park nearby and the reception in a catering hall far grander than anything the Elks might have dreamed up, even if they did have a member they declared the Grand Exalted Ruler, which I knew because the parking space was clearly marked in the lot outside. There would be a rehearsal dinner after the, you know, rehearsal, but right now Angie was contenting herself with tiny pizzas on a tray. She was biting into one when Patrick and I approached.

'Who have you seen?' I demanded. This wasn't just going to be a family affair. Most of the people we knew from Westfield High School would be there, too.

'Everybody we don't want to,' Angie answered. 'Don McBride, Sarah Panico and your cousin Skinny, so far.'

'I saw Skinny,' I said. 'She's the reason we're here.' But Sarah Panico? I'd barely seen Sarah Panico in high school because I had the (ahem!) advanced classes, but she was my nemesis in grade school, and I had no interest in finding out she was now the CEO of some huge corporation or something. 'Can you make sure I don't have to talk to her?'

'What am I, the social director?'

Patrick was being waylaid by a group of people who, after years of carrying nothing but a mobile phone, had found scraps of paper and writing implements to get his autograph. But that didn't stop them from taking out phones for selfies. This happens a lot in his life, and I'd hoped the New Jersey crowd would be cooler, but they weren't.

I'd have tried to rescue him, but I was ambushed by my mother and sister, who were touring the room and visiting with everyone but had, alas, reached us again. Mom was drinking white wine from a plastic cup, which was probably the most undignified thing she'd done in ten years. Delia, having eschewed all things that might in any way impact her figure, was abstaining.

They were leading a woman I just about recognized over toward us, and the closer they got, the more my stomach dropped. I tried to avert my glance and saw Stephanie walk through the swinging doors into the kitchen, and I wondered what business she had in there. The dinner tonight would be held elsewhere. 'Snacks,' we had been told, would be served this afternoon.

'Sandra!' My mother, of course. 'Look who we found, and she's dying to see you!'

Sarah Panico. Leave it to my mother to deposit Sarah Panico directly in front of me after all the times she heard me complain about her superior attitude, her smug condescension and her complete lack of sense ('She's so bossy!') until I entered junior year of high school and didn't have to deal with Sarah anymore. Until now.

'Sandy!' Sarah belted out. Everyone seemed to think that shouting some version of my name was the best way to communicate today. 'You look amazing!'

Now, I have seen myself in the mirror (and had that very morning) and I have seen how I am described by Patrick's fans on Twitter ('mousy,' 'plain,' 'boring' and those are the polite ones), so I knew I did not look amazing. I looked fine for me. 'So do you, Sarah,' I said. 'How have you been?' (Since I last paid attention to you twenty-five years ago.)

'Oh, you know,' she said. 'Husband, two kids. I stay at home with the little ones because it's so important when they're young, you know. I'm only here today because Stephanie and I are so close.'

What? Sarah Panico was besties with my cousin Stephanie? How did I miss that one?

'Of course,' I said, because that's what you say when you can't think of anything else.

'How about you? I hear you have a famous boyfriend.' She looked blank.

I don't brag about Patrick, but the fact was at that very moment he was signing autographs and taking fan selfies less than fifteen feet away. Either Sarah was being obtuse as a way to amuse herself or she was as dense as concrete. My money was on the latter possibility.

Angie, bless her, has no compunction about such things. 'He's *right over there*,' she said, pointing.

Sarah looked, did the same kind of surprised take many people do and then said, 'That's Sandy's boyfriend?'

'I'm right here,' I pointed out.

Apparently, that wasn't relevant. Sarah looked back over at Patrick and then fixed her gaze on Angie. 'What's his name, again?'

There was a noticeable pause. My mother, who by now had adopted Patrick as the only evidence that I was worthwhile, coughed lightly and said, 'Patrick McNabb.' My mother has blue eyes that can be piercing whenever she wants them to be, which is much of the time. I'll say no more on the subject.

'Oh, yeah.' Sometimes the eye thing works and sometimes it doesn't. It depends on the audience. Sarah might have truly never heard of Patrick. It happens. Or she might have been a good enough actress to sell the attitude. If you'd have asked me in fifth grade, I'd have been able to tell you definitively which it was. Now that I was a practicing criminal defense/ family law attorney my priorities had shifted a bit. 'That's great, Sandy.' So she did remember I was in the room. I heard a buzz, then Sarah removed a phone from her jacket pocket. 'Oh, sorry. Stephanie needs me.' She walked off in the direction of the kitchen doors. Apparently, the kitchen was where everything was happening today.

I shook my head a little just to clear it out. Mom finished her cup of wine and went looking for a server to hand it back. I thought it was more likely she'd amble over to the bar and get another. Family gatherings are difficult for everyone.

Patrick, holding up both hands in surrender, escaped from the hordes of admirers and made his way back to Angie and me, making sure to give me a light kiss just in case there were some who didn't believe the rumors. Patrick didn't make it in Hollywood by *not* paying attention to appearances.

'Has anyone seen the groom yet?' he asked. 'The poor man is invisible at his own wedding.'

'Rehearsal,' I corrected. I have no idea why.

Patrick nodded. 'The groom is always somewhat ignored at a wedding,' he said.

'Won't be when you get married,' Angie said. Thanks a heap, Angie.

I saw a strapping man about our age, handsome (but not Patrick-handsome) and wearing jeans with suspenders, of all things, walk into the kitchen. I got the sense that there was a better party going on in the next room, but I had absolutely no desire to attend. I held on to Patrick's arm and reminded myself that he had never once complained about having to travel to New Jersey for a wedding featuring people he had never even heard about before. He looked at me and smiled.

I nudged Angie with my other hand and gestured toward the guy heading into the kitchen version of the celebration. 'Who's Paul Bunyan?' I asked.

She gave him her beneath-my-notice glance. 'The best man, Brandon Starkey,' she said. 'Nobody loves him as much as he does.'

Patrick nodded, not at the description but at the idea that Angie would just know who everybody in the room might be. She does that for him on a professional basis and never has to refer to notes. Angie has superpowers that never appear on a movie screen; she doesn't have to hold out her hands, palms forward, to generate lightning bolts of energy.

'You seen Michael?' I asked her. She looked blank. 'The groom?'

'A man with the personality of an elm tree,' she said.

'I didn't ask for a thumbnail,' I reminded her, although the information had at least been entertaining. 'I wanted to know if you've seen him.'

'Ever?'

I tried to remember the reason I'd asked the question in the first place. 'Today.'

'Yeah. He's here,' Angie said. 'Watch out for the guy who looks like he should have branches and you'll find him.'

Much as I wanted to stay among the people I felt were on my side, I decided it was best to tour the room and not so much mingle as observe. If I saw someone who resembled a large plant, I'd guess he was Michael the Groom, and if not, I'd likely run into those I'd known all my life or at least met before. Aunts and uncles, other cousins and the occasional cousin-once-removed – which doesn't mean anything in real life but pads the guest list at events like this one – would all be present. If

I could get all my appearances in early, I could cocoon with Patrick and Angie the rest of the weekend and hide as much as possible from my mother, Delia and Sarah Panico.

'I'm gonna do the tour,' I said. 'If I'm not back in fifteen minutes, alert the National Guard.'

'Godspeed,' Angie said.

'Do you want me to come with you?' Patrick said as yet another anonymous wedding guest shuffled over with a mobile phone in hand, set to camera.

'No, that's OK, but thanks,' I told him. 'You tend to attract a crowd.'

'Hazard of the job, love.' He put on the smile he reserves for fans and turned toward the skinny guy.

'You're a pro,' I told him and squeezed his arm.

I gathered my breath and set my sights on the far side of the room, where a guy I thought I knew from high school (Rob Sherrell, maybe?) was standing alone and drinking his soda out of a clear plastic cup. He looked lonely. I could make him a destination. The gauntlet between us was the problem.

Of course, I hadn't gotten ten feet from my comfort zone when Stephanie's brother Stephen (not Steve), who had grown up never leaving her shadow, walked toward me. Now, I have nothing at all against Stephen and I know what it's like to be the younger sibling of someone everybody thinks is amazing. But he's always been just a tiny bit (and I want to emphasize that *tiny* bit) creepy. It's not that I think Stephen is violent or dangerous. It's that I think he would like to be if he could muster the courage, but he never will.

'Sandy.' That was it. That was the tweet.

'How are you, Stephen?' I asked. It's what you ask. I didn't really want a detailed description of his medical profile. 'Been a long time.'

'Since what?' He had those dead eyes, as if he had recently been under anesthesia.

'Since we saw each other.'

Rob Sherrell – if that was his name – smiled as a gorgeous woman approached him and kissed him with as much passion as is acceptable in a room full of spectators, unless you're currently acting the part of Juliet. So much for my efforts to rescue him from solitude. And good for Rob, by the way. Too bad for Angie, who I had figured I'd fix him up with.

'Yes.' Stephen was in one of his talkative moods. But he'd approached me, so I figured there had been a point at the time.

'I've never met Stephanie's fiancé,' I said. 'What can you tell me about him?'

No hesitation from Stephen. 'He's very loyal.'

So were most cocker spaniels. 'Loyal?'

'Yes.'

It's always a thrill to talk to Stephen. 'Have you seen him around here?' I asked. 'I thought it might be a good idea to meet him before he marries Stephanie. Warn him off, maybe.'

Maybe Stephen was *still* under anesthesia. 'Warn him?'

'It was a joke, Stephen.'

Stephen nodded, absorbing the concept of a joke. 'Yes.' It appeared that *yes* was Stephen's hot new catchphrase. No doubt you'd be hearing all the late-night comedians repeating it within a week.

'So can you point Michael out to me?' I didn't see anyone sprouting leaves, so I figured I'd need a little help.

'Michael?' This was definitely not a high-intelligence day on Stephen's biorhythm chart.

'Yes. The groom. Where is he?'

'I'll look.' And before I knew it, Stephen was heading for the kitchen as well. I was starting to think that this was the 1980s and there might just be a little white powder being distributed in the kitchen where the Grand Exalted Leader might stop for a ham sandwich.

Without the destination of Rob Sherrell left to me, I briefly considered chickening out and retreating to my personal posse, but no, Delia was heading in my direction, and no matter how complicated my feelings toward her might be, she was my sister and that meant two things without question: one, I loved her and, two, I knew who she was. In this situation, those were two very valuable characteristics to have.

She stopped when she reached me. 'Where's Stephanie?' she asked. We're not great at small talk, my sister and I.

'There seems to be a gathering of the cool kids in the kitchen,' I told her. 'If you hurry, you might be able to grab an invite.'

Delia let out her breath slowly. She does that a lot around me. 'You know, I get that you don't like me. You don't have to make a point of repeating it every time we speak to each other.'

I stopped to think about that. *Did* I dislike my sister? Or was I legitimately jealous of her, having the life we'd been told was perfect since we were born? 'That's not true,' I said as a way to buy myself time. I could have been saying it wasn't true that I didn't like Delia *or* I could have been saying that it wasn't true I made a point of it whenever I talked to her. I was weighing my options.

'Sure it is. You've made it plain since you were ten.'

I closed my eyes for a second. I mean, I literally counted to one in my mind. 'We have some stuff we should say to each other, but this isn't the place,' I said. 'Let's just leave it that you're wrong about how I feel.'

'Stephanie's in the kitchen?' Delia wasn't going to let my saying that we should work out our issues become, you know, an issue.

I glanced over as a natural reflex when the kitchen was mentioned and saw Stephen exiting the place, looking less implacable than usual. He was followed soon after by Sarah Panico, who looked a touch miffed. I considered that a good sign.

'Yeah. People have been coming and going from there for about ten minutes. I think that, as an officer of the court, it would be best if I didn't go in to see what's been taking place.'

Delia gave me the side-eye. 'You're not an officer of the court here anymore. You work in California.' She said, 'California,' as if it were a new strain of virus for which a vaccine had not yet been developed.

'Actually, I've maintained my license in Jersey,' I corrected her. 'You never know when you're going to need it.' Like if I had to negotiate a divorce between our cousin Stephanie and a forest attraction. 'Have you seen the groom?'

'Michael?' Everyone I'd asked had said the same thing. Was there another groom at this wedding about whom I hadn't been informed?

But I didn't get to acknowledge that yes, Michael was the

groom in question. From the vicinity of – you guessed it – the kitchen, there came what I can't help but describe as a blood-curdling scream. Because I'm fairly sure my blood curdled.

The kitchen door swung open as absolutely everyone in the room, a good hundred people (well, OK, a good thirty-five people and sixty-five of questionable quality) turned to see what might be the cause of such a disturbing sound. And they all got a look at the person they'd come to see – my cousin Stephanie, exiting the kitchen, her dress torn in a couple of places and her hair completely disheveled.

She was also covered from shoulders to knees in blood.

'Oh, Skinny,' I said to myself.

FOUR

As you might imagine, after that the events of the afternoon picked up speed pretty seriously.

At least sixteen people ran toward Stephanie. I was not one of them. I honestly didn't have the capacity to process what I'd just seen and just reached out my left hand, a little behind me. I didn't have to look and I didn't have to think about it. Patrick's hand took mine immediately and held it gently. I said, 'Thank you,' in a low voice.

'What just happened?' That was Angie. Why she would think I'd have an answer to that question remains a mystery to this day.

'Just watch,' I said. It sounded authoritative, which I have found is the best way to cover the fact that you have no idea what you're talking about. Watch any politician on television and you'll know what I mean.

Stephanie pretty much fell to her knees with the crowd closing in around her. I looked toward the kitchen door because I couldn't remember whether there was anyone else I'd seen enter who was no longer there. It was becoming evident despite my cousin kneeling on the floor that the hemoglobin covering her was not her own.

Several among the crowd had already produced phones and called 911, which had probably caused the Woodbridge Police Department to overload its switchboard, if they still have switchboards. I heard my Aunt Grace somewhere behind me say, 'The cops are on their way.' At least four other voices added, 'I know. I called them.'

I could hear the sirens in the distance already. And given my experience, I felt it was important to make my voice heard. 'Don't anybody touch the kitchen door or go in there,' I said. 'Don't contaminate the crime scene.'

Immediately, four people rushed for the kitchen door. But one of them was Angie, and she stood in front of it with an expression of such fierceness that the other three guests (including my cousin Stephen) stopped in their tracks.

'She said *don't* contaminate the scene,' Angie said. Everyone standing there who wasn't her dropped their heads in agreement.

Angie stood at the kitchen door for the three minutes it took the entrance to open and for two uniformed cops to walk in looking confused. Then they spotted Stephanie and her newly decorated dress and rushed to her, already asking questions.

'Can you tell me what happened?' said the older cop, maybe forty-five, greying and gaining a bit of a bulge around his middle.

Stephanie, her eyes still wide, had managed to raise herself from a kneeling position but was shaking her head and making incoherent noises. No. She couldn't tell him. She probably *knew*, but she couldn't tell him.

I touched Patrick's hand, and he understood and let go of mine. I walked over to the cops and tried as hard as I could not to fixate on the already-drying blood on Stephanie's outfit. 'Stephanie,' I said, staring her in the face, where her makeup was remarkably intact, 'let us know what happened in the kitchen. Someone's obviously hurt. Is it you?'

The younger cop, who looked to be in his mid-thirties and a little more full of himself than his more seasoned partner, tried to get between Stephanie and me. 'Let us handle this, ma'am,' he said.

Ma'am?

But his partner shook his head. 'Let the lady talk, Bobby,' he said. He looked at me. His nametag read *Crawford*. 'Are you a friend of this woman?' he asked.

That was a really good question. Probably not. 'I'm her cousin,' I said. 'We're here for her wedding rehearsal.' Bobby the cop actually let out a rueful laugh at that.

'This took place in the kitchen?' Officer Crawford asked. Then I looked at his sleeve. Oops. Make that *Sergeant* Crawford.

'Yes, but I wasn't in there,' I pointed out. I was just there to calm Stephanie down to the point that she could speak, not to become a suspect in . . . whatever this was. Crawford gestured toward Stephanie, indicating I should continue talking to her. 'Is whoever it is –' I made sure not to say 'was' – 'still in there?' I said.

She could nod affirmatively. Crawford quickly gestured to Bobby, who rushed to the kitchen door and opened it.

Then he fell to his knees. I hoped against hope he was not about to vomit. But he was.

'So it's OK if *he* contaminates the crime scene?' Stephen said.

Bobby managed to look at Crawford and say, 'Backup. Now. And EMS.'

Crawford nodded. He walked past his partner while speaking into his shoulder comm unit. He looked into the kitchen, stopped, and then entered. The door closed behind him, which made me grateful.

But Bobby had recovered to the point that he could stand and walk over to Stephanie. He spoke gruffly. 'OK, what happened?'

Stephanie turned toward the kitchen door, which was now the entrance not only to what must have been an awful crime but also to what was left of Officer Bobby's lunch. 'Someone stabbed him,' she said. 'Stabbed.'

Bobby, who could have used a whole package of breath mints, was determined to do his job. 'Stabbed who?' he asked.

Her forehead wrinkled and her eyes watered. 'Brandon,' she squeaked out.

'Brandon Starkey,' Stephen said. 'The best man. I saw him in there, but he wasn't bleeding or anything then.' That was the most I'd heard Stephen say all in a row in at least fifteen years.

I heard a few people in the crowd gasp, and a woman actually sobbed. 'Brandon!' she said. The best man, after all, would be the best friend of the . . .

'Where's the groom?' I asked in general. Nobody answered me. Not even a, 'Michael?'

Crawford stuck his head out from the kitchen. 'Are those EMTs here yet?'

Bobby shook his head. 'Any second. I can hear the sirens. Can you save the guy?'

Crawford flashed an annoyed glance at his partner. 'Let me know when they're here. And don't let *anybody* leave, understand?' He didn't wait for Bobby to answer and ducked back into what was readily becoming the crime scene.

'Oh my GOD!' The scream came from the kitchen, and almost immediately Crawford opened the door again and escorted out a tall, sturdy-looking man with a wide head and a square body. A man who, if he'd had leaves, would have been . . . well, you know.

The groom. 'What happened?' he insisted. Then he took in the Eli Roth spectacle his bride-to-be had become and said, 'Steffie! What did you do?'

Stephanie looked positively lost. Her face was stunned, and the man she had come to rely upon for support was accusing her of . . . something. I wasn't prepared yet to say what had gone on in the kitchen. I'm a lawyer. I need proof.

I didn't have to wait long. Stephanie didn't answer Michael (that must have been Michael). The building's entrance opened and in rushed three EMTs with a gurney. They looked around. 'Where's the patient?' one of the two women asked.

Stephanie seemed to be responding to questions. She raised her right hand and pointed in the direction of the kitchen. 'There,' she said.

The only problem (well, the most immediate problem, anyway) was that her right hand, which had been obscured by her drenched outfit, was holding a six-inch kitchen knife. I bet you can imagine what was dripping off of it.

The whole room froze. Even Bobby.

But not the EMTs. They couldn't care less who had done what to whom; their job was to get inside and provide the necessary aid and transport. They rushed right past the stunned crowd and hit the swinging door to the kitchen with savagery. The rest of the gathered assemblage, though, didn't so much as blink. There was no other movement in the room.

That held for about five seconds. Then Bobby pulled an evidence bag out of one pocket and a latex glove from another and used them to gently relieve my cousin Stephanie of the knife and place it in the bag. She offered less than no resistance.

One of the EMTs, looking a little dazed, emerged from the kitchen wiping his hands with a towel. He'd clearly been trying to provide first aid to Brandon Starkey, and from the look of his uniform and his face, he had not been successful. Crawford, behind him, walked directly to Bobby. 'The detectives are on their way, along with a CSI team from the county,' he said. Then he got a look at the bag Bobby was holding and, more to the point, what was in it. 'Where'd you get that?'

Bobby was still a little wobbly (sorry for the rhyme) and just pointed at Stephanie. 'From her.'

Crawford didn't hesitate. 'The guy's dead,' he said. 'This is a murder.'

There were sobs from the crowd and my Aunt Fern, Stephanie's mother, appeared from whatever perch she'd been occupying to close ranks with her daughter. 'I'm so sorry,' she said, wanting to hug Stephanie but not seeing a way to do that without first putting on a hazmat suit.

'It's more than that, I'm afraid,' Crawford said. He looked at Stephanie. 'You're going to have to come with us, young lady.' He sounded as though he was admonishing her for eating an extra cookie from the jar. 'We need to ask you some questions.'

I took a step toward him. 'Are you arresting her?' I asked.

Crawford shook his head. 'Not up to me. But it's pretty clear she was in the room when this happened and she had the knife, so we're taking her in for questioning.' Without the same queasiness Aunt Fern was exhibiting, he took Stephanie's hand – the left one, I noticed, not the one that had held the knife – and tugged to lead her away.

But Stephanie was not moving. 'I want a lawyer,' she said.

'You're not being arrested yet,' Crawford explained again.

'I don't care. I want a lawyer.' Then she looked straight at me and said, 'I want *her*.'

What came out of me was something between a sigh and a groan. 'Oh, Skinny,' I said again.

FIVE

Detective Lester Schultz of the Woodbridge Police Department was a somewhat disheveled man, tall, with clothes that hung off him like he was a coat hanger and not a mannequin. His hair was sort of wavy in the way that it would be in a man who didn't comb his hair very often. And his manner was world-weary and flat. I'd never worked with Detective Schultz when I was a prosecutor with Middlesex County, so my resume was not impressing him in the least. And his shirt, with a blue checked pattern and a chocolate stain on the left sleeve, was not impressing me much, either.

I'd never missed Lieutenant K.C. Trench of the Los Angeles Police Department so much in my life. And I'd only known Trench for a couple of years.

We'd arrived in Schultz's somewhat dubious presence by way of Crawford and Bobby (whose last name turned out to be Puglia), who had stuffed Stephanie into the back of their cruiser (no handcuffs, which I thought was humane of them), shivering not from cold but from trauma, and beckoning for me to follow them, as if I didn't know where the Woodbridge municipal complex was situated. One of the (few, I was realizing) advantages to being (temporarily) back in New Jersey was that, unlike in my new home, I knew all the roads. Just to be brazen, I didn't even use the GPS in the rental car to get here.

Stephanie had not been processed because she was technically not being arrested. The county investigators, who were no doubt at the scene of the crime at this moment, would make a determination and a recommendation, and if they found no evidence that anyone else might have killed this Brandon Starkey guy (whom I had never actually met), they would no doubt see to it that Skinny was arrested and arraigned. I was expecting that to happen at any minute. She was still doing her deer-in-the-headlights thing, but the front of her dress was making her look, let's say, less innocent than a newborn faun.

I barely knew any of the people involved besides Stephanie, so I had no clue what the dynamic between and among them might be. I knew Skinny, and the idea that she'd take a kitchen knife to her future husband's best friend seemed highly unlikely.

But then I wasn't her lawyer. I kept telling myself that. I lived in Los Angeles, California, now and I worked for Seaton, Taylor, Evans and Wentworth (especially Wentworth, who was my immediate supervisor). I was mostly a family law attorney and only occasionally took on a criminal defense. And if I *were* to accept a case involving a murder, it would unquestionably not be one that also involved my family, to which I was at least technically a witness, and which had taken place three thousand miles from my apartment. Not to mention the house Patrick and I were buying together.

Nope, I wasn't Stephanie's lawyer. That was clear.

'Are you her lawyer?' Schultz asked me while Stephanie sat in the predictable interrogation room, a police department jacket someone had offered draped around her shoulders.

'Yes,' Stephanie said, her voice taking on more authority than I'd heard since she'd stumbled out of the Elks kitchen.

'Not really,' I told him. 'I'm here to help with the questioning, but if she's charged with anything, we will be hiring a lawyer from around here. I live in Los Angeles.' There was a real sense of relief in being able to say my home was a continent away from here.

'Sandy!' Stephanie's eyes, which had been glazed over, were now showing fear. 'You're my lawyer.' Definitive.

'I'm your cousin,' I corrected her. 'But let's hope you're not being charged with anything and so this conversation will be moot.'

'How can a conversation be mute? ASL?' Nobody ever accused Stephanie of ducking out of Mensa meetings because she was bored with the pedestrian company.

Schultz, clearly trying to regain a sense of authority in this conversation, cleared his throat and it had the desired effect; we looked at him. 'Why don't you just tell me what happened in that kitchen,' he said.

'I wasn't in the kitchen,' I noted.

'Not you,' he said.

Stephanie nodded; she was getting that she was the star attraction in this room and was trying to decide how she felt about it. Clearly, she'd have preferred not to be in this situation, but then she'd always been the one that nobody looked at in a group. Had things been different, she might be feeling that way because she'd be getting married tomorrow. Had things been different.

(It should be noted that out in the waiting area, a small army of people had undoubtedly gathered by now, one that would include Patrick, Angie, Michael, my mother, who wouldn't be denied, my sister, who wouldn't let my mother out of her sight, Aunt Fern, probably members of the victim's family and I could only imagine how many members of what we laughingly call 'the press,' which would have included anyone who had been in the room and owned a smartphone. I was weirdly glad to be in this part of the police station.)

'Stephanie,' Schultz said. He was doing the buddy-cop thing where he tried to get the suspect (guess who) to believe he's her friend and will do all he can to help her out of this impossible situation. When, in fact, he's looking for a fast collar and a case he can move to the county prosecutor that will get him noticed and into position for promotion. Don't believe a cop when he tells you he's your friend. Unless, you know, he's your actual friend. 'Just tell me what happened so I can help.' See?

I had been given no time to confer with my client, but this was a questioning and not an arraignment, so I said nothing. I, too, looked at Stephanie because, frankly, I was pretty interested in what she was going to say.

'I went into the kitchen and Brandon was sitting on one of the prep tables, which I thought was rude,' she began. 'I mean, people have to cook food on there. People are going to eat off of there, basically.'

'Why did you go into the kitchen?' Schultz obviously thought that hygiene violations were the least of anybody's problems here, and he probably had a point.

Stephanie, roused out of the daydream she was beginning to relate, stopped and blinked. 'Brandon texted me and asked me to come in,' she said.

'Brandon Starkey? The victim?' Schultz knew who she meant. This was an attempt to get her to say so on whatever record was being created. I understood why Schultz was operating the way he was, but that didn't make me like it – or him – any better.

Stephanie's lower lip quivered a little at the word 'victim.' 'Yes.' She took a moment to compose herself. 'He didn't say why I needed to go meet him there, but I went.'

'What happened when you got there?' Schultz seemed to be getting impatient with the way Stephanie, who was still wearing *that dress*, was answering questions. I decided right then and there not to invite him to my next birthday party.

'He said he had to talk to me,' she told him. Before he could express his impatience again, she added, 'Brandon said he had to get it off his chest. He said he was in love with me and that I needed to know that before I married Michael.'

Schultz clearly wanted to say, 'So you stabbed him?' but he was a cop in an interrogation room and knew better than to jump the gun. The knife. Whatever. 'So did that make you angry?' he asked.

If it was a court of law, I would have objected that he was leading the witness, but it wasn't and, again, I was going back to LA on Monday, so I let this be someone else's problem. I started thinking of defense attorneys I knew in the area to recommend to Stephanie and Aunt Fern if my cousin was charged. And from what I could see in Schultz's face, he wanted to charge her.

Stephanie looked startled. 'Angry? Why would that make me angry?' Then she saw the steel bars closing around her, and her eyes widened almost to the point they'd been when she'd stumbled out with the murder weapon (let's be real) in her right hand. 'You think I killed Brandon because he said he loved me?'

'I don't know. You have to tell me how he got stabbed.'

Schultz was trying again to get on Skinny's good side but that wasn't going to work anymore.

'I don't *know* how he got stabbed. I told Brandon I was very flattered but that I'm in love with Michael, because I *am*, and that he'd have to learn to deal with it. I told him he'd find someone to love probably very soon, and I meant it. I mean, he just broke up with Lucia and that must have made him a little depressed or something, right?'

This offered an insight into the mind of Schultz, who was taking notes furiously on his iPad. Would he ask who Lucia was or would he stick with the incident in question? If he didn't ask about Lucia (who clearly was Brandon's ex), that could mean he'd already decided Stephanie was guilty and he didn't need to consider alternative suspects.

'Are you suggesting that the victim stabbed himself with that kitchen knife?' he asked. Bingo. He'd concluded his considerations and made up his mind. He was going after Stephanie.

'Are you going to arrest my cousin?' I said. I wanted to break his line of questioning and head off any problems that might arise if Stephanie thought she could just speak freely. She hadn't been read her rights yet, which meant nothing could be used in court, but there was no sense in giving Schultz more fodder than he believed he already had.

He looked at me as the annoyance I was sincerely hoping I had become. 'That hasn't been decided yet. At the moment, I'm just asking some questions and—'

'Trying to help her. I get that. Except you're not interested in who Lucia might be? A recent ex? Someone who might have a grudge against the victim? Why are you focusing only on Stephanie?' I believe I get points for not saying, 'Stephanie here.'

'I was going to ask that later,' he said through clenched teeth. 'Right now, I'm trying to establish what happened. And since there are no charges leveled at your cousin, keep in mind that there's no legal reason for you to be here.'

Well, that was a complete and utter lie, and I was about to tell him that when Skinny touched me on the arm. Luckily, they'd let her wash her hands before putting her in this room. 'It's OK, Sandy,' she said. 'I want to help the detective.'

Frustrated, I sat back and folded my arms because there's nothing I like better than body language clichés. I said nothing.

'Of course I don't think Brandon killed himself with a knife,' she said, ostensibly answering a question Schultz had meant to be sarcastic. 'I think someone else came in while I was out of the room and killed him.' Her eyes welled up a bit again.

'You left the room?' That was, after all, new information, and I had to admit that I had not seen Stephanie back in the main part of the Elks hall after she'd walked into the kitchen. I *had* seen Sarah Panico and my cousin Stephen go into the kitchen and both come out, but I wasn't here to accuse anyone else.

On the other hand, if it turned out Sarah Panico had killed Brandon, would I really be all that upset?

'Yeah,' Stephanie said. 'I figured I'd better leave Brandon to himself because he just had that breakup, and now he thought I was sort of dumping him, so I took a minute and went into the employee bathroom they have back there. I looked over my emails and some other stuff, and when I came out, that's when I saw . . .' She didn't finish the sentence but her hands flapped a little on the table. It was still a good thing that they weren't handcuffed.

'And you didn't hear anything in there? You didn't hear the . . . Brandon yell out or anything?' We weren't in court yet and Schultz wanted to rip holes in my client's – no – my *cousin's* story.

'I had my headphones in,' Stephanie told him. 'I was listening to a Taylor Swift album. I figured if Brandon broke down crying over me or something, I'd give him his privacy.'

Even I was having trouble buying this story, although the retreating-to-the-bathroom thing was definitely plausible with Stephanie. Once when we were kids, she ducked out on a Passover seder to watch a basketball game and it took an hour and a half before anyone thought to look for her.

'Uh-huh.' I wasn't sure if Schultz was commenting or just trying to type out notes and converse at the same time. Either way, I didn't care for the tone of his voice. 'Was there anyone else in the kitchen when you came out of the restroom?'

Stephanie's face soured. 'Yeah. I saw someone kill him and

just forgot to mention it. No, Detective, there wasn't anybody there.' She was from New Jersey after all.

But Schultz was a Garden Stater, too. 'OK, then, since you're so observant,' he said, 'how did you get covered in Brandon Starkey's blood?'

Now her voice had a sharper edge than it had since we'd arrived. '*Obviously*, I tried to help him. I was trying to do CPR. But I think he was already dead.' No hesitation that time.

Schultz came right back after her. 'And how did you get the knife in your hand?' he asked.

That stopped Skinny short. She opened her mouth as if to reply and then closed it again. She blinked a couple of times.

'I honestly have no idea,' she said.

SIX

Stephanie was released without charges being filed, but that was just a formality. The assistant prosecutor placed in charge of the case, whichever former colleague of mine that turned out to be, would make a determination based on the report of Schultz and other detectives as well as the incident report filed by the uniformed cops. And then, in all likelihood, they'd charge Stephanie because they didn't have any other suspects (I could think of at least four off the top of my head) and liked to take the easy path.

But that was not going to be my problem, or at least not my professional problem. I was already packing for the return trip to Los Angeles and I'd never been so glad to have moved to a huge city that had millions of people all of whom wanted to be movie stars or work with them. Until they *did* work with movie stars, and then it was too late.

(Except you, Patrick!)

After the civilized festival of leaving the police station surrounded by wedding (probably not) guests, cops (two), bridal party (who thought it was part of their sworn duty), reporters, vloggers, video technicians, Patrick, Angie, Mom and Delia (the Four Tops) and one protestor with a clearly improvised sign that read *FREE*, and had no name because she didn't know who had been arrested yet, Patrick had made sure the rental car was 'brought round' and we headed into it like the Beatles in *A Hard Day's Night*. There were no screaming fans, but there was plenty of screaming.

Inside the car, which bordered on limo but did not, alas, have Esteban behind the wheel – which I think disappointed Angie but she wouldn't say it – the scene wasn't as loud but it was just as tense. For one thing, Aunt Fern had brought Stephanie a T-shirt and sweats to wear because the cops had confiscated her Carrie-after-the-prom outfit for evidence. The rest of us were choosing not to make an issue of her ensemble.

In fact, there had been almost no conversation in the car at all. Patrick arranged for the driver (this one's name was Robert) to drop Stephanie off at her apartment, where her mother, her fiancé and her brother Stephen (if he was finished being questioned) were awaiting her. She hadn't said anything at all until she stepped out of the car, turned to look directly at my face and intoned, 'You're my lawyer.' Then, before I could protest, she had turned and walked toward the two-family house whose top floor was her home.

I had decided I'd text her from the tarmac of whatever flight we were taking home and recommend some defense attorneys I knew. There was no sense in a phone call or a text while it was still possible to change my course. I was determined. I was going back to California to my actual life. I was very sorry Stephanie was in such awful trouble, but it wasn't my responsibility to get her out of it.

And I told that to Mom, Delia, Angie and especially Patrick as they watched me repack my suitcase in our hotel room.

'Your cousin *specifically* asked for you,' my mother said. 'You can't run out on her in her time of need.'

'Think of it, Sandy,' Delia chimed in. Delia was great at chiming in. I think she majored in it in college before she took the MCATs and decided to heal the sick so people would tell her what a great humanitarian she was while they paid her bill. 'Stephanie was preparing for the most magical day of her life and now she's facing the gallows.' Seriously. My sister talks like that. Nobody has been executed in New Jersey in at least twenty years, and the gallows was last used here in 1963. I know; I was surprised it was that late, too.

But there was no purpose in pointing that out to my two female relatives. They were operating on pure emotion, most of which was that they wanted me to come riding to Stephanie's rescue, something I had no intention of trying and no confidence I could do. 'She hasn't been charged with anything,' I said. 'The cops might be out finding another suspect as we speak.'

Angie, of all people, put her hand on her left hip and looked at me with even more attitude than usual. 'You know perfectly well they're going to charge her,' she said. I stopped sorting my socks (I had planned to be here for three days and I was sorting socks – I'm very meticulous about my packing) and stared at her.

'*Et tu*, Angela?' I said. '*You* know perfectly well that a murder trial and the process leading up to one, if that's going to happen, could take months if not years, and I live in Los Angeles. There's no chance I could do it.' The only sane person in the room, it seemed (besides me) was Patrick, and that's a real leap. I've seen him dive out of (slowly) moving cars when he saw something on the side of the road he wanted to examine more closely. Once he did that when he was driving.

I turned to him now for some words of reason. 'You know what I'm saying, don't you, Patrick? You wouldn't want me away for months at a time, would you?'

'Well, no.' Thank goodness for Patrick. But then he shifted his left foot a bit. 'But I could stay here with you for a time if necessary. In fact, I'd rather enjoy it.'

Now there were no sane people in the room. Including me.

'What?' Patrick worked in television. He was between seasons on *Torn*, his streaming series about a private investigator with Dissociative Identity Disorder (DID), but he always had something lined up when he was 'on hiatus,' didn't he? Why would he want to stay in New Jersey for an extended period?

'I have reasons that mean staying in New York for a while wouldn't be a problem,' he said sheepishly, by which I mean he looked like a lost lamb and wouldn't make eye contact with me. 'I've been thinking it over. It wouldn't be bad to rent an apartment there and stay for a while, perhaps.'

This was a conversation for another time, when Patrick and I were alone. Angie's expression indicated she'd known about these 'reasons' because she is basically Patrick's enforcer and nothing happens in his business life that she doesn't know about. And neither of them had told me. I was definitely going to sit the two of them down and read them the Riot Act.

Maybe I'd do it on the plane. I folded a T-shirt and put it in the suitcase.

'Sandra.' My mother was putting as much weight into her voice as she could manage. 'Your cousin Stephanie needs you.'

'I agree she needs a good lawyer, but she can do way better than me,' I told her. 'I haven't worked in this system for years. I'm mostly a family law practitioner now. *If* Stephanie is charged – and that's a big *if* – she'll need someone who knows every judge, every assistant prosecutor and every change in the code, and I'm not up on those things anymore. Besides, and I can't emphasize this enough, I live in *Los Angeles* now.'

Nobody said anything for a long moment. Then, as if I hadn't said a word, my mother repeated, 'Stephanie needs you.'

I zipped up the suitcase and took it off the bed. It rolled a little but I steadied it. All I needed to do now was book a new flight, at least a day earlier than the one I'd been planning on taking.

I don't want you to think that I had no sympathy for Skinny, because I did. But if, as I suspected, she was eventually charged (days or weeks from now) with Brandon's murder, the logistics of my taking her case and defending her successfully would be almost impossible to navigate.

Besides, having to defend a family member against a murder charge while under the scrutiny of my mother was way more than I was willing to take on. In fact, just being in the same state as my mother for all that time was something of a deal breaker. I glanced at Angie, who was sprawled on the inevitable easy chair hotels like to think you need in a room you're using for two nights. But then, there was Angie in the chair, so maybe they were right. Still, the point right now was the look on her face, which indicated she was thinking in the same direction that I was, and understood. She looked between me and my mother a few times, then made eye contact with me and nodded. She got it.

'Sandy probably couldn't handle the case,' she told the room. That wasn't exactly what I was looking for in terms of support, but at least it was an attempt. 'It's three thousand miles away and you guys would be breathing down her neck the whole time. That would make it tougher.' I made a mental note to buy Angie a filter to go between her brain and her mouth. Maybe for Christmas.

'Oh, we would not,' Delia said before my mother's head could explode and increase the fee we'd be paying for cleaning the room. Remember when hotels used to do that automatically? But I digress. 'Mom and I have always been completely supportive of everything Sandy did and that wouldn't change now. We want her to stay *because* we think she's the best lawyer for Stephanie. Poor Stephanie.'

I started to regret not having called my father and put him on speaker because he could certainly have disputed at the very least the first part of that last statement. But he was living in Saskatchewan now with his girlfriend Lena and was blissfully unaware of anything that had happened in the past . . . Was it really only about six hours?

'Let's forget about that part of it,' I suggested, mostly because I wanted Angie to never have said anything about my neck or who might have been breathing down it. 'It doesn't make sense for me to defend Stephanie, and I'll be back in LA for days before we even find out if she'll need a defense at all.'

Because the universe likes to amuse itself with me, that was the very moment my phone rang, and the caller was Aunt Fern. That couldn't be good.

I had no choice but to take the call. Everyone in the room was watching, and I really cared about what some of them thought about me. 'Um, hi.' I don't know why I didn't want to say, 'Aunt Fern' out loud, but I didn't.

'Sandy, I need you to come over here right away.' My family is so warm and sentimental. 'There's a man here trying to arrest Stephanie.'

One man? That didn't make any sense. Cops travel in pairs,

generally, and in a situation like this, at least Schultz would show up with his partner and maybe the two uniformed officers who had brought Skinny in, to begin with. 'What man?' I asked.

'I don't know. A prosecutor or something.'

They sent an assistant prosecutor out to do the arrest? This was getting weirder and weirder. I had never been called to such an event in the eight years I'd worked for Middlesex County.

'Is Stephanie there at your house?' I said. We'd dropped Stephanie off at her apartment not all that long before.

'No.' Fern sounded puzzled, like she was wondering why I didn't know that. 'We're at her apartment.'

Better to get to business. 'There's just the one man there?' I asked Aunt Fern. Patrick was looking at me curiously, but my mother was already practicing her stern look, which was pretty much her resting face anyway.

'No, there are a couple of police officers, too.' Luckily, Aunt Fern knew better than to call them *cops*. Cops don't like that.

Maybe the assistant prosecutor they'd sent was someone I knew or, better, had worked with. I might be able to clear this up on the phone. 'Let me talk to the prosecutor,' I instructed my aunt. I looked at the suitcase longingly. I should have booked that flight sooner.

'OK.' Fern sounded skeptical, but you couldn't blame her for that. There was the usual sound of a mobile phone being handed from one person to another, which roughly resembles crinkling a newspaper in someone's ear.

'Sandy Moss,' the voice said. 'Never thought I'd hear from you again.'

Oh, no.

'Richard,' I said. 'It would be so much better if you hadn't. Are you arresting my cousin?'

'No,' he said. I could hear the smug sneer in his voice. 'I'm not. These two nice police officers are doing that at my suggestion.'

Richard Chapman. Without knowing why, I glanced at Patrick, who was looking concerned. Richard Chapman, after all, was the reason I'd met Patrick at all.

He was the man I'd left New Jersey to escape.

SEVEN

'My client does not waive her right to an attorney and will not answer any questions until I'm present,' I told my ex, who technically wasn't my ex because he'd been married (without my knowledge) the whole time we were dating. 'Now put her on the phone so I can tell her that.'

Patrick looked at me with at least seven questions in his eyes, and I couldn't answer any of them for him yet because I was on the phone with a massive jerk, trying to keep my cousin Skinny out of jail. It was, as we say in the legal business, a complicated situation.

But Angie had started at the name 'Richard.' She could probably tell by the look on my face exactly which Richard this was, and she knew how that would make me feel, which mostly bordered on the homicidal.

'In a minute,' he answered. 'Don't worry. Nothing's going to be done that you won't know about.'

'Since when does the county prosecutor get involved directly?' I said, doing my very best to maintain my authority and change the subject. 'Why didn't you assign my successor to the job?'

Richard used the tone he had cultivated into a voice recorder for those occasions when he had to talk to the media, which was more often than anyone except Richard wanted. 'When someone is brutally murdered in my county, it's an affront to me, an affront to law enforcement and an affront to every citizen,' he said. No. Seriously. I'm not making a word of it up.

'CNN isn't on the line,' I said. 'You don't have to sound like you're running for office. You're not, are you? Because I might have a story or two to tell.' OK, so that was unprofessional. Report me to the Middlesex County Bar Association. I'll still be able to work in Los Angeles.

'It's the truth,' Richard lied.

'Uh-huh. Put Stephanie on the phone now.'

Surprisingly, Richard did as I'd asked, so the next voice I heard was Stephanie's and she sounded just as scared as before. I was hoping she'd at least had the chance to shower.

'Sandy?' She sounded like a four-year-old trying to remember what a tulip was called. As though she wasn't so much trying to prove it was me as to re-establish her sanity by identifying me correctly. As though she thought the prosecutor and the cops might be lying to her. Because they can. It's legal.

'It's me, Stephanie. Have you told them anything I didn't hear before in the police station?'

'No.' She said it proudly, the little girl in the class pleased with herself for getting a question she knew how to answer.

'That's good. That's very good. Now listen to me, Skinny.'

'You're not going to call me that in court, are you?'

'No. With any luck at all, we won't be in court for anything but an arraignment and then you'll come home. But you have to listen to me right now and do exactly what I say.'

'I will.' She was paying attention now and seeing me as an authority figure. That was exactly what I needed.

'Good. From now until I get there, you don't say *anything* to the cops, the prosecutor or anyone else that talks to you. You only talk to me.'

'But what if they ask me a question?' Stephanie said.

'You say what I'm about to tell you. Ready?'

'Yes.'

'You say, "I'm waiting until my attorney is here." That's it. No matter what they say or how they promise they're going to help you and it's bad to wait for me, assume they're lying. The only thing you say is "I'm waiting until my attorney is here." Got that?'

'Yeah. I'm not stupid, Sandy.'

'I don't think you are. Now repeat it back to me. What do you say when they talk to you about anything?'

'I'm waiting until my attorney is here.'

My mother was, for some perverse reason, smiling. Because she thought this meant I'd be representing Skinny all the way through a trial. She was wrong, but go tell her that.

'Perfect. You say that to everybody about everything. Someone asks you why you killed Brandon and you say . . .'

'I didn't—'

'No. You don't say that. What *do* you say?'

'I'm waiting until my attorney is here.'

'That's it. If someone asks you if you want a cup of coffee, what do you say?'

'I'm waiting until my attorney is here.'

I exhaled. 'Now you have it. I'll be where they're taking you probably before you get there. Just say nothing or say your line until you see me.'

'I'm waiting until my attorney is here,' she said.

'Excellent. Hand the prosecutor your phone but try to do it without touching him in any way.' I would have told her to wipe the phone but her fingerprints on her phone weren't going to convict her of anything. 'I'll see you soon.'

The next voice you hear will be that of the Prince of Darkness. 'It's a loser, Sandy,' Richard said. 'It's a slam dunk. She had the murder weapon in her hand, she was in the room alone with the victim and she was covered in his blood.'

'Are you trying to convince me not to take the case or are you enjoying making my cousin feel terrified?' I asked. 'Never mind answering that. Where are you taking her? Are you partnering with the Woodbridge cops?' Sometimes the county investigators will work with the municipal police to work a case and then the headquarters will be with the town police instead of the county prosecutor.

'Oh, no,' Richard said. 'We'll be taking Stephanie to my office in New Brunswick and you can meet us there if you're the attorney of record.'

Have you ever felt like walls were springing up around you, confining you to a place and there was no way to escape? It's hard to feel like that in a hotel suite, but I was managing. 'We'll talk about that,' I said. Then I disconnected the call.

I unpacked my bag.

EIGHT

'I'm not staying for the whole trial,' I told Stephanie.

We were sitting in an 'interview room' in the prosecutor's office where I had spent eight years before slapping Richard Chapman in the face and booking a flight to Los Angeles and a firm called Seaton, Taylor, Evans and Bach (at the time). It was decidedly uncomfortable being back here, although a few of the people I'd known during my tenure had given me warm welcomes on my entrance, even if they looked a little confused as to what the hell I was doing there, to begin with.

We had very little time. Richard would, I knew, be making a grand entrance into the interrogation room to best intimidate my client (Skinny) and me (good luck with that). So I had to make sure Stephanie knew how this was going to go and that she should not, under any circumstances, expect me to suspend my California career for the better part of a year – at least – to try her case for her.

'But you're my lawyer,' she said. It had equal parts ignorance of the criminal justice system and passive aggression in it, which made it the most my-family thing I'd heard all day. And that was saying something.

'I am today,' I assured her. 'I'll see you through the arraignment, which, it appears, will be necessary, and get something started in discovery, but I'm going to refer you to a very good defense attorney I know who will be able to concentrate on your case in ways that I can't from three thousand miles away.' (And whose name I would definitely decide upon as soon as the arraignment was over.) 'But I don't want you thinking that I can stay here in New Jersey for the whole time this trial might take because I can't. I work, and live, in Los Angeles.' I was getting so tired of telling people where I lived, especially the ones who already knew where I lived.

'Sandy—' Stephanie said, but she was interrupted by Richard, who threw the door to the room open as dramatically as he could. They're on suspension hinges which means they don't open very fast, which was good because he might have hit my client in the face if the door had swung freely.

Richard looked exactly as he'd looked when we were dating. He was handsome, although I was happy to remind myself that Patrick was not only more handsome (and that could be verified objectively by his many fan clubs) but six times a better person than Richard. I made a mental note to kiss Patrick extra passionately when I got back to the hotel.

Patrick had heard about Richard, of course, but neither of us had expected to see him on this trip. Being Patrick, he had not shown any sign of jealousy, which was wise of him, or resentment, largely because I resented Richard enough for both of us. Angie had offered to come along with me to this conference, but I felt that it would be too much for me to have to defend her on charges of assault while I was trying to keep Stephanie out of jail for murder.

My mother, of course, had nothing good to say about Richard other than that I should have known he was married despite his never wearing a wedding ring. Delia had already been out of the house and busy turning out grandchildren for Mom when I was dating Richard, so she had not been paying attention, which now seemed like a real sisterly gesture on her part. She offered no opinions.

'So, Ms Silverstone' – that was Stephanie because, yes, Aunt Fern had married Lester Silverstone, who was currently dead of natural causes – 'can you tell us why you killed Brandon Starkey?' Wow. Richard was being even more of a jerk than usual. This was probably residual anger aimed at me, and that was totally unprofessional. I tucked away an idea to petition the court to have him removed from the case. He clearly could not act with any objectivity while a member of my family was the defendant.

If it came to that.

Before Stephanie could protest, I raised a finger, something Richard knew meant I was being serious. 'I think maybe you want to start off with something just a little less confrontational, Mr Prosecutor, or my client will refuse to answer any of your questions and you'll be forced to actually investigate the case through your office to find evidence that does not exist, because she will be pleading not guilty.'

He'd anticipated that reaction, of course. 'Certainly, *Counselor*,' he said. 'Not that we don't already have enough evidence to convict, but let's play it your way for a while.' He sat down across from us and looked Stephanie in the eye. 'Ms Silverstone. Did you have any animosity toward Mr Starkey?'

I had instructed Skinny quite clearly on how to respond to questions from a hostile source, like my ex-boyfriend the county prosecutor. 'No,' she said.

'None?' Was Richard cross-examining already? Shouldn't he wait for, I don't know, a *trial* for that? 'I'll be honest with you.' (I doubted that.) 'We already have a few witnesses who say that you and the *victim* were, let's say, in the midst of a very close relationship right before he was killed.'

It took me a moment, and I think Skinny was trying to decipher the supposed subtlety Richard had exercised, too. But I recovered first. 'Are you suggesting that my client and the deceased were intimate in the kitchen of the Elks Lodge?' I asked. And yes, it sounded just that ridiculous when I said it, even to me.

'I'm not suggesting it,' the big jerk said. 'I have *a witness* who's suggesting it.'

'Who said that?' Stephanie demanded. 'Who told you that?' It wasn't the response I would have hoped for after that little bombshell. She didn't immediately say it wasn't true or that she was horribly offended. She didn't want vindication; she wanted revenge. Not the best look when someone is being charged with a violent crime.

I gave Skinny a sharp look and she caught it. She stopped talking.

(I know; you've noticed that sometimes I call my cousin 'Skinny' and sometimes I call her 'Stephanie.' It's mostly random but sometimes it relates to how irritated I am with her. Because she really doesn't like my calling her 'Skinny.')

'Did you have a physical relationship with the victim?' Richard (who always wants to be called Richard, although 'Dick' would not be inaccurate) said. He wanted motive and he wanted Stephanie to supply one to him for free.

'Don't answer that,' I instructed her. 'We need to know what charges are being brought and what the current status of her case is. Has a hearing on pre-trial release been arranged? How soon can she leave custody?'

Richard did his it-wasn't-me face, which was the one I hit when I found out about his wife. 'The charges were made clear when Ms Silverstone was given her Miranda warning,' he said.

'Oddly, nobody waited for me to show up when that was happening, despite my client saying she wouldn't speak until I arrived,' I said with as little inflection in my voice as I could muster while still wanting to throttle someone. 'So how about you repeat that little detail with her attorney present.'

To his credit, Richard did not roll his eyes. That's the last time I'll mention something to his credit, and it ain't much. He never broke eye contact with me as he said, 'The charges are first-degree murder, manslaughter, assault, aggravated assault, and I'm sure there are a few health code violations about stabbing a man's chest seventeen times in the kitchen of a public accommodation. As for a pre-trial release, the judge will be in session Monday morning at nine a.m. Your client' – he did not even emphasize the word 'client' to get to me, which got to me – 'will be spending the weekend in county lockup.'

I wanted to ask which judge because I still had a few in my contacts.

But Stephanie's eyes opened to the size of silver dollar pancakes at the IHOP, where silver dollars are apparently the size of the 45-rpm vinyl records my father used to play for me. 'Sandy,' she said. Her voice quivered.

I wished I had a casebook in front of me so I could snap it shut as I stood. 'My client will be doing no such thing,' I said to Richard. Then I turned to my cousin. 'Stephanie, you go where they take you, but I'll be working to have you home as soon as possible, understand? Don't worry. This is what I'm good at.'

Actually, I was good at putting low-level drug dealers in jail and, as it turned out, getting celebrities acquitted of murder charges, but those last ones were flukes and I knew it. I could make some phone calls and wake a few people up if it got that late, but I was going to have Stephanie out of jail before she went to sleep tonight.

'Sandy, I really can't go to prison,' she said, as if it were up to me. Because it kind of was now.

'I know. Don't answer any questions, just like before, unless I'm in the room with you. Keep your head down. I'm on it. It won't be long.' I wished I was even half as certain about any of this as I sounded. I turned toward Richard. 'Do you need anything else from me?' I asked.

'Other than an apology? I don't think so.'

I waited for a uniformed cop to lead Stephanie out of the room before I answered him. 'I owe *you* an apology?' I said.

'Given the effect you had on my life, I'd say it's the very least I should expect.' Ego and arrogance aren't necessarily the same thing, but most people with too much of one had an ample supply of the other. Richard was the East Coast distributor of both.

'If I could go back and tell your wife about our affair again, not only would I do it but I'd bring pictures,' I said.

Having thought I'd delivered a withering exit line, I headed for the door and didn't even break stride as I heard him ask, 'There are pictures?'

Men!

NINE

I spent about two hours on the phone, first to identify the judge who might be presiding over Stephanie's case and then to convince that judge that it was an emergency to hear the case immediately. Luckily, I knew Judge Rivera, who was assigned this month, and he still thought of me as a prosecutor, so he liked me. All the law enforcement types think they share a mindset, although that is hardly a given. Rivera agreed to hold the hearing that evening and had his office contact Richard's, which must have caused some degree of hysteria in my old neck of the woods. Good.

Then I went back to the hotel to see Patrick and change clothes before the hearing. The clothes, because I had been dressed for packing and leaving and *not* for a court appearance, and Patrick because I needed to remind myself that all males were not Richard, which admittedly was setting the bar pretty low.

'So what's this about an offer in New York?' I asked him after a very long and supportive hug had disengaged. I looked into the drawers of the hotel's dresser and then into the closet for something that I could wear to work and not to a wedding or a baseball game at Yankee Stadium (which had been on the agenda for this trip) and coming up fairly dry.

'Do you really want to hear about it now?' Patrick said. 'It's been a very difficult day and you have a pretty difficult evening ahead of you.'

'I do,' I said. 'I need to hear about something else.'

Patrick considered that and nodded. He sat down on the edge of the bed to get a better angle watching me move from the closet to the dresser and back again in a frantic search to find the right outfit, which, let's be real, wasn't there.

'It's a play on Broadway,' he said. 'Well, it'll start at the Public Theater but there's talk it'll go to Broadway. A young playwright being produced with a reimagined version of Macbeth.'

'Don't you have to say, "The Scottish Play"?' I asked.

'Not if you're not in a theater, and frankly, I think that superstition is silly. But this one is a modern version, played as a comedy, without Shakespeare's language but with the bare bones of the plot. It's even called *The Scottish Play*. I've read it and it's very interesting. I think I could do a lot with it.'

'You'd be playing Macbeth?' I asked.

Patrick took on an odd grin. 'Actually, Lady Macbeth. The roles have been gender-reversed for this version. I get to goad an actress into taking over the bowling league.'

I stopped and regarded him a moment. 'The bowling league?'

He chuckled. 'The stakes are not quite as high as in the original. It's a commentary on the concept that power is a dangerous thing, no matter how low the level might be.'

OK. That might make sense. What did I know about putting

on a play, anyway? 'So you won't have to memorize all that iambic pentameter? Probably a relief for you, huh?'

Patrick cocked an eyebrow to indicate I might have touched a nerve. Then, with a voice I'd never heard come from him before, he said, 'There would have been a time for such a word. Tomorrow, and tomorrow, and tomorrow, creeps in this petty pace from day to day to the last syllable of recorded time, and all our yesterdays have lighted fools the way to dusty death. Out, out, brief candle! Life's but a walking shadow, a poor player that struts and frets his hour upon the stage and then is heard no more: it is a tale told by an idiot, full of sound and fury, signifying nothing.'

He was mesmerizing. It took me a moment, but I said, 'My apologies. I should never have underestimated you, of all people.'

Then he was back to Patrick again. 'No worries, love. You've only seen me in television shows, an idiotic action movie and that blasted soap opera you were watching on the plane. I do have some background, you know.'

Still, I felt the need to walk over and give him a hug, which he accepted. We held there for a moment, and I even forgot to worry about my wardrobe for Stephanie's pre-trial hearing. But it didn't last. We let go of each other and I headed back to the closet. 'Can you be away from *Torn* long enough to do this play? And now that I'm thinking about it, why didn't you tell me about this before we left?'

'*Torn* is on hiatus between seasons, and we never really know if they're going to renew us or not,' he said. 'I could be out of work for a while. It's one of the factors going into my decision to do the play or not. And as for why I didn't mention it, that's one superstition I *do* believe in: I never tell you about any project until I'm sure it has integrity and that I won't embarrass myself in it.'

The hell with it; I'd just wear the outfit I was going to wear to the brunch the day after the wedding, which had been scheduled for right before when I'd planned to light out for the airport at warp speed. 'Why not?' I asked. 'I could help you decide if you want an opinion. I mean, I know I'm completely ignorant when it comes to show business, but—'

Patrick cut me off. 'It's because I don't want to do anything that will make you think less of me,' he said. Then he sat there and looked at me, as if he was unsure what my reaction might be, like he had bared a part of his soul he'd been concealing through our whole relationship.

I resisted the urge to go over and hug him again, lest he think that was my answer to everything. 'Oh, Patrick,' I said. 'There is nothing you can do that will make me think less of you, especially nothing you can do professionally.'

Again, there was the slightest nod and a longer moment in which neither of us spoke. Then he looked over at the closet. 'Right,' Patrick said. 'You should wear the green one.'

I wore the green one. After all that, how could I not? Standing in the familiar courtroom but on the opposite side of the aisle from my former domain, I watched as Judge Rivera entered, then sat down. The rest of us followed suit.

Stephanie, thankfully not in a prison jumpsuit (they probably had not had time to issue her one), sat to my right. Patrick (who had signed numerous autographs), with Angie in tow, was one row behind us, as were Aunt Fern, Stephen, my mother, Delia and Sarah Panico. Sarah was probably preparing a podcast on the murder and the ensuing legal proceedings as seen from the perspective of . . . Sarah Panico.

Michael the Groom was nowhere to be seen. Probably hanging out in the forest with the rest of his family.

Across the aisle, looking as peeved as he could while still behaving professionally, Richard glared at me whenever the judge wasn't speaking. Which, since Judge Rivera speaks very slowly, was more in the area of pauses than breaks.

'Having seen the defense's petition for release pending trial, I am inclined to grant it if the prosecution has no objections,' the judge said.

'The prosecution has many objections,' Richard countered. Sitting next to him was a pretty young blonde assistant prosecutor I didn't know. He'd moved on quickly. After all, he was a divorcé now and eligible to 'play the field.' I know because I used to be the field. 'For one thing, we believe the defendant is a flight risk.'

I didn't even have to ask because Rivera did. 'Based on what evidence, Mr Chapman?'

Richard wasn't a great guy, no matter how well he could pretend, but he was a very good lawyer. 'The defendant has not held an address for more than six months in the past five years, Your Honor. She has traveled out of the country twice in the past two years. She has relatives in Venezuela and Poland. It would be easy enough for her to vanish and find asylum in a country that has no extradition treaty or will not return a prisoner to a country that employs capital punishment.'

Stephanie blanched a little.

I stood up. 'Your Honor, the defendant has moved all those times because she was trying to pay her rent and it kept going up, so she moved to less expensive housing each time. She has traveled twice in two years on vacation. As for her relatives overseas, they are for the most part the same as mine, and you can believe me when I say that they will be happy to pack Ms Silverstone up and send her back rather than keep her indefinitely. As for capital punishment, you know certainly well – and so does the prosecutor – that this state hasn't had it since 2007, when it was abolished by the governor. And even before that, it hadn't been used since 1963.'

'All that is true, Ms Moss,' Rivera said. 'What other objections do you have, Mr Prosecutor?'

Richard didn't so much as twitch. He was prepared. 'The defendant left the room where the murder was committed, covered in blood and carrying the weapon that had been used to kill Mr Starkey,' he said. 'Since we do not yet have a clear view of her motive, we can assume, pending an examination, that there might be a factor of mental illness and that means she could be a danger to herself or others if left in the general population. For everyone's protection, she is best left in custody.'

It is considered something of a faux pas to roll your eyes at a prosecutor, but I'll admit it took effort not to do so. 'Mr Chapman is indulging in the worst kind of stereotyping and speculation,' I told Rivera. 'My client has no history of violence, no history of mental illness and no history of suicide attempts. She is a danger to no one, and since she has *not* been proven to have committed any violent act at all, the prosecutor's suggestions are not relevant. He has no proof for anything he just said.'

That was the moment I looked over at Skinny and she was avoiding my glance.

Richard did not telegraph his mood. He simply reached his left hand out and allowed the blonde to hand him a document. 'Your Honor, I'd like to submit a copy of a report dated seventeen months ago from St. Peter's University Hospital in New Brunswick, where the defendant Ms Silverstone was admitted after having ingested twelve Xanax tablets in an attempt to end her own life.'

One thing I had learned while working under . . . *for* Richard was to maintain a steady demeanor in court at all times. I did not swivel to stare at Skinny in her seat. I did not widen my eyes in stunned surprise. I did not cough, stammer, groan or ask for a moment to visit the restroom. I watched as Richard handed the printout to Rivera and saw the judge put on reading glasses to peruse it.

'This appears to be genuine,' he said. 'Ms Moss?'

'It's the first mention I've heard of that incident, Your Honor.' You can't lie to a judge. Write that down. 'If I might have a moment to confer with my client.'

Rivera, his estimation of me clearly lowered at least half a step, nodded. 'Just one moment, Ms Moss.'

I sat down hard in the chair next to Skinny. 'Why didn't I know about this?' I hissed at her.

'My mother didn't want it to get around.' She was almost in tears.

'I mean, why didn't I know about this *now*?'

Stephanie looked surprised. 'I didn't know it would come up.'

I was going to fly back to Los Angeles after this hearing. I had to keep reminding myself of that. This was going to be some other lawyer's problem very soon. I maintained my calm. 'OK. What happened?'

'It was before I met Michael,' she said, as if that were important. 'My boyfriend broke up with me, I was out of a job, I was going to have to move back in with my mom and I just couldn't handle it. So I took some pills because I thought that wouldn't hurt.'

'Did it hurt?' I asked.

'It wasn't great when they pumped my stomach,' Stephanie answered.

'All right. What happened after?'

She told me, and I stood up. 'Your Honor,' I said.

Rivera took off the reading glasses and looked at me.

'It is true that my client tried to end her life by suicide seventeen months ago during a period of extreme stress. But you'll also note, if it's on those records, that she completed three separate courses of treatment with therapists and psychiatrists and is now taking anti-depressant medication. She is engaged to be married, has steady employment and has managed to live on her own, in one apartment, for the past six months and has no intention of moving until she and her fiancé marry. She has turned her life around, and that incident should not be used against her given all her efforts to overcome the behavior she exhibited at that time. She should be commended for having rebounded so well.'

'She stands accused of stabbing the best man at her wedding in the kitchen of a catering hall,' Rivera pointed out. 'Let's not petition the Nobel committee just yet.'

'I'd say not,' Richard said. Sometimes he talks like a retired colonel in a Noel Coward play.

'Of course, Your Honor,' I said. The best way to deal with Richard is to pretend he's not there. Makes life so much more enjoyable. 'But I think we have shown that the prosecution's attempts to justify keeping my client in custody are not relevant. She should be free to leave under her own recognizance.'

Rivera gave that some thought and spoke, as always, slowly. 'I am inclined to rule in the defense's favor. Any further arguments, Mr Chapman?'

Richard did not look outraged. Even if he *was* outraged, and he probably wasn't given the weak case he'd presented, he wouldn't have allowed it to show. 'I would request that the court confiscate the defendant's REAL ID and passport so she may not leave the state while awaiting trial,' he said, in a tone that would indicate he was deciding which of two pipe wrenches to buy at the local hardware store. But I knew for a fact that Richard would hire a handyman to change the light bulb in his entrance hall because he refused to get on a ladder.

'I think that is reasonable,' Rivera noted. 'Objection, Ms Moss?'

Having once had a client awaiting trial skip to Mexico for an evening (I haven't forgotten, Patrick!), I didn't see any harm in the proposal. I wanted Skinny to stay put in New Jersey for the duration, too. In fact, I'd be happy if she never left her apartment until her new lawyer had gotten her acquitted. Because judging from the look on her face right now, she wanted to get far, far away as quickly as she could. I'd save her defense team a ton of aggravation this way.

'No objections, Your Honor.' Stephanie looked annoyed. I considered how happy it would make Aunt Fern to spend some time with her daughter again and figured I had just alienated most of my family on my mother's side.

My father was in Canada and would not be flying in to smooth all the ruffled feathers. But I had a ticket to Los Angeles.

'One more request, Judge.' I tensed up because Richard likes to save his little bombshells in court for the last second. Something else I learned from him that I don't always use.

'Mr Chapman?' Rivera said.

'I'd like to request that the defendant be held in Ms Moss's custody, or at least under her supervision, until trial, to curb the possibility of flight.' Wow. I knew he was mad at me but I didn't know he was *that* mad.

'You think that's necessary?' Rivera, bless him, sounded skeptical.

'It's not, and it's also impossible, Your Honor,' I said. 'I am returning to my home in California in a matter of days and will not be representing Ms Silverstone at trial. I am here just for this proceeding and nothing more.'

Stephanie's jaw dropped open. I swear. After the fifty times I'd told her I was going to go home but that I'd find her a good lawyer.

'You don't intend to defend Ms Silverstone when her trial begins?' Rivera now sounded incredulous, wondering why the hell I had called him to convene a special pre-trial hearing for someone I was prepared to skip out on at the first possible opportunity.

'No, Your Honor. My practice is with Seaton, Taylor, Evans and Wentworth in Los Angeles.' The offices were much nicer than the ones in the prosecutor's office, too. Even Richard's.

'Your Honor.' Of all people, Stephanie stood up to address the judge. And I couldn't rush over to put my hand over her mouth just now. It would have looked unprofessional.

'Ms Silverstone, you have something to add for the court?'

'Yeah. Your Honor, can you make it so Sandy – Ms Moss – is required to be my lawyer? I've never been in a situation like this before and I really need to have someone I can trust. I don't know any other lawyers.' She looked as though she might tear up. Skinny had always been able to summon up fake tears when she needed them, but I had to allow that these might actually be real. It's so hard to tell with tears.

Rivera shook his head. 'I'm sorry, Ms Silverstone, but I can't compel someone to represent a defendant if they prefer not to take the case. But if you can't afford an attorney, we can certainly make arrangements—'

Now Stephanie looked downright offended. 'I can afford a lawyer,' she said with more of an edge than I believe she had intended. 'But I want Sandy.' Honestly. I should have put her on billboards on Sepulveda Boulevard to drum up business. If I got enough clients, I might make partner. If I'd wanted anything other than to be a family attorney.

'My apologies, Ms Silverstone.' The judge was apologizing to the woman accused of murder. 'But the courts are not set up to force an attorney to take a case against her will.'

'Doesn't seem fair,' Skinny muttered, but she sat down again. She glared at me. 'You just don't want to,' she said.

I was now officially ignoring everyone in the courtroom except the judge. 'As you see, Your Honor, this is a family matter for me and one best handled by someone less personally involved,' I told him. 'So I can't take responsibility for Ms Silverstone's whereabouts because I will be three thousand miles away.'

Rivera, ever to his credit a realist, nodded. 'It is ordered that the defendant must surrender her REAL ID and passport and may not leave the state of New Jersey for the duration of this matter without the expressed permission of this court.' He looked at Richard. 'Any further restrictions are not being set at this time but can be revisited if a need arises. Agreed, Mr Prosecutor?'

Richard admitted that he couldn't override a judge, no matter how much he wanted to, and we were back out on the street in a half hour after Stephanie, now not talking to me at all, filled out the requisite forms and was given the necessary paperwork in return. Every now and then, she would stare at me with accusations (unfounded ones) in her eyes. We got to the parking lot where Patrick's rental car, a plug-in convertible (naturally) was waiting, and I gestured toward my cousin to get in.

She turned her back and followed Aunt Fern back to her thirteen-year-old Corolla. Yup, she was pissed, all right.

I got in on the passenger side as Angie inserted herself into the back seat. Patrick started the engine and then waited, looking into his rearview mirror. 'Sandy,' he said.

I didn't even have the time to turn around and look before my sister Delia opened the back door on Patrick's side and sat down in the convertible. Angie, sitting next to her, looked stunned.

'Delia?' I said. I want to be clear that I was not questioning her identity. It was a request for clarification.

'I need to talk to you without Mom,' she said. 'Can you drop me off at her house? That's where my car is.'

Great. Not only did we now have to drive back to my mother's place, but we'd have her favorite undercover operative with us for the whole trip. 'Of course,' Patrick said. I couldn't blame him because I didn't have an alternate answer (like, 'Hell, no, take a cab'), but he didn't have to agree so quickly, I thought.

Patrick pulled out of the Paterson Street parking deck, where jurors park for the week they're required (or for the duration of the trial if they're unlucky and actually get empaneled) and out on to the streets of New Brunswick, heading for Mom's house.

'What did you want to talk about?' I asked Delia after a few long seconds. If she wasn't going to volunteer, I guessed I'd have to start the whole thing rolling myself. Patrick looked intently at the GPS despite his having driven here from the hotel, and Angie had suddenly become terribly interested in what was going on outside her window. Her neck would be stiff later from not having moved an inch the whole ride.

'Stephanie,' my sister said. 'I think she might have killed that guy.'

TEN

'Don't tell me,' I said. 'Tell the cops. Tell her lawyer. I'm not her lawyer.'

Delia did the thing where she just sort of lets a breath out of her throat and puts her hands up in front of her, which indicates that the person (usually me) talking to her is being unreasonable and should just do as they are told. 'Oh, you are so,' she said.

I waited. 'That's it? That was your argument? I should uproot my entire life that I've spent the past few years finally building for myself and move back here to defend our cousin, to whom I was never especially close, for months on end, possibly lose my job and my boyfriend . . .'

'No chance,' Patrick noted from the driver's seat. 'Tell her about the play.'

I was *not* going to tell her about the play. So I picked up just where I'd left off as if Patrick had not spoken. I'd make it up to him later. 'Just because you said, "Oh, you are so"?'

'Everyone wants you to defend her,' Delia said, as if explaining the simplest basics of the English alphabet. A is for Always, B is for Be, C is for Compliant . . . 'Mom wants you to, Aunt Fern wants you to, even Stephen wants you to. You're a defense attorney and you still have your New Jersey license. What is the problem?'

Well, everything I'd just told her, but that didn't seem to be getting through, so I said, 'I don't want to, especially if you really believe Skinny killed that Brandon guy.'

I was looking my sister directly in the eye to make sure she'd gotten my point. She blinked then shook her head as if waking herself up. 'Of course,' she said. Good. I'd gotten through to her. 'Skinny is Stephanie. I forgot you called her that.' So maybe I *hadn't* made that connection. 'But don't you see, the whole family is sure you're going to be her lawyer. You can't just fly back to Los Angeles and forget about that.'

Watch me. 'I will make absolutely certain that Stephanie' – and it took some effort to call her that – 'will have legal counsel in this case that I promise you – and the *entire family* – will be better than I would have been. But it's just not possible for me to stay here for all the months it will take for her to stand trial. I'll start making phone calls first thing in the morning.'

'It's Sunday,' Angie said, gaze still fixed on the roads she'd seen a thousand times before.

That wasn't helping. 'They'll answer my call,' I said.

Delia did, in fact, roll her eyes in what I'm sure she thought was frustration with my stubbornness. 'Fine,' she said. And that was it.

'Now tell me why,' I said after it was clear she'd said her piece.

'I told you why. The family—'

'No. Not why you want me to represent Stephanie. Why do you think she killed the best man at her sort-of wedding?'

'Because I know her story is bogus,' Delia answered. 'She was having a fling with Brandon. At least that's what she told me. Now, I wasn't in the kitchen with her when this happened—'

'No,' Angie said. 'But Stephen was, and Sarah Panico, and who knows who else?'

'Stephen?' That rather than all the rest seemed to upset Delia.

'Yeah,' I told her. 'I saw him go in after Stephanie, and then Sarah Panico later. We thought they were having a wild sub-party in there, to tell you the truth.'

Delia absorbed that information silently and then tapped me on the shoulder to get my attention because turning toward the back seat had finally gotten my neck stiff and I'd decided to sit straight and look through the windshield. I knew what Angie and Delia looked like, after all. 'I can hear you,' I said.

'I know you can but I need you to look at me,' she said.

My neck, in particular the right side, disagreed, but she was my sister and these circumstances were not typical. 'I was looking for Stephanie because Mom wanted to give her a gift,' she said. A lot of people would wait until the wedding itself or give a gift on the couple's online account, but then a lot of people – more than you might think – are not my mother. 'So I took a look in the kitchen because I couldn't find her in the main room. And none of those people were in there when I opened the door.'

'Who was?' I asked. Now I felt like I couldn't turn back to face ahead even though my right trapezius was begging me to do so. Poor trapezius.

'Stephanie and Brandon, the best man. And they were . . .' Delia's voice trailed off. I waited until it was either say something or relieve my trapezius.

Sorry for my neck, talking won. 'They were what?' Like she wouldn't have eventually finished the sentence anyway.

Delia looked away, which I felt gave me license to relieve my neck and look ahead. But after a prolonged moment, I heard her say, 'They were doing it.'

Now, it's a little sad when a grown woman says, 'doing it' to mean sex. I mean, she had two children and a medical degree so she clearly understood the procedure. But Delia has always been the good girl and wouldn't, as far as I knew, ever do anything that would cause my mother embarrassment, even when Mom wasn't there. Because our mother would sense it like Spider-Man.

On the other hand, the semantics seemed beside the point at this moment. Luckily, Angie was along for the ride (literally). She let a laugh that sounded like an air compressor spitting out emit from her lips. 'Skinny and the best man?' Even with Brandon Starkey dead and Stephanie accused of the crime, Angie could not help but find the circumstance amusing. This is one of the reasons I love Angie.

'You sure you saw right?' I asked Delia when I could keep a chuckle out of my voice. 'It couldn't have been the fiancé? What's his name?'

'Michael,' Patrick contributed from the driver's seat.

'Right.' Not sure why I felt it necessary to point out that he was correct, but it was interesting that he was the first one in the car to remember that name. 'Could it have been Michael?' I asked Delia.

'Not a chance,' she answered.

'No trunk,' Angie muttered.

'And they were having sex right there in the kitchen?' I mean, that had been what she'd said, but it seemed so improbable I figured it would be good to confirm the claim. Maybe 'doing it' meant they were filleting a salmon. I don't keep up with the slang.

'Right there on the prep table,' Delia said. We still hadn't ruled out the salmon thing. 'I mean, I only looked for a *second*, but it was pretty clear. I don't think I misinterpreted.' Well, once she put it like *that*, I was pretty sure she hadn't, either.

'So what makes you think she killed him?' I asked, in defense attorney mode. 'Did she bite his head off like a praying mantis?' I tried to picture that, but at the very least Stephanie would have had to unhinge her jaw and in all the years I'd known her she'd never exhibited that particular talent.

'Well, I didn't *watch*,' my sister said, a defensive air to her voice. 'As soon as I saw what was going on, I backed out and didn't look back inside again.'

'Not even after she came out looking like Lady Macbeth?' Angie asked. Angie once saw a version of *Macbeth*, the very play Patrick was thinking of kind of doing in the city (New Jerseyans call New York 'the city,' and we really only mean Manhattan), performed by one man, who voiced each of the characters in the play with a voice from *The Simpsons*. So she thinks she knows *Macbeth*.

I wasn't looking at Delia but I could almost hear her shudder. 'Especially not then,' she said.

'So how do you know she killed him?' Angie is relentless in a literal way. She will not stop until she gets the answer she wants.

'I don't *know*.' Delia's voice was showing the stress. 'But there she was with him, the day before she was supposed to marry another man, and then she comes out holding the knife while he's in the same room, you know . . .'

'Minced,' Angie suggested.

For some reason, Delia and Angie have never really meshed.

'All I'm saying is, he had a lot of leverage with her at that moment, and it wouldn't be the first time a physical affair ended in violence.' I did turn to look at Delia, trapezius be damned, and she looked brutalized. I mean, every hair was still in place (of course), but the pain and anger in her eyes alone were enough to convince me there was more going on than she was saying.

But she was my sister, and I did love her, even if we didn't like each other all the time.

'Did you talk to the prosecutor?' I said. 'He said witnesses told him Skinny was involved with the best man.'

'No, I didn't talk to the prosecutor,' Delia said, still with enough nerve to sound annoyed. 'Who do you think I am?'

'From the way you're talking, it sounds like you want to prosecute the case yourself.'

'I'm not trying to convict Stephanie,' Delia said, her focus back on her task, which she saw as getting me to do what she (and by extension my mother) wanted me to do. 'I'm trying to give you all the information you need to help her.'

'I'm going back to LA the day after tomorrow,' I told her with intent in my voice. Then I exhaled. 'I'll run the defense from there.'

ELEVEN

We flew out Monday morning, after a Sunday during which Patrick met with the producers of *The Scottish Play*, the script of which he'd shown me on Saturday night. I'd only read through about thirty pages before falling asleep, but that wasn't the play's fault. It was funny and smart and the part for Patrick was likely to show an audience sides of him they hadn't seen before. I could see why he wanted to do it. And I couldn't argue with that, or decide to stay and run Skinny's defense from the New York area. I had a job in Los Angeles that I wanted to keep after Stephanie's trial was over, and that meant I'd stay in LA.

But Patrick's months spent away in New York weren't a pleasant prospect, even if I was in the area periodically to deal with Stephanie's case. I was going to get a crash course in being the long-distance significant other of an actor who was in demand.

I wasn't sure I was going to like it.

The other thing that happened Sunday was that word got around my family and Skinny's wedding guests that I had agreed (under extreme duress, although that part might not have been circulated) to represent her in her case. My phone had rarely been quite so busy, even when I was defending two famous actors and a film director. There's fame and then there's your home town. Neither is necessarily desirable.

My mother had deigned to come to our hotel suite to confer on the case, despite not being asked to do so. She didn't express any gratitude for what I was doing, or even confidence that I could pull it off successfully, but she did suggest that I make sure to bring some more 'appropriate' clothing to wear in court when I returned for the next hearing, which was all about procedure and would take place in about four weeks. I was considering skipping it entirely and letting a local attorney handle it. But the idea that I might have some knowledge of what to wear in a courtroom after eleven years of practice had apparently eluded Mom.

I met briefly (again, in the hotel because the trip to Yankee Stadium had been canceled in favor of Patrick, Angie and me hightailing it out of town as quickly as possible under the guise of preparing for Stephanie's defense) with the defendant – Skinny – and her somewhat plantlike fiancé Michael, who had managed to pry himself away for this and not for her pre-trial hearing the night before, something he'd have to work hard to make up to me. What was going on between him and Stephanie was not something I cared to speculate about. Yet.

'What you have to understand is that you're going to be seeing me only when there's a court appearance scheduled,' I told them (mostly her). They were seated in two of the luxurious-but-corporate armchairs as I faced them from the somewhat more comfortable sofa. They had chosen the seating arrangements. Perhaps being on something that could be defined as a 'loveseat' might have been a little too ironic for the couple at this point. 'I'm calling a few much more local attorneys to act as my second chair on this case and you'll see them most of the time. I'll be on Zoom for the most part. Of course, you'll have approval over which of the New Jersey lawyers we choose, but you should probably take my advice because I know them all and have seen them in court. You haven't.'

Stephanie and Michael nodded dutifully, and at that moment I knew they'd be arguing with me about the second chair every step of the way. You get a sense of a client, and now my cousin Skinny had become my client. To say I wasn't looking forward to this experience would be a gross understatement, and there were scores of reasons that was true.

'Do you have any questions before we get started?' I asked. Because I had a *lot* of questions so it would be best to get theirs out of the way first.

'How much is this going to cost?' Michael asked. Not the first thing I'd have expected from the almost-husband of a woman accused of killing his best friend, but certainly a legitimate concern for most people.

'I'm not going to charge you my full fee, largely because I won't be here most of the time.' Best to emphasize that as much as possible. 'But my firm in Los Angeles will be budgeting me for things like investigators, the second chair and general expenses, and those I can't negotiate. It will not be cheap, I'm afraid.'

Michael sat back looking displeased. He no doubt had seen movies where lawyers waived their fees because the accused was so pure and innocent. He'd probably also seen movies where men could take on the qualities of spiders or dress in a bat suit and act as municipally condoned vigilantes, and he'd undoubtedly found those just as credible.

Stephanie read his face and looked equally unhappy. I was starting to see that she was watching him for all of her emotional cues. How she should feel seemed to be coming from Michael, which was weird, especially given that they were barely making eye contact otherwise. 'Why can't you stay here and run your other cases from your phone?' she asked.

Really? 'If for no other reason, because I have twenty-six open files on my desk right now in California and one here,'

I said. 'Also because Patrick and I are in the process of renovating the house we're going to live in and that will take a couple of months. And because that's where my life is now, Stephanie. Living here to see to your case just isn't practical for me, and with the help of a good New Jersey attorney, I'll be able to do just as strong a job as I could if I were here all the time.' That last part might not have been a hundred percent true, but then I'd never tried such a thing before, so how would I know?

'I would think I would be a higher priority,' Skinny said, pouting. It was the first of many times I almost resigned her case.

'Those are my terms,' I said finally. There was no point in losing my job over a case that someone who actually lived in Middlesex County – and I already had someone in mind – could handle better. 'Take them or leave them.'

Stephanie had the unmitigated gall to look surprised. Michael, tall, thick (in more ways than one) and not terribly animated, just sat there waiting for a new layer of bark to form on his body. I remained as impassive as I could because I knew I'd made my last offer, and if they didn't take it, I could fly home and keep living my California life. I'd check in on Skinny once in a while to see if she'd been convicted.

But she was not stupid and she knew exactly what position she was in right now. What she didn't appear to understand was that I might not be her best option in terms of a defense attorney. She clenched her jaw tightly but managed to squeeze 'I'll take it' out through her teeth.

'OK,' I said, because 'Good' would have been lying. 'I'll give you a list of three names before I leave tomorrow and you can choose which one you'd prefer.'

'Tomorrow?' Skinny's voice sounded hoarse. 'You're leaving tomorrow?'

'There's not much else I can do here right now,' I assured her. 'I'll make some phone calls to lawyers and see which ones are available to handle your case with me and then I'll give you that list.' *Available* here was a euphemism for *willing*, since a lot of the lawyers I knew would consider this case a sure loser and be, let's say, reluctant to get involved.

'I really wish you'd reconsider,' Stephanie said. She seemed to believe that I wasn't adequately grasping the seriousness of her situation. I believed, on the other hand, that I had a far better grasp of the gravity here than she did, but that I was handling it as well as someone could who lived an entire continent away from the courtroom.

'That's not an option, Stephanie.' I rarely called her 'Skinny' to her face anymore. That was something I kept for my own thoughts. Angie forgot sometimes and just used the names interchangeably, which caused Stephanie to cringe. 'Why don't you go ahead and start getting things as close to normal as you can? This is going to be a long process and you're going to have to get used to it. So am I.' I stood up to indicate that they should get out of my hotel suite as soon as possible because I was getting a stress headache, a possible indication that my mother was in the area.

But Stephanie and the large houseplant would not budge. 'How long a process?' Michael asked. He was probably concerned that this process might last until football season and he would be asked to give up his Giants tickets on occasion.

'At least six months and probably longer,' I said. 'Prepare for the long haul. Try to live your lives and only deal with the legal proceedings when I tell you it's necessary.'

Michael's eyes got harder and meaner. 'I have to go to my best friend's funeral on Wednesday,' he said. 'I'm not sure I can just go on living my regular life right now.' He didn't look at Stephanie when he said it, but you could be sure that his comment wasn't aimed at me.

Michael thought Stephanie had killed Brandon Starkey. Everyone I was talking to thought that Stephanie had killed Brandon Starkey. I hadn't polled Patrick and Angie yet, but I'm sure the sight of Skinny drenched in blood and carrying a kitchen knife couldn't have been a terrific selling point for her innocence. What would a jury of strangers think? Should I file for a change of venue?

Finally, Stephanie, her eyes glazed over, stood up and walked toward the door. She might have been thinking along the same lines as I was (other than the change of venue, which I doubted she would have considered at this point) because she kept glancing back at Michael as he followed her out, looking grumpy.

Just when she touched the doorknob, she stopped and looked at me. 'I was supposed to get married today,' she said.

TWELVE

P atrick had offered to charter a private jet for the trip home, but I was unaccustomed enough to first-class seats in a commercial jet that I felt anything more would have been obscenely bourgeois. It was uncomfortable enough when coach passengers trooped by after we'd already been seated and a flight attendant had taken our drink orders.

It's possible I wasn't born to travel in first class.

I wanted to sleep on the plane. I wish I could sleep on planes. Angie's butt hits the seat and she's out like a light, but she can always tell when we're close to landing and she wakes up refreshed. She says the vibration of the flight comforts her. I think being 35,000 feet in the air is anything but comforting.

So I watch movies or talk on flights, and since I didn't feel like dragging out my laptop (it would require me to start thinking about work), I rested my head on Patrick's shoulder. He was in his don't-notice-me mode, wearing dark sunglasses and a baseball cap (Dodgers, naturally) pulled down almost to his eyes. But he put his arm around me and stroked my upper arm. 'This isn't going to be easy on you, is it?' he asked.

I made an involuntary sound in my throat that sounded disturbingly like gargling. 'No. I'm going to have to fly back and forth a lot, and I'm not even sure I think my cousin isn't guilty of the crime, but no matter what happens, my family will blame me and that's just more than I was bargaining for when I sent back the RSVP card. Last week.'

Patrick looked slightly confused. 'Of course,' he said. 'It will be difficult for you that I won't be home as much.'

Well, yes, but that wasn't what I was talking about. 'Where does it stand with the play right now?' I asked. Might as well talk about his work. I had just resolved not to think about my own until I was home. In Los Angeles.

'Josh will hear the offer from the producers, and no matter what it is, if the company will pay my expenses while I'm in New York, I'll probably take it,' he answered. He was still using the soothing tone he had before, but it sounded weird talking business. Josh was his manager, Josh Moran of Moran Associates. Patrick could have moved to one of the humongous agencies when *Legality* happened, but he's loyal and Josh has been very helpful to him. They've become good friends who also work together.

How did I feel about him being away for months when I'd be commuting back and forth to work on Skinny's case? It wasn't my favorite idea, of course, but it meant that I'd be staying at the apartment Angie and I shared, because even when the ongoing renovations of our new (to us) house were completed, I definitely wasn't moving into that place by myself. I'd wait for Patrick to be ready to live there full-time.

'It's a good play,' I told him, although I still hadn't finished reading it. 'I think you'll be wonderful in it.'

'We'll see,' he said. Patrick's tone was a little guarded. 'Comedy is so difficult to pull off. I'll want to talk to the director once all the papers are signed. Everyone on board needs to be trying to do the same kind of comedy.' I'd never heard him speak about his work tentatively before; he had the confidence of ten men and they were all named Spike.

'You sure you want to do it?' I asked.

Patrick stiffened up in his seat. 'Do you think I shouldn't?'

'No. I just told you I think it's a good play and you'll be wonderful in it. Remember?'

He smiled and I felt his arm relax. 'I will miss you.'

'I know. I'll miss you too.'

Patrick squeezed my upper arm again and it felt like a snuggle. Then, perhaps to show that he was as supportive as they come, boyfriend-wise, he said, 'How difficult will it be to run a criminal defense from across the country?'

I probably let out a long breath; I honestly don't remember. But it feels like I should have. 'I'd rather be playing Macbeth in a comedy,' I said. 'And I can't act even a little bit.'

'Lady Macbeth,' he corrected me. 'What about a New Jersey attorney to help you? Certainly, it can't all be done from Los Angeles.'

He'd heard me suggest that very thing at least three times, and I had brought it up a few more when Patrick wasn't around. But the thing about Patrick is that he'll absorb information and ideas, which will coalesce into what he thinks was his own original notion. Actors, in case you hadn't heard, are not without ego. His warm heart counterweighs it well.

'I talked to a couple on the phone yesterday,' I told him. Patrick had been in New York with the theater people while I was working on the case. 'I think Jessica Berliner is my best bet and I think she'll do it. Jess is a sucker for an underdog story.'

I had, in fact, talked to Jess the day before. I knew her from my days as a prosecutor and she was one of the most conscientious defense attorneys I'd ever known. She'd defend people who she knew were guilty – all criminal defense lawyers do – but she always found a legitimate basis for the defense and never just phoned one in. When I'd told her about Skinny's predicament and was completely candid about it ('I'm not a hundred percent sure she didn't do it'), she was on board almost immediately. We'd just have to work out the details of our agreement and figure out Jess's fee for me to pass on to Stephanie. Maybe I could get Josh the manager to negotiate for me.

That's a joke.

'She'll do a good job?' Patrick asked, not having been privy to my chain of thought right then.

'She definitely will do all she can,' I said. 'I don't even know what can be done yet. I'll need an investigator in Jersey, too, because I'm not paying Nate Garrigan' – the investigator I'd worked with on all my California criminal trials – 'to fly back and forth for the next year or so.'

'You are a very good lawyer,' Patrick said. He was being careful. There was a time he couldn't resist telling me I was 'brilliant,' which I'm not. 'Very good' I could accept.

'And you are an excellent actor,' I told him in return.

'Well, then, what have we got to worry about?'

We sat that way for about an hour before Patrick's arm fell

asleep and by then we were heading for our 'final destination,' which seemed more ominous than usual. LA with a New Jersey homicide case pending in the distance. It was going to be a fun summer.

THIRTEEN

'How often will you have to take time off?' Holiday Wentworth asked.

Holly is my direct superior (that is, my boss) at Seaton, Taylor, and in terms of criminal matters, she had, to this point, left me almost entirely on my own, which was the way I wanted it. But now I was telling her that I needed some time in the future to travel back and forth to New Jersey to conduct a defense of a woman who, to the naked eye, looked a lot like someone who had stabbed a man multiple times in the chest after having sex with him in the kitchen of an Elks Lodge. Most bosses are not open-minded on matters like that, but this was Holly.

We were sitting in Holly's office, which was naturally a lot nicer than mine since she's a partner and I have . . . met all the partners. I think. At an office holiday party last year, maybe. She was sitting behind a blonde wood desk that had two computer monitors and her laptop on it. The view out the window did not include the HOLLYWOOD sign but did have a lovely view of the hills. We were on a high enough floor that you could choose not to look straight down and see the bustle of corporate employees and lawyers, although there still weren't as many milling around as there had been before the pandemic. Some people were still working at home.

'I can't be sure,' I answered. 'You know how trials go.'

'I know how family law trials and custody hearings go in Los Angeles County,' Holly said. 'I don't know how homicide trials go in New Jersey.' There was an unusual edge to her voice, as if my situation was more of an issue from her perspective than I might have expected.

'There'll be a preliminary hearing probably within the next month when the plea will be entered formally and the judge will set up a schedule for the trial,' I told her. 'I expect that the trial itself will take about two weeks and probably won't start for at least six months, maybe more. The courts shut down during the state's lockdown and never really caught up again, so everything's taking a little longer. I'll have my associate in New Jersey doing most of the statements, and I'll have an investigator I still need to hire out there for discovery and witness interviews. Probably the only one I'll have to attend is when the investigator interviews me.'

'How will it affect your workload here?' Holly asked. I felt suddenly like I was being interviewed for my job again, except that Holly had been more comforting the first time.

'I'm hoping it won't until I have to go back to be at the trial,' I said. 'But my client—'

'Your cousin,' Holly said.

Whoa. 'Yes. My cousin is, understandably, very shaken and wants me there as much as possible. I'm thinking the more I stay away, the more she'll get used to having Jessica there in my place and it won't be an issue.'

'Could you recuse yourself because you're a member of the defendant's family?' There was something Holly wasn't saying, and I couldn't figure out what it might be.

'I could try, but I've already promised virtually my entire family I'd do it, and the judge who held the pre-trial hearing didn't seem to have a problem with me handling the defense,' I said with a tone of suspicion I was trying to keep out of my voice not so much being kept out of my voice. 'Holly, is there some particular reason you don't want me to be involved with this?'

Holly let the air out of her lungs slowly, considering. 'Not right now,' she said.

'Not right now? What does that mean?' Usually, I could be informal with Holly because she was a relaxed boss, but this new dynamic between the two of us, which I couldn't understand, was giving me a queasy feeling.

She smiled what would under normal circumstances have

been a conspiratorial smile. 'I could tell you, but then I'd have to kill you,' she said.

That didn't sound promising. 'Well, then, don't tell me.'

Holly leaned forward in her chair. 'I'm not saying you shouldn't handle this case,' she said finally. 'But as a friend and as a lawyer who admires your work, I'd advise you not to let it take over your life. Don't let your workload here suffer any more than it absolutely has to. Keep the divorces and the criminal matters you have moving forward. I don't want as much as one client to complain that they can't get you on the phone or meet with you when they need to. OK?'

That had been my plan anyway. The fact was, no matter how close I was to Stephanie's case, I cared deeply about my job here at Seaton, Taylor and would do nothing to jeopardize it. It was just that I'd never seriously expected my job might really be jeopardized and now Holly was making it sound as if that were the case.

'Should I be worried?' I asked her.

That smile came back. 'You don't want me to have to kill you, right?'

Right.

Having gotten the message, I spent the rest of the day working on my three current divorce matters, a criminal charge of breaking and entering that had stemmed from one of those divorce cases, and the matter of a man stupid enough to have embezzled funds from his father-in-law's investment firm, a place in which accountants outnumbered normal people by a six-to-one ratio. I was negotiating a plea on that last one.

Once I was at home in the apartment with Angie, though, I could take advantage of the three-hour time difference and call Jessica Berliner at home. I knew Jess had a couple of kids but they weren't little, and if it was six in the evening in LA, it was nine at Jess's house. She'd already told me it was OK to call before ten.

'Do you have anyone in mind to do the investigating for us?' I asked. I'd worked with the county investigators when I was a prosecutor and most of them were still working in that job.

Better not to let the prosecutor, that low-down, rotten . . .
Richard . . . in on everything I was doing.

'I know someone,' Jess said. 'I've worked with her a couple
of times and she's not intimidated if the client seems almost
certainly guilty when you look at the circumstantial stuff.'
Subtle. But I knew how bad it looked for Skinny and I didn't
mind Jess acknowledging it.

'What's her name and what's her background?' I asked.

'It's Mae Tennyson,' she said. 'Do you know her?'

I searched my memory and came up with a time I had a really
good Reuben at a deli in Montclair. 'I don't think so,' I said. 'All
the investigators I knew worked for the prosecutor's office.'

'Mae's really good,' Jess answered. 'Everybody immediately
likes her, so witnesses open up as soon as she calls or drops
by. But she never misses anything and won't give up on a lead
until she finds what she needs.'

'If we can afford her, I'm fine with it,' I said. 'We're going
to need a copy of the police report and anything that comes out
of Richard Chapman's office. I'd like to have as little to do
with Chapman as possible, so if you can handle that, I'd
appreciate it.'

There was a momentary pause. 'Yeah, I sort of figured you'd
want to stay away from him,' Jess said.

Swell. She knew about my past with Richard. 'You heard?'
I asked.

'Yeah. Pretty much everybody has. But I hear your new
boyfriend is a movie star.' They say LA is a company town.
The problem is everybody thinks they're in the company no
matter where they live.

'Something like that,' I said. 'I'll have to be there when actual
court appearances are required, and for the trial itself, but I
imagine he'll send his nastiest deputy to oppose me in court.
We should be prepared for that.'

Another pause. 'I don't think that's going to be the case,
Sandy,' Jess said.

That sounded odd. 'You think he'll send someone easy to
this trial?'

'No. According to the paperwork I've seen, Chapman plans
to handle the case himself.'

What? So my vindictive ex-boyfriend, whose wife divorced him based on my telling her what had happened between us, the man who blamed me for losing half his money to his (now) ex-wife? *He* was coming to court to try to beat me and my cousin on a murder charge (and who knows what else he'd throw in the pot)?

If I hadn't been sitting down, I would have sat down. Maybe I should stand up so I could sit down. I felt beads of sweat on my forehead. 'Oh, boy,' I said reflexively.

'Yeah.' Jess knew exactly what I was thinking.

I had to get my head back in the game. 'OK. Make sure Mae gets started as soon as possible. Don't worry about the fee; I'll make sure it gets paid. Tell her to get in touch with me over any expenses that she thinks are too much and I'll tell her they're not. But there's one thing we have to do as soon as we're all working,' I said.

'What's that?'

I was going to tell her whether she'd said that or not, but I appreciated it. 'We have to make sure my cousin isn't guilty.'

FOURTEEN

'How long will you be away?' I asked Patrick.

Three weeks after we'd arrived home, Patrick was packing up to leave. This wouldn't be a long trip, I thought. *The Scottish Play* wouldn't be starting rehearsals for another two months, he'd said.

'Only about five days,' Patrick answered. 'Some of it, frankly, is stuff that could have been done from here, but I want to meet with the director again now that we're sure I'm going to play the role. It's a comedy, but I don't want the joke to be that I look ridiculous.'

'Fair enough.' I walked over and leaned toward the bed, where he was packing, to kiss him. 'I will miss you.'

'As I will you, love. But you're not rid of me that easily. I'll call at least once a day and will no doubt be texting you to the point of insanity. You know how I am when I'm on my own.'

I smiled. 'I'm not sure whether I'll miss you or Angie more,' I teased. As the management executive for Dunwoody Productions – a title that still hadn't been adequately defined for me *or* for Angie – she'd be required on this trip. That probably wouldn't be the case once the show opened and was running, but it would be for business meetings and possibly when Patrick went for weeks of rehearsals. It was going to be a lonely summer for me in Los Angeles.

Patrick held up his hands like he was being robbed in a western. 'Oh, Angie, of course,' he said.

I pulled him close to me. 'Don't bet on it,' I said.

Eventually, we let go of each other, if only because Patrick had a flight to catch in four hours, and when you're driving to LAX that means you leave in less than an hour. 'Do you want me to check in on your cousin or your sister?' Patrick asked. He knew better than to approach my mother alone.

'I don't think it would be a good idea to establish that as a pattern,' I told him. 'You're going to be in New York for quite some time. Don't make yourself a habit with my mom or Delia. But if you want to call on Stephanie and find out how she's holding up, you're welcome to do so. She won't open up to me because she can't get it through her head that I'm not the one prosecuting her. She keeps thinking I'm trying to catch her in a lie.'

Patrick zipped up his suitcase and placed it on the floor. Men can pack so easily it's infuriating to even watch them prepare to travel. But I bravely tamped down the urge to throttle him, because he was leaving and I loved him. 'Do you think she is lying about the murder?' he asked.

'That is an excellent question. I've seen the police report and it doesn't tell me much beyond what we saw. Whoever did kill Brandon was neater than you might imagine about it. Only Stephanie's footprints from the, you know, blood are on the floor.'

'That doesn't sound ideal,' Patrick said. 'What about finger-prints on the knife?'

I let out a small sigh. 'As you might imagine, Stephanie's prints are all over the handle,' I told him. 'That's not up for dispute. You and I and everyone else in that room saw her walking out of the kitchen with that knife – and yes, forensics confirmed it is the murder weapon, as if anyone would doubt it – in her right hand.'

I'd conducted a Zoom interview with my cousin, and she'd told me everything she told the cops. She went into the kitchen because Brandon texted her. He wanted her to run away with him instead of marrying Michael. She fled to the restroom and came out to find him stabbed. She'd tried to do CPR and failed miserably, and she didn't remember how the knife showed up in her hand.

In all, I'd had easier cases.

'The plot thickens,' Patrick said.

In the weeks since I'd returned to LA, I'd been in touch with Mae through Zoom, email and (mostly) texts. She was as advertised by Jessica: organized, thorough and indomitable. So far, though, all we'd gotten were the two incident reports (municipal and county) and the medical examiner's report, which offered the shocking information that Brandon Starkey had died of stab wounds, mostly to the chest, specifically to the heart and lungs. I knew that before the paramedics had arrived at the Elks Lodge.

To be honest, it felt weird to be preparing a case for trial and mostly letting other people do even the important work. I was in touch with the court from my California office but hadn't gotten a trial date yet. That wasn't unusual but it was annoying.

I had managed, so far, to avoid any contact with Richard, but I knew that winning streak wasn't going to last. The thought of dealing with him made my stomach clench, and what was even more infuriating was knowing that if he heard me say that, he would enjoy it. (Spoiler alert: He would never hear me say that.)

'If it gets any thicker, I'll need a food processor to handle it,' I said. I know nothing about cooking. That's something Patrick and Angie are much better at than I am.

He smiled a genuine smile – I've come to recognize the actor ones – and shook his head just a little. 'You're a breath of fresh air, you are.'

'So why not stay here and breathe instead of going all the way to New York? I don't remember if they have air there.' I was sounding so much like a clinging girlfriend I wanted to unfriend myself on Facebook.

'You know why,' he answered.

'Yes, I do. I'm sorry I said that.' I was even sorry I'd had to hear myself say it.

Patrick straightened himself up as his phone buzzed. He took a look and said, 'The car is here. I have to get going, I'm afraid.'

'Don't be afraid,' I said, and I got very close to him and kissed him the way I felt. I hoped it was encouraging at the very least.

He wasn't in the car for more than ten seconds when I got a text from Angie.

I'll keep him away from women.

Angie's heart was in the right place, but I knew Patrick and I knew that wasn't going to be a problem. I just wanted something to think about that didn't involve what looked for all the world like a losing case in which my cousin would be lucky to avoid a life sentence without parole.

There was no escaping it; I had to establish that someone else could have killed Brandon and I needed to interview witnesses, particularly a select few. Because Mae and Jess wouldn't know the cues and wouldn't know the coping mechanisms. They wouldn't be able to spot a lie under any circumstances. On our team, I was the only one who could do that, but I really didn't want to. So this was going to be extra difficult.

I was going to have to talk to my mother and my sister.

FIFTEEN

'It's the middle of the night,' my mother said.

The thing was, she wasn't completely wrong. I had called her at seven o'clock my time, meaning it was ten p.m. where she was, and where Patrick and Angie were heading. But the only thing to do was call Mom and interview her about what she knew that I could use in Stephanie's defense. I had thought that rationale would be persuasive enough to make her more eager to talk. I had, as often is the case regarding my mother, been wrong.

'Yes, I'm sorry about that, but it's three hours earlier here in LA,' I told her. Even when deluding myself, I knew that tactic wouldn't stand up very long.

'Why couldn't you call during the day?' Time zones meant little to a woman who taught me about sex by buying me a book and instructing me to read it. At age eight.

'Because I was working in my office on cases that don't take place in New Jersey,' I explained, even as I wondered why I was still trying. 'If it's a really bad time for you, we can do this another night.'

'Why can't it be during the day?' My mother is not stupid. She is impossible to get off a point.

I explained again that there was a three-hour difference between the coasts and that I had a full-time job in the one with the earlier time zone, but she didn't want to hear about it. As I had throughout my teenage years, I simply plowed ahead because I couldn't think of anything else to do. 'Did you know anything about Brandon Starkey before the rehearsal party?' I asked.

As I'd learned during high school, my mother has little defense against the direct approach. 'No, I didn't know him,' she said, pronouncing every consonant clearly. 'Why would I know the best man for your cousin's wedding? I don't think I'd ever even met the groom before.'

'You'd remember,' I suggested. 'He's not a riveting personality, but he does look a lot like a giant redwood.'

'I don't know what you mean.' Yes, she did. Trust me.

'It's not important,' I said. 'So you didn't know the best man and you hadn't met the groom. Had you heard about them?'

Before she could inform me that it *was so important* and that I should explain, Mom had been distracted by another bright shiny question. 'Of course, Aunt Fern told me about Michael,' she said. 'He works for a tech firm and he's very loyal to Stephanie.'

I waited, but that was it.

'Loyal? Are you describing a potential husband or a German shepherd?' It slipped out. I don't know what I was thinking.

'That's not funny, Sandra.' Wait. Now I knew what I'd been thinking, and it wasn't helpful. Enough of the wise-ass stuff.

'Is that all Aunt Fern told you?' Get the witness to elaborate whenever possible. Without attempting to, many will stumble across something useful.

Mom took a moment, no doubt to pause what she was watching on TV. She wasn't fooling me with the 'it's so late' argument. She was heavily into *NCIS* and didn't want to be interrupted. I'd gotten her to watch one episode of *Torn* once so she could see Patrick at work. But she didn't subscribe to the streaming service that offered it and so she watched only the one that she could get on a free trial. My mother has the divorce money and a pension from her years working at a financial firm but she won't spring seven dollars a month to watch her . . . daughter's boyfriend and a host of other entertainment options. She's not cheap. She's stubborn. Television means CBS.

Anyway, what she said was, 'I suppose so. I mean, we talk regularly about our children and grandchildren, you know, but Stephanie's wedding seemed to be happening so fast. You know, they only met a couple of months ago.'

That's what I mean by stumbling over something useful. 'Is that right? How did they meet?'

'One of those online dating things you do with your phone,' Mom said. I would have bet $1000 she knew the names of at least three just from watching Stephen Colbert at night but she was determined to be thought of as a doddering old lady so she could stun you with her up-to-date knowledge when it was strategically advantageous.

Look, I didn't become a trial lawyer by accident.

'Does Aunt Fern know more about Brandon Starkey?' I asked.

'Wouldn't it make more sense to ask your Aunt Fern about that?' She was itching to hit PLAY on the remote. And besides, she did have a point.

But even three hours earlier than where Mom was, I was too tired to try to take on Aunt Fern tonight.

'One more thing and I'll let you go,' I started.

'You don't have to release me,' my mother told me. 'You're my daughter.' That was in case I'd forgotten.

Barrel on through, Sandy. 'How well do you know Stephanie?' I said, just barely avoiding calling her by the nickname I'd given her.

'She's my niece.' I think that one had confused Mom. But maybe I was being strategically foolish.

'I'm well aware of that,' I assured her. 'But you can really know someone in your family or you can sort of be an acquaintance. Stephanie's the generation after you. You and Aunt Fern are very close, but from what I can remember growing up, Stephanie was kind of a special guest around our house. She didn't come for sleepovers or anything. I don't remember her coming to my birthday parties. I know about *my* relationship with her, but I don't know anything about yours, especially since I moved out here. How well do you know Stephanie?'

My apartment was looking lonely. It had never looked lonely before. (This was my *second* place in Los Angeles, the one Angie and I rented together. The first one had looked lonely for a little bit before Angie came out to save my life. It's a long story.) Maybe that was why I was calling my mother, because I'd never expected her to have any dynamite about Stephanie, Michael, Brandon or anyone else involved in this tragic fiasco.

'I know she had a drug problem when she was in high school and that she was in a rehab facility for three months about two years ago,' my mother said, with a tone that suggested I'd been challenging her somehow. And that was, to be fair, information I hadn't had before, largely because I hadn't paid much attention to Skinny from the time I was twelve until I had to fill out that last-minute RSVP card.

'I didn't know that,' I said. 'What was she addicted to?'

'Heroin. It was touch and go there for a while as to whether she'd survive, frankly. She was in the hospital for a week before she went to rehab.'

'And nobody thought it was a good idea to tell me about this?' I asked.

'Well, it's not the kind of thing the family wanted to get around.' There is this odd entity out there my mother calls 'The Family,' as if it were the Corleone bunch, that seems to have meetings to which I've never been invited or even gotten an email newsletter, but which makes decisions for all of us all the time. My hunch is that it is comprised of Mom and Aunt Fern.

'That's not the point,' I said while the top of my head threatened to blow off. 'Why didn't anybody tell me about it *now*?'

I could hear her looking surprised. 'I just did.'

There was no point. 'OK, I'm going to need the name of the rehab facility and the dates when Stephanie was there,' I said. 'Should I ask her or Aunt Fern for that information, or do you have it in your database right there?' OK, so that last part was snarky.

'I don't think that's the kind of thing that should get out in a courtroom.' Mom sounded downright matronly, like she was going to offer me a sweet tea and fan herself with, you know, a fan.

'It really doesn't matter whether we think it should be public; it's going to be public,' I said. 'The prosecutor will exploit it to the most extreme extent, and I need to have a plan to defend Stephanie against what he'll say. So I'm asking again: Who do I ask about this information?'

She practically sniffed in disgust at my insolence. 'I don't know. I suppose Stephanie should know you're going to bring it up at her trial, so ask her. Now I'm sorry, Sandra, but I need to get to bed.' And fifteen seconds later, she hung up.

Bed. *NCIS*.

SIXTEEN

Patrick and Angie arrived in New York at ten forty-seven p.m. and Angie was texting me at ten forty-nine. Patrick took all the way until ten fifty-five. He doesn't believe you've arrived until the plane stops taxiing and parks at a gate.

The fact that where I was living (and where they lived most of the time) it was almost two in the morning didn't seem to be a serious factor for either of them. Luckily, I turn the buzzer off on my phone at eleven.

I could have called them when I got out of bed at seven, but that would have been cruel. I just texted back.

The whole Stephanie thing was going to have to wait. I certainly wasn't going to call *her* at four in the morning, and I had a day of actual work to do. (I should note that Skinny's case was indeed actual law work, but I was thinking of it as something of a sideline because it was so far away and a number of months from needing my full attention. So don't think I'm being flip, even though I probably am.) I got showered and dressed after a short morning run because it was Los Angeles in the summer and a long morning run would have required medical transport home. I settled in at my office after the drive there – the only one I can actually navigate without a GPS but I used it anyway – put my head down and got through files at a record pace. There wasn't much of an unusual nature in my workload right then.

Once I'd waded hip-deep into the pile on my desk, it was after noon and Jon Irvin appeared in my doorway. 'Lunch?' Jon and I have lunch on days when Holly and I aren't having lunch, which is most of the time.

I'll spare you the mechanics of the conversation and tell you we were at what passes in Los Angeles for a Jewish deli about twenty minutes later, my ordering half a pastrami sandwich on 'rye' bread and Jon an omelet because he's Jon.

By leaving for lunch together, Jon and I had left the criminal law division at Seaton, Taylor completely unmanned (or unwomanned). We weren't generating enough business to hire another associate to handle criminal cases and, frankly, we weren't trying that hard. Jon likes the drama of a criminal case, and I was sort of cornered into heading the division after winning Patrick's murder case because nobody thought I could do that. Once they found out I could, there was suddenly a new division at the firm.

'You're dying to tell me about this case back in New Jersey, aren't you?' he asked as soon as the waiter (who claimed his name was Moe, but who should have just been honest and said it was Mohammed because then we'd know what to call him) took our menus and walked away. 'So what's it about?'

'What makes you think I'm dying to talk about it?' I said. 'I don't want to talk about it.'

'Yes, you do,' Jon said. He's gotten to know me pretty well over the past couple of years. 'It's burning a hole in your mouth.'

'That was always there. It's how I eat.'

'Spill, Sandy.' He took a very leisurely sip of water and put it down on the paper tablecloth. (Tablepaper? I was in a weird mood today.)

'No, I'm interested. How can you tell when I want to discuss a case?' I could match him sip for sip.

Jon smiled. 'When I mentioned it, the right side of your mouth twitched. You didn't exactly wink but your right eye closed a tiny bit. That's not what you look like when something bothers you. It's what you do when you want to tell me something. Like when you told me about them making a criminal law division just for us and putting you in charge.'

'Does it bother you that I'm in charge?'

'*No!* Now tell me about the case in New Jersey.'

So I did. Jon clearly had gotten *some* background, mostly from the news reports he must have found online, but he knew better than to believe the stupid ones that claimed Skinny had killed Brandon after seducing him and eating his heart. Jon asked intelligent questions and listened to my answers carefully.

Jon is a good listener and didn't even blink when I told him about the scene in the Elks Lodge, particularly Stephanie's spectacular entrance from the kitchen. To him, it was part of the case. To me, it was an image I could never unsee.

'OK,' he said when I was finished stating the extremely limited facts as I knew them. 'Knowing you and knowing how much you relish dealing with your family, I'm going to assume that you have not yet interviewed your cousin other than when she was being held and charged. Am I right so far?'

Luckily, that was when the pastrami sandwich arrived so I didn't have to make eye contact with Jon. I spent some time applying mustard while saying, 'I did but she didn't tell me anything useful.' I looked away. I am a walking cliché.

'I'm not challenging you, Sandy,' Jon said. 'You have your process and it works well for you. And it's always more difficult when the client is someone you know, let alone a member of your family. But have you asked your New Jersey associate to talk to her yet?'

The pastrami was great. The rye bread . . . this was California. I shook my head. 'I can't ask Jessica to talk to Skinny,' I said. 'My family's already on top of me because I'm not there running the case. I can't let it look like I'm passing her along to an assistant.' Mentally, I apologized to Jess for using that word, however much it was meant as a problem of appearance and not a real thing.

My phone buzzed with a text from Angie, who, it appeared, was always going to contact me before Patrick did. *Hotel is amazing. Bidet!* It was accompanied by a picture of the appliance in question, in case I didn't know what a bidet looked like. I send back a quizzical-looking emoji and looked at Jon.

'You have to be able to separate the merits of your case from the expectations of your family,' Jon said.

'What's your advice, then? Because I don't know how to do that.'

Jon raised an eyebrow like Mr Spock, whom he resembles temperamentally, except Jon has a sly sense of humor. 'I would have advised you not to take the case.'

I made a gravelly sound in my throat, and it wasn't because of the rye. 'Believe me, I tried,' I told him.

'OK. That ship has sailed. So going forward, if it were me, I'd do the visible stuff. Contact your cousin and set up a Zoom meeting with a lot of time in it to talk about her case. Get a moment-by-moment statement of what she says happened that day. Of course, record it. Don't give it to the prosecutor.'

I know it *sounded* as if I burped but that's just the noise I make when I am forced to think about Richard. 'There's something I need to tell you about the prosecutor,' I told Jon. And then I told him *that* whole insanity. Jon, bless him, did not look at me as if I must be a major-league nut case, which was surely what he had to be thinking.

He let out a long breath. Luckily, it wasn't an onion omelet. It was a small table. 'Well. That's a thing.'

'That's one way of putting it,' I admitted.

'And I take it this guy is making it something of a personal vendetta against you to not only convict your cousin but to make it as painful as possible every step of the way.'

'That's all true except the "something of,"' I said.

'It's not good, Sandy.' Jon must have been the captain of his high school Stating the Obvious team. 'But your inclination is going to be to avoid this guy and you can't. He's the opposition in a trial you need to win. You have to work against your own nature and charge right at him with everything you've got.'

'That's the problem,' I said. 'I haven't got very much.'

'Talk to your cousin.'

The phone buzzed again and invariably it was going to be Patrick. Except it wasn't.

It was a text from Richard Chapman, whose ears (or thumbs, since he texted) must have been burning from 3,000 miles away.

Plea will be entered in court this Thursday.

Today was Monday. I *could* ask Jessica Berliner to handle it. I probably *should* ask Jess to do it. That would be the practical thing.

'Let's finish as soon as we can,' I said to Jon. 'When we get back to the office, I need to make airline reservations.'

SEVENTEEN

Air travel is never going to appeal to me. Maybe in the 1960s, when people dressed up to get on a plane, when food was free and entertainment was, well, a book, I might have found something enjoyable about it. Now it's like going to a processing station in the hope of quickly being stuck at the DMV for six hours on the way to another processing station that will send you to a car that will eventually take you to a place you might want to be. At least Disney has added 'pre-shows' to its lines that attempt to make the waiting less excruciating. The airlines will do that for you, but they charge you extra.

It doesn't matter what time of year I travel, I exit a plane feeling as if I need a shower. And this was summer. New Jersey isn't famous for its humidity, but not for lack of trying, so as soon as I got to Patrick's suite in Manhattan and found him out at a meeting about *The Scottish Play*, I made a beeline for the luxurious bathroom and washed everything on me that I could get my hands on. The jet lag would kick in later, but right now I was ready to attack Stephanie's case and prepare for tomorrow's hearing.

First I called Jessica and told her I'd arrived. 'Glad you called,' she said. 'The hearing is simple enough – you know that – but I want to make sure there are no bumps in the road.'

'I don't expect any,' I told her. 'But I want to make sure you know that I need to talk to Stephanie myself, and I probably need to have a meeting with Chapman, too. That's not a reflection on anything you're doing; it's for me.'

Jess and I had met only once on a case where I was the prosecutor, so it had been a few years ago. Even so, I could practically hear the smile on her face. 'Don't worry about my ego, Sandy,' she said. 'I have two children. They're capable of much worse than anything you could dream up.'

So I could talk to Jessica *or* my sister about why it wasn't good to have children. Awesome. 'Thanks for understanding. I assume there's nothing to the hearing other than to register a plea of not guilty and make sure the judge continues the pre-trial finding,' I said.

'Pretty much. I'm sure Chapman is going to try some trick to get Stephanie put in jail until the trial just because he's mean, but I can't imagine anything that would work on that count.'

I agreed, but I felt it was necessary to fill Jess in on Skinny's fight with addiction and her stint in rehab. 'He might want to use that if he's found out about it.' I was sure my mother's Spidey-sense was tingling even as I spilled the beans, but there was no alternative.

She was clearly taking notes, maybe on a tablet. 'Clearly, although I don't see how that makes her more of a danger to anyone or a flight risk. She's been sober for two years.'

'Richard will find a way,' I said. 'It'll be unreasonable but it won't sound unreasonable.'

Jess took a moment. 'Got ya,' she said. 'I'll have something to counter before the hearing.'

I thanked her and hung up just in time to hear my phone ring and see that the caller was 'Office of the County Prosecutor.' Probably a confirmation of some sort that would be unusual but not unheard of. I picked it up and regretted it immediately.

'Counselor.' Richard's voice can, I can attest, sound charming and warm. At this moment, it was like getting ice poured down your pants. 'I'm calling about your murder case.'

'No kidding. I didn't think you wanted me to come along for a game of snooker. What is it, Richard?'

There have been people more smug than Richard in history, but most of them died of smugness and the others star in caper movies. I always watch those things and consider how I'd prosecute our 'heroes' and send them away for decades. I suppose these days I should be working up a strong defense in my head, but I can't get past the whole idea that the good guys are the ones committing a crime.

He ignored my snooker comment, for which I did not blame him. It wasn't my A material. 'I'm calling to suggest in a friendly way that you consider entering a plea of guilty tomorrow,' he said. 'We could possibly reduce the charge to manslaughter and shorten the sentence to, say, fifteen years?'

'Say "no years" and it'll be more attractive but we'll still say no,' I said. Imagine the nerve of the man trying to make me recommend a plea bargain to my own cousin, especially one as feeble as that! 'Stephanie Silverstone did not kill Brandon Starkey and therefore will not plead guilty to anything tomorrow. But thanks for the call and please do sleep badly tonight.'

I was about to hang up, but Richard cut in. 'You really should confer with your client first.'

'Should I? The fact that you're calling me today to offer a deal indicates that you know you have nothing and you don't want to go to court and lose. You want me to recommend a fifteen-year prison sentence to my own cousin? Shove your deal, Richard, and make sure it goes up really far so nobody will ever see it again.'

He was trying to interject again, but this time I disconnected quickly enough to ignore him.

But just on an ethical basis, I did need to report the offer to my client, so I went to the suite's refrigerator and got out a Toblerone, the candy nobody eats anywhere but in hotel suites because that means someone else is generally paying the ridiculously inflated price. I sat down and ate one and then gathered my strength and picked up my phone again to call Skinny.

Oddly, she was texting me even before I could hit a button on the screen.

DA says they're offering a deal and you turned it down.

I refrained from informing her that in New Jersey we don't have district attorneys but county prosecutors, or that it was wildly unethical for him to get in touch with her without me at least present on the call. I'd deal with that in a letter to the bar association and the county commissioners, who I sincerely hoped would pass it on to the governor of the state of New Jersey and have Richard fired.

Instead, I decided I'd call instead of texting back, and Stephanie picked up on the first ring. 'Did you turn down the offer?' she said before I could say hello and ask how her mother was holding up.

'Yes. It was a bad deal and the fact that he offered it is a sign he thinks we'll win at trial.' See what a good lawyer I am for you?

'Stop, Sandy,' Stephanie said. There was a very strange quality to her voice that worried me. Had she fallen off the wagon? That would be extremely bad for our case. 'I want you to take the deal.'

EIGHTEEN

Clients can be flighty. That's to be understood and expected. Sometimes, as with Skinny, they're facing trouble the like of which they've never seen before. That leads to justifiable fear, and fear leads to rash decisions. She probably thought Richard was offering her a lifeboat when he was really throwing her an anchor.

On the other hand, I had recently dealt with a client who had decided he was guilty of the crime (which was false) while in prison for the crime. Don't even ask; I did it for his daughter.

'What are you telling me?' I asked my cousin. 'You want to plead guilty? Wait. I'm coming over.'

'Sandy . . .' But she didn't add anything after that, and I was already texting Patrick to say I was going to Jersey and I'd see him the instant I could.

I hadn't rented a car for the trip because I was going to be staying in Manhattan and the bus from New York to Westfield is impossible and time-consuming. I could have taken a New Jersey Transit train and changed to another line somewhere in the middle, but if you've ever done that, you're already laughing at the very suggestion, so I took into account my salary, the fee for Stephanie's defense (to which I would definitely charge the trip) and Patrick's last paycheck from *Torn* and simply app-ed myself a Lyft, which was in front of the hotel in ten minutes.

It wasn't rush hour and New York/New Jersey traffic is bad, but I was now used to Los Angeles so this was nothing. I was knocking on Skinny's door in less than an hour, which is how long it takes to get from LA to, say, Santa Monica.

For those of you who don't want to consult an atlas, that second trip should be a lot shorter in duration and it's not. Just take my word for it.

Stephanie was dressed in cutoff jeans and a tank top when I arrived, leading me to believe that she thought the 1980s had returned and she was living on a farm. Her speech was not slurred and her gait was steady, but then I haven't had a ton of experience with people on heroin so I wouldn't know what to look for. She let me in but clearly wasn't happy about it; the first thing she said was 'We could have done this on the phone.'

'I wanted you to look me directly in the eye and tell me why you want to take a bad deal that would send you to prison for fifteen years,' I said in my sternest lawyer tone. 'When you were charged, you practically had a nervous breakdown at the prospect of two nights in county lockup and I moved heaven and earth to keep you from having to do that. Now I flew three thousand miles across the country just to enter a plea for you and you're saying I could have just filed some papers from my comfy office in California and that would have done the trick. Your mother will never forgive me – not you – and my mother will likely disown me. I want to know why all that's true. So you look me in the eye and you tell me. What changed your mind, Skinny?'

She hates when I call her that and I knew it. I keep it in my back pocket for special occasions and this was the most special yet. She knew I was irritated and she knew that I meant business.

Good.

'My name is Stephanie.' But already the fire in her eye was dimming. I was having the effect I wanted. This was not the time to let up on the gas pedal.

'And mine is Sandra Moss, esquire,' I said. 'Do you actually need my services, or do you just want someone to do what you say without questioning your completely unexplainable motives? Why. Did. You. Change. Your. Mind?'

'Because I could get life in prison if I don't take the deal,' she said. Tears were already falling. 'Because maybe fifteen years isn't so bad. The DA said I might get out in three or four if I behave, and I'm gonna behave, Sandy, believe me.'

She was staring down at the floor, so I walked over to her, took her face in my hands and tilted it up until she was looking into my eyes. 'Stephanie,' I said, establishing that we were back on friendly terms. 'The county prosecutor is a liar. He tells people anything he thinks they want to hear to get what he wants. He pretends to care but trust me, all he cares about is putting you in jail for as long as he can. He cheats on his wife. Don't question that. I know it for a fact. And he is *not* on your side. He wants you in jail and he wants to beat *me* in court. Believe absolutely nothing he tells you. Believe Jessica, believe Mae, believe me. Those are the only people whose advice you accept. Understand?'

Her eyes, still tearing, were so squinted that I could barely tell if they were open at all, but she seemed to be capable of seeing me (which was good because I was all of two feet away). She sniffed several times. Then, very slowly, she nodded. 'OK,' she managed to choke out.

I held my client close, something I'd never done before (OK, so I've held Patrick close many times but never when he was my client). I patted her back. It's possible I even stroked her hair for a short time.

'I'm going to win this case for you,' I said. 'I'm going to keep you out of jail.'

And immediately I began wondering why I would say something that ludicrous.

Back in the hotel suite in time to meet my boyfriend (thanks to Lyft), I was holding Patrick as close to me as I could as if he had been away for weeks. It had been two days. I was fighting the urge to become the clingy, needy girlfriend I had always sworn I would not be. So far, I thought, I was holding my own. I would not define myself based on the man in my life. The problem was, the job I was trying to do was making me feel inadequate and Patrick was not, so I was focusing on him.

Maybe it was the reality of Skinny's case setting in and the absurd promise I'd made her, but I was stressed out as I'd never been on a case before. And if you know me, you're aware that's saying a lot. My stomach was never not clenched. My hands, while not shaking, were clumsy; I was dropping things like pens and credit cards (not to worry, I always picked them up immediately).

'You're in a cast with beautiful women,' I said.

'I'm always in a cast with beautiful women,' Patrick told me. 'It's a hazard of the profession.'

'I know,' I told him. 'I honestly *don't* think you're going to dump me for a beautiful actress. You could have done that seventeen times since we got together. And the fact is, I actually do trust you. I just don't believe I'm necessarily in your class.' Years of thinking like a sixth grader were coming home to roost.

Patrick's smile on the other pillow was warm and a little incredulous. 'You, Sandra Moss, are so far above my class that it's hard for me to see you from here.' Then he kissed me and everything was all right except Skinny's case.

'That's not true,' I said when we came up for air. 'You're a great big movie star and I'm a divorce lawyer.'

'You are Sandra Moss and I'm Patrick Dunwoody,' he countered. 'And if you're asking my opinion, I don't think we should compete.'

So we didn't. We did other things until it was time for me

to call Mae Tennyson, something I'd set up even before I'd left for LAX.

I was freshly but casually dressed from the waist up, which is all you need on Zoom, and Mae, I assumed, was the same. It was a hot day, even in an air-conditioned suite. But hey, it's a wet heat.

'I've got something on the knife,' Mae said as soon as the inevitable pleasantries were out of the way. 'It appears that it was not from the Elks kitchen. I checked with the person in charge of their catering business. It was not in his inventory.'

OK, that was weird. 'So someone brought it in from outside?' I asked. That was the only logical explanation, but it was hard to figure how that could have worked.

'That's the only way it makes any sense, but it doesn't make sense,' Mae said. 'That was not a small knife. You'd think it would have been seen on the way in.'

'Is there any evidence other than fingerprints that ties Stephanie to the knife?'

Mae looked at me a moment as if I'd suggested that an elephant had just flown into the room. 'It's not like knives are registered,' she said. 'But I am checking on the manufacturer and model and maybe I can trace it back to the place it was purchased.'

'Any way we can get credit card records if you do?' It was a long shot and only a bit questionable ethically.

'I'll let you know,' she said. Mae didn't know me well. She wasn't ready to discuss any even slightly shady practices just yet. And that was good for me. It's not that credit card information isn't sensitive, because it is. But if the cops can get it, we should be able to get it, and somehow I wasn't comfortable trusting Richard to share. I know; I'm paranoid. But he was a real Richard.

'You know, the prosecutor offered Stephanie a plea deal,' I told her, then elaborated on the intrigue with Richard that I'd just barely managed to quell.

'Wow,' Mae said. 'He must really think he has a weak case.'

'Does he?' I said.

'Well, she walked out of the kitchen covered in blood and

carrying the murder weapon,' she said. 'That ain't nothing, especially when a jury gets a hold of it.'

She wasn't wrong. 'But it's all he has,' I suggested. 'He doesn't have anything strong on motive and he doesn't have anything that indicates premeditation.'

Mae thought about that and nodded in a sort of noncommittal way. Mae wasn't the type who gave anything away, emotionally or practically. 'Unless he figures out how she got the knife into the building without being seen. It's not as easy as it sounds.'

It wasn't? 'I just figured the person could carry it in a bag or hide it in their clothes,' I said. 'What am I missing?'

'It was a very sharp knife,' Mae said. 'Probably had been sharpened or purchased that morning. So carrying it in under your clothes would be dangerous at best. As for a bag, it's possible, but it would at the very least have to be a canvas bag and more likely something like a case. The kind of thing a chef might have.'

I was sifting the information as it came in. 'OK, that's helpful,' I said. 'It narrows things down and gives us something to look for, all of which is good.'

'You're discounting the possibility that our client did kill the guy,' she told me.

'It doesn't help me to think that way. If she did it, my job would be to cast doubt. It's better if I have the doubt myself.'

Mae took that in, and although her expression indicated she didn't completely grasp the concept, she nodded, acknowledging that I was a lawyer and she wasn't. I like to extend the same courtesy to the people I work with, like, for example, investigators, because they have an area of professional expertise that I lack.

'I think I should check into this ex-girlfriend of the victim, Lucia D'Alessandro,' she said.

'You already know more than I do,' I told her. 'I didn't have a last name for her.'

'It's amazing what you can learn when you talk to people,' Mae said without irony. 'This Lucia and our old friend Brandon were quite the couple there for a little over a year. Then one day, according to their friends and Brandon's mom, Lucia just ups and leaves him without explanation. Brandon was devastated, they said.'

'So devastated he was going at it with Stephanie on a prep table in the Elks kitchen on the day of her wedding rehearsal?'

There was a moment of hesitation on Mae's end of the call. 'So far, your sister is the only person who has any direct knowledge of that.'

Uh-oh. My voice sounded dry, as if I had just drained it. 'The only one?' It wasn't great conversation and it certainly wasn't terrific legal work. It was a placeholder until I could manage to process what I'd just heard.

'Yeah, and the medical examiner's report doesn't offer any evidence that the victim had just . . . completed any sexual activity before he died,' Mae said.

Uh-oh twice. 'Why would Delia lie about that?' I asked myself, except that Mae could hear me. Patrick, lying on the sofa in the suite and reading (again) the script of *The Scottish Play*, looked up, not so much alarmed as intrigued.

'Should I ask her or do you want to?' Mae asked.

'I think maybe I'd better.' Now my voice sounded like I'd just sandpapered it. 'But I don't *want* to.'

NINETEEN

I'd like to state right off the top that it had *not* been my idea for Patrick and me to go out to dinner in New Brunswick with Angie, Mom and Delia the night before Stephanie's plea hearing. Patrick had asked Angie to arrange it once he'd heard I was flying in on the red-eye that morning. I'm sure it seemed like a good idea to Patrick, to help ingratiate him with my mother and sister, but Angie of all people should have known better.

Still, she is the management executive for his production company, and since nobody had figured out what that meant yet, Angie was still functioning essentially as his primary assistant, just at twice the salary she'd had before. There are worse compromises. But it meant that when Patrick asked her to do something, she generally did it without argument.

I thought it was slightly suspicious because there's nothing Angie likes better than a good argument.

We went to Catherine Lombardi, a wildly upscale Italian restaurant in a state full of less upscale Italian restaurants, and I was having lasagna because we weren't in LA right now, and to hell with the calories. It was delicious, for the record, but my appetite while contemplating asking my sister why she might be lying about what she saw just before Stephanie had presented herself as a walking tableau from *The Masque of the Red Death* was, let's say, not up to its usual standards.

'So this play is *Macbeth* and you are *not* playing Macbeth? Is there a bigger star in that role?' my mother asked Patrick, because she and tact are not on speaking terms.

Angie's eyes opened to the size of hubcaps, but Patrick merely wiped a little of his chicken scarpariello off his chin with a red napkin. 'It's not actually *Macbeth*,' he said. 'It's a comical take on the original play and I am, in fact, playing *Lady* Macbeth, in another form, of course.'

My mother's eyes narrowed as if Patrick were very far away. 'You'll be in a dress?' she asked.

'That's still under negotiation,' Patrick answered. He looked at me with amusement in his eye. There had never been so much as a suggestion that Patrick play the part of Laddie, the revised Mrs Macbeth, in drag. He was just having fun with Mom, something no one had done in fifteen years.

'It all sounds pretty weird,' she said, shaking her head in bewilderment.

I chose that moment to shift the conversation toward Delia, which was not something that normally required doing by anyone other than Delia. But the fact that she'd been invited to dinner and that the invitation had included her husband and children made it curious that they were not here, especially given that Patrick was picking up the exorbitant check. 'Is everybody OK at home?' I asked her.

You know when people say you've been 'given the side-eye'? Delia literally looked at me through the side of her eye. The right side, if you're keeping score at home. Angie, on the other hand, looked surprised, and I hadn't surprised Angie since the eleventh grade.

'Yes,' Delia said carefully. 'Why do you ask?'

'I just thought, you know, given that they could have come and had dinner with us . . .' My voice just sort of trailed off. I had given up that whole convention of speaking in complete sentences just from seeing the expression on my sister's face.

'I thought it would be nice to be just adults only in a place like this,' she said, sweeping her hand because we might have now thought we were at a Burger King and she needed to remind us we were not. 'And since it was short notice, we couldn't find a sitter in time.'

'I'm usually the sitter,' my mother said. Because she had decided she was a wonderful grandmother and an even more helpful parent. You didn't see my *father* coming to watch Delia's kids for an evening, although the commute from Saskatoon would have been extravagant. (Divorces never really end.)

'And the children love you,' Delia assured her, patting her hand. It was all I could do to keep from shaking my head. Mom wasn't *that* old.

The trick here was to avoid looking like I was questioning Delia about saying she'd seen Stephanie and the best man Brandon 'doing it' right before Stephanie came out of the kitchen and Brandon, you know, didn't. That *was* what I was going to be doing, of course, but I knew Delia, and if she felt like I was somehow accusing her of . . . anything . . . she'd get defensive and my ability to glean any information from her for my case would be permanently shut off. Delia could be the co-captain of the Olympic grudge-holding team. My mother would be the captain emeritus.

Luckily, there is Angie. I'd spoken to her on the way to the restaurant and mentioned just in passing what Mae had told me about Delia being the only witness to the supposed tryst. That had been all I'd needed to do.

'So, Delia,' she started, 'did you really see Stephanie and Brandon going at it in the Elks kitchen? I mean, holy god, right?' Angie once passed subtlety in the street, but I don't think they even nodded at each other.

My mother winced because anything even remotely

referencing sex is kryptonite for her. How she managed to have two daughters is probably something that could be written up in the *New England Journal of Medicine.* I've never asked, and I never will. She tried to gasp but couldn't quite manage it, so she put her hand to her mouth and it looked like she was yawning. She'd never betray a true feeling in front of strangers, and to her, Patrick was still a stranger.

Delia, the center of the issue at this moment, looked more irritated than anything else. She stole a glance at my mother to see if she needed any smelling salts (which I would have bet money Delia carried on her person) and then regarded Angie with an expression that was only slightly less poisonous than the one she undoubtedly would have used on me.

'I just glanced in, and when I saw what was going on, I looked away,' she said. 'It's not something I enjoyed seeing, believe me.'

'I'm just asking because you're the only one who saw it.' Never let it be said Angie didn't plow right on ahead whenever she was given the chance, and sometimes when she wasn't. 'I mean, the cops talked to everybody and no one else mentioned that.'

'I can't speak for anyone else,' Delia said with an edge in her voice she could have used to cut the veal scallopini on her plate. 'I didn't see anyone else in the kitchen, but then I really only looked for half a second. I'm not sure I saw everything.'

Patrick, who never doesn't want to help, joined in and, skilled actor that he is, made it sound like a normal casual conversation. 'So it's possible there was someone else in the kitchen when you popped in, then?'

'Yes, Patrick. It's possible.' Delia looked from one side of the restaurant to the other, no doubt noting that some of the other patrons were stealing glances at our table to see if that really was the famous TV actor having dinner. But this being Catherine Lombardi, they were way too classy a bunch to approach and ask for a selfie. Until we were outside the restaurant, I was sure. A few were very surreptitiously holding their phones up to take video and others were texting their relatives or friends about who they saw at the place in New Brunswick. ('Can you believe it?') Then Delia looked at me.

'But I'm not testifying at the moment, am I, Sandy?' Some sarcasm dripped off her words and seasoned her veal.

'I'm not planning on calling you as a witness, if that's what you're asking,' I said. The last thing I needed was my sister on the stand telling a jury she'd seen the defendant *shtupping* the victim right before he was murdered. That was going to be Richard's play if he'd heard about Delia's little voyeuristic moment, and I had to plan that he had.

'I *mean*, you're treating me like a suspect in Brandon's murder,' she said, balling up her cloth napkin and tossing it onto her plate. 'You're acting like *I* was the one on the prep table with that guy. And I don't have to put up with it.' She stood and marched – because there is no other word for it – to the exit. Before anyone could say anything, Delia was gone.

And that was when I knew my sister was having trouble in her marriage.

My mother, ever the pragmatist, gave herself a moment to look appalled, no doubt at the way I'd treated her daughter, and then looked over at me. 'I'm going to need a ride home, I guess,' she said.

TWENTY

Richard Chapman was, as I've chronicled, an awful man, a terrible boyfriend, a worse husband and an untrustworthy friend. But he could rock a business suit as well as any man I knew (with one exception), and he was in his best finery for Stephanie's plea hearing.

I sat with my client (Skinny) at the defense table and kept feeding her encouragement like 'This is all routine' and 'Don't worry about a thing, it'll be over before you know it.' All of which was true. This was just a plea hearing and not the start of what I was certain was going to be an ordeal of a trial.

Stephanie was less communicative than usual, which worried me. I didn't know the status of her rehab or her recovery, and she was wearing long sleeves, even in the July heat, which made me wonder whether there were marks on her arms she didn't want anyone to see. All she'd said to me was 'What if I did something else?' which didn't make sense or have any relevance. When I asked what she meant, she repeated the same question. I decided to chalk it all up to her nerves, which were understandable.

'I don't think that's a great idea,' I said, having no clue what she was talking about. It probably wasn't a great idea. I felt like I was on solid ground in this argument.

Richard, at his seat, might as well have been smoking a pipe and warming a brandy snifter with his right hand. If he were any more comfortable in this courtroom, he'd have been wearing pajamas with feet and drinking a cup of cocoa. I'll bet the chair he was sitting in was trained to his specific butt.

Judge Constantino Martinez entered, heralded as ever by the bailiff, and we stood up because he was a judge and we weren't. Some things are just that simple. Once everyone was seated again and Stephanie's case number was read aloud, the business of the court could begin.

I stood again when prompted and told the judge we were willing to forgo the reading of the charges. Almost everyone does that because, frankly, we know why we're here and we don't especially care to have everyone in earshot hear what wrongdoing they think my client should be punished for doing.

Martinez nodded. 'Having waived the reading of the charges, all that is required is for the defendant to enter a plea for each of them.'

'Yes, Your Honor.' Judges like it when you call them 'Your Honor.' I've known some who were far from honorable, but I don't suppose it's meant to be taken literally in all cases. Any way you look at it, that's the person who's going to preside over your trial and you're better off not getting them annoyed.

I tensed up immediately when Richard raised a hand as he stood. Either he was going to ask to use the bathroom or he was raising his hand to hide whatever he had up his sleeve. 'If I may, Your Honor,' he began.

Martinez, understandably puzzled by this, looked down at Richard and took off his readers. 'You are not being asked to enter a plea for the defendant, Mr Chapman.'

'I'm aware of that, Your Honor. And I have no intention of doing so, but the defendant and my office have reached an agreement on the plea, and I'd like to file it with the court before we proceed.'

Huh? I stood up. 'Your Honor, the defendant has entered into no agreement with the prosecutor's office. There hasn't even been a formal offer of an agreement, but when one was discussed, we rejected it without further discussion.'

Stephanie pulled on my outstretched sleeve. 'Sandy,' she said. Then nothing more. Just a sort of blank stare.

I took a quick peek at Richard but all I could see in my mind's eye was the word *NEFARIOUS* in a very bold font and a very large point size. 'Tell me you didn't sign anything, Skinny,' I hissed at her.

Two rows back, Aunt Fern looked as if she might faint. For once I couldn't blame her. I was thinking of doing the same.

'I'm sorry,' Stephanie said.

'Let me see the document,' Martinez said. He reached out his hand, and Richard was about to extend his to pass over whatever insane piece of paper he'd gotten Skinny to sign. I saw no choice other than to pretty much launch myself into the space between them and prevent the exchange. I looked up at the judge.

'Your Honor,' I said, feeling as if I'd just stepped onstage at an improv comedy show without even being told the situation the audience had suggested. 'I was given no prior notice of this supposed agreement and have had absolutely no time to examine it. May I request a postponement of this hearing until such time as I can confer with my client and advise her as to her rights?'

Martinez once again regarded Richard with a skeptical expression. 'You didn't share this information with the defense attorney?' he asked. If nothing else, he was at least half as pissed off at Richard as I was, and that was saying a lot.

Richard, though, was the very picture of cool confidence. He waved a hand in my general direction in order to declare my objection frivolous and unwarranted. 'Judge, I personally called Ms Moss to discuss the agreement. She was well aware of it yesterday. If she hasn't been able to stay on top of the case from Los Angeles, I don't see why that should invalidate something both sides have agreed to in principle.'

Just in case you're wondering, standing in a courtroom in front of a judge and at least thirty witnesses (many of whom were wondering why this simple hearing was taking so long and making them wait longer) is an extremely bad place to kill someone. But you may rest assured that I did at least briefly contemplate the idea and decided against it for the time being.

'As I said, Your Honor, the plea deal – it's not an agreement because we have not agreed to it – was mentioned to me yesterday and was turned down without any ambiguity. Mr Chapman has been conferring with my client without alerting me, and she needs the advice of her counsel to make an informed decision that could have such an enormous impact on her life. May I please have a postponement?'

Martinez, possibly having had enough of both attorneys before him, waved us back to our tables. Once there, we sat and he put his readers back on to consult the calendar in front of him on an iPad.

'This hearing is adjourned and will be resumed on . . . Monday, four days from now. At that time, I will expect that both parties will be up to date on the state of negotiations and the status of this matter. Is that understood?'

Richard and I each assured him we were conversant in English and therefore had grasped the meaning of his words. I wanted to object, but then there was the matter of strangling my client as soon as no one could witness the act, so I nodded and the judge banged his gavel (which is not nearly as suggestive as it sounds) and I turned and started back toward the defense table.

'It's going to be this way all the way until the day I see your cousin go to jail for the rest of her life, which will probably be Monday,' Richard hissed at me as we walked. 'Just know it's your fault for snitching on me to my wife.'

I didn't stop but I did regard him with a look. '*Snitching?*' I hissed right back.

That was, thankfully, the end of our conversation. I didn't change the outraged expression on my face as I approached Stephanie. The idea that she'd agreed to – and signed – a plea agreement without so much as notifying me was beyond disrespectful and ill-advised. It bordered on egregious. I had a very strong urge to tell Skinny's mother on her.

She stood up warily, if such a thing is possible, watching me near the table. 'Sandy?' The voice was from my memory. I was around seven and Skinny was about eleven. But it wasn't going to save her from my wrath. (Yes, you heard me. I said 'wrath.')

'We're going to talk. Now,' I told her. Then I turned and walked toward the exit without looking back because I knew for a fact that she didn't have the nerve not to follow me.

And all I could think was *I have to be here another four days.*

TWENTY-ONE

There isn't a cafeteria or a public area where you can avoid being seen in the Middlesex County courthouse, so we walked down a block to George Street and ended up in a bar called Tavern on George that thankfully was a little more creative than its name might indicate. But I wasn't really hungry (they have a complete menu) and didn't need any alcohol at the moment. So I ordered a diet soda and looked at Skinny.

'Are you OK in a bar?' It had just occurred to me that I'd steered an addict into a saloon, probably not the best strategy, but what with being blinded by rage at her, Stephanie's welfare wasn't my top priority. Except that it was exactly what we were going to be talking about.

She had the nerve to look annoyed at me. 'I'm not an alcoholic; I'm a junkie,' she said and ordered a beer. For now, I was taking her word on that.

As soon as the server walked away from our table, I let out the words I'd been holding in for a half hour or so. 'Are you out of your mind? You sign a plea agreement that would send you to prison for decades, and you don't even consult with me before you give up your freedom? What are you thinking? Did you kill Brandon and you've had a change of heart? What's going on, Skinny?'

I'll give Stephanie this: She didn't cry this time. She looked determined, like she was aware we were going to go nose-to-nose and she didn't intend to come in second. 'I was trying to avoid spending *the rest of my life* in prison, Sandy, and you weren't willing to hear my side of it. You just told me to trust you. Well, you're my cousin and that's something, but this is my life and you want me to just go on *trust*? You're not even here most of the time. You're off in Hollywood dating movie stars and handling expensive divorces. Why should I trust you?'

I had asked her, time and again, to let me recommend a more experienced defense attorney who was based in New Jersey. Go back some pages and look; you'll see where I did. But each time I was practically begged to handle this case against my better judgment and I caved in, only now to be told that I wasn't trustworthy for all the same reasons I had previously argued someone else should handle Stephanie's defense. I would like that on the record, Your Honor.

But I didn't say any of that at this moment because it would have fallen on deaf ears. 'It doesn't matter who your attorney is in this case. No matter who you hired to defend you in court – and I'm perfectly happy to step aside if you want someone else – when a plea offer is made, you absolutely must tell your lawyer about it, Stephanie. That's just basic. I could have talked you out of signing that ridiculous paper or maybe I couldn't, but either way, I would have known about it before I walked into that courtroom and looked like an idiot today.'

Our drinks were placed in front of us. Skinny took a long pull on the bottle of Blue Moon she had ordered, put it down with a beer-commercial clunk and regarded me with a condescending sneer (as if there were another kind). 'So that's what this is about? Your ego?'

'No. This is about your consistent attempts to get yourself behind bars for a very long time.' The diet soda, as at most bars and restaurants, was too sweet and somewhat flat. They'll give you a bottle of beer but not a can of Diet Coke. 'This is about my ability to help you avoid that, which I used to believe you wanted, but my *in*ability to help you if you don't let me.

I haven't had the chance to read this agreement yet, so why don't you tell me what's so damned attractive about it?'

She broke eye contact. 'I told you. It's about fifteen years instead of life. If you're at a car dealership and they give you a sixty percent discount, you take it, don't you?'

'Not if you can get away without paying a dime, no. I can still help you, Stephanie. The judge will dismiss the agreement based strictly on the prosecutor not informing me of its existence. But you have to come clean about *everything* that led to Brandon Starkey being dead, and you have to do it now.'

Stephanie heaved a sigh that would have killed a lesser woman. 'I've already *told* you everything I know!' If we hadn't been seated in a tavern among other New Jerseyans, I am certain she would have put her head on the table in weary frustration.

'No, you haven't. I've heard from a relatively reliable source that you were' – and I promise I lowered my voice here out of a sense of civility for the other patrons of the tavern – 'having sex with Brandon just minutes before he was skewered with that knife you were carrying. So let's start there.'

Stephanie's face immediately sharpened and she leaned forward across the table, very nearly upsetting her bottle of beer. 'What are you talking about?' she demanded.

'Someone told me that you and the best man were finding out whether he *was* the best man and then ten minutes later you were painted in his blood. So let's hear it all, step by step, one more time, and in this telling you don't leave anything out. Start.' I pointed at her so the man eating a burger at the next table, who was trying very hard to appear like he wasn't listening, didn't think I was talking to him. I did give him a dirty look and he pretended to be engrossed in his phone.

'Nothing like that happened,' Stephanie said. 'I'm in love with Michael. I had no interest in his best friend. I told you what went on: Brandon said he loved me and that I should leave Michael, and I told him no. Then I went to the bathroom to get my head back together and when I came out he was . . . you know . . .'

'Dead, or dying,' I said for her. The fact was the fact; there was no point in not saying the words. 'Then how come someone

thinks they saw the two of you going at it on the prep table?'
Look, getting a word picture out of Delia had not been easy.
She is, I'd say, a little prudish on the subject.

'How the hell should I know?' OK, that was a good question.
'I tried to CPR him. Maybe they saw that.'

'Tell me about your relationship with Brandon,' I said.

'We didn't have one.' Petulant now. Try to help people
sometime and see what it gets you.

'Not a romantic relationship. Were you friends? Did he resent
you for taking his friend away? How well did you know the
guy?' I immediately regretted giving her options to choose from.
Ask a person an open-ended question and you'll get the answer
they think of, true or false. Give them a multiple-choice question and they'll take one of the choices, which generally is not
as helpful to getting the truth or, as I hoped, building a legal
case.

'We weren't friends, exactly,' she said, ticking off one of my
suggestions. 'I mean, he was the guy that Michael had to clear
me with. If I hadn't passed Brandon's approval, we probably
wouldn't have gotten past a third date.'

I'd heard about people like that, but I'd thought they only
existed in bad television shows, much worse than the ones
Patrick produces or acts in.

'OK, so that's what you weren't,' I said. 'What were you?'
No easy options to pick from this time.

Stephanie, to her credit, took some time to think that over.
'I guess we were like in-laws, you know? Like, you are both
devoted to the one person but you have to deal with the other
one, so you . . . I was going to say you make the best of it, but
it wasn't like that. I didn't dislike Brandon. He was just kind
of there.'

I figured it was time to dredge up the murder again, seeing
as how she was accused of it. 'When you were in that bathroom,
you didn't hear anything? Anyone? We have to prove that you
didn't kill Brandon. One way to do that – and it's not the only
way by any means – is to prove that someone else did, or at
least could have. So if you heard *anything*, no matter how
insignificant it seemed then, let me know and Mae will track
it down.'

'Who's Mae?' Of course. Mae hadn't talked to Skinny, and likely never would unless she had a theory that needed testing.

'She's the investigator we're using for your case. Actually, she runs the investigation agency and has four investigators who are working on your case.' It was mostly Mae on her own – that's who we were paying for – but it impresses the client to mention the other people in the agency, and for all I knew, Mae might send one of them to follow a possible suspect, if we ever had one.

Skinny closed her eyes in what I initially took for annoyance but soon realized was an attempt to think back to the moment I was asking about. After about ten seconds, she opened them again and looked at the beer bottle. 'I didn't hear anything. I was listening to music with my earbuds specifically because I didn't want to hear anything that was going on out there. I don't have anything to tell Mae about that.' Sometimes it's a good thing when your client starts to think of themselves as part of the team. With Patrick, it had not been a good thing. With Stephanie, it was still too early to tell.

'Tell me this: Who do *you* think killed Brandon Starkey?' I like to ask. The people on the inside of the (usually) tangled relationships that lead to a crime – or for that matter, a divorce – are the ones who probably have the best insights.

She didn't hesitate at all. 'If I had to guess, I'd say it was Sarah Panico,' she said.

Music to my ears.

TWENTY-TWO

'Forget Sarah Panico,' Mae Tennyson said.

Dammit.

'Why?' I asked.

Mae and I had met for lunch in a Venezuelan place called Merey in Highland Park, which is just over the Raritan River from New Brunswick. It's a lovely, tiny restaurant that thankfully has outdoor seating when it's not winter, and it wasn't. I was having an arepa with chicken and Mae had opted for the beef empanada, both of which I'd had before and were excellent.

It was Mae who had suggested we meet. We'd Zoomed a few times and texted frequently but never met. Now she was telling me that my childhood nemesis couldn't be the person who stabbed Brandon Starkey, and frankly, that was putting a crimp in my afternoon.

'Because she came out of the kitchen, by your own account, *before* the murder took place. I've checked out that building and yes, it has a back entrance that goes to the kitchen, but it was locked that day because the food was being brought in by an outside caterer. Apparently, the staff at the Elks Lodge wasn't fancy enough for your cousin. Oh, and by the way, Sarah has no motive to kill Brandon.'

'Who had a key to the back door?' It was a long shot, but suppose Sarah Panico had gone into the locksmith business now or was in a common law relationship with an Elk. Things happen.

She took a bite and washed it down with some diet ginger ale. Merey does not have a liquor license. 'I don't know all of them for sure yet, but the main chef who works events for the Elks is a guy named Tony Angelino, but he's a contractor. He has a key. The grand amazing poohbah or whatever has a key.'

'Exalted Ruler,' I said.

'Yup. The building superintendent, a man named Larry Mandrake, has a key, of course. Larry works in the real estate business and he belongs to the Elks for the same reason most of them do, which is to make business connections. He's as much a building superintendent as any suburban homeowner who's ever tried to change the washer on his kitchen sink and ended up calling a plumber.'

'It's nice you're not judgmental,' I teased.

Mae's voice dropped to what she considered a male range. 'I call 'em as I see 'em,' she said.

'So we don't have a connection yet to any of those men opening the back door to the Lodge on the day Brandon was killed,' I said.

Mae shook her head while finishing off the empanada. 'No,

even the grand exalted whatever – who's a woman, by the way – was in Cape Cod for the weekend and didn't come down just to let someone into the kitchen so she could shish-kabob a guy.'

I thought that day over, which was something I'd been doing constantly since, well, that day. 'I saw a few people go into the kitchen and I still don't have an explanation as to why any of them were there except Stephanie, and her story is shaky,' I told Mae. 'Sarah Panico was in there. My cousin Stephen was in there. My sister says she peeked inside and recoiled at the horror of seeing two people having sex. And Stephanie was in there. She says Brandon texted her because he wanted to tell her he was madly in love with her. I don't think he texted Stephen or Sarah with the same message. Do you have any idea why they were gathering in the kitchen?'

Mae pointed at me like a stadium vendor asking if you were the one who wanted the seventeen-dollar beer. 'Your sister,' she said.

My guard went up. Delia and I have our issues, to be sure, but we are sisters and we do look out for each other whenever we're not sniping at one another. You know. Sisters. 'What about her?' I asked.

Mae must have sensed my immediate tension. 'Ease up, Sandy. I'm not suggesting your sister killed Brandon Starkey. There's absolutely no evidence she was even in the room. I'm just saying, she's the one who told us she saw Stephanie and Brandon going at it like a couple of wildcats in the kitchen. But she only peeked for a second. Suppose Brandon was, you know, working out his frustration with someone else?'

It was possible, but something was nagging at me. 'I can't imagine they were completely undressed in there. There just wasn't enough time,' I said. 'Stephanie says she was in the restroom listening to Taylor Swift for about ten minutes.'

'That's long enough for a lot of men,' Mae said.

'Yes, but by the time Stephanie came out, the other woman, if there was one, was gone. She'd have had to walk in, suggest to Brandon that this was a good idea, which probably didn't take tons of convincing, then go ahead, finish and get redressed to the point that nobody would have noticed anything askew, in ten minutes. I suppose it's possible, but it would have to be really well planned, in my opinion.'

Mae shrugged. 'OK. So they were partially dressed. That cuts down on the time considerably.'

'Except for one thing,' I told her. 'That was my sister Delia doing the peeking. And if that woman in the kitchen was anyone but Stephanie, she would have known it from any distance. My sister has never not taken note of another woman's clothing in her life. Unless there was another woman in that party wearing the exact same dress as Stephanie, then the person Delia saw was, in fact, Stephanie.'

'This ain't looking good, Sandy,' Mae said.

'No. It's not.'

TWENTY-THREE

Angie had her feet up on the couch in the suite. That wasn't very unusual, but the rest of her body was on the floor. Angie was doing sit-ups. Angie has dedicated her life to being the fittest woman in the world and, unintentionally (I think), making me feel inadequate.

'It's all about the plea agreement right now,' I was telling her. 'All I have to do is make certain that Skinny's not going to flake out on me again and then tell the judge we are not going ahead with the agreement; he'll strike it and move on with the not-guilty plea.'

Angie leaned back and started doing bicycle legs, her absolute favorite exercise because it's really difficult and she does it perfectly without breaking a sweat. It's a good thing I love Angie or else I'd have to kill her. 'Why did Stephanie agree to the deal in the first place?' she asked, not breathing hard. 'What's the upside for her? Fifteen years in jail?'

I looked over at Patrick, who was on the phone with his manager Josh Moran, going over the details of his *Scottish Play* contract. He smiled at me, and I felt guilty for hoping the contract would fall through so he wouldn't be away from LA for months.

'That's the explanation Skinny's trying to sell, but I'm not buying it,' I answered. 'I think the most logical conclusion is that she's covering for someone.'

'The elm tree?' Angie said, still 'pedaling' in the air while lying on her back, hands on her hips.

'Michael would be the obvious choice, yes. But there are other possible candidates, including my cousin Stephen, who was in the kitchen just before Brandon was stabbed.'

Angie rolled herself up into a sitting position and despite having not appeared to have exerted herself, got up to get a bottle of water from the suite's refrigerator. Used to be I would stare at the contents of a hotel room's refrigerator in horror at the thought of being charged seven dollars for a bag of M&Ms. Life had taken an interesting turn once I moved to LA and met Patrick.

'Yeah, but you and I were both watching that door to figure out what was going on at the cocaine party inside, and we both know the Ent never went in there and Stephen left before there was any sign of, you know, a bloody murder.'

That was true, but it didn't help my case. 'Skinny says she was in a bathroom and couldn't hear anything. It's possible someone killed Brandon and then walked out and she never knew it.'

Then Angie brought up the one point I'd thought of that I didn't want to consider. 'Stephanie's the only one who came out looking like she'd just survived a Stephen King book,' she said. 'If, say, Sarah Panico had slashed Brandon to bits, how come she was clean as a whistle the whole rest of the day?'

I groaned. 'Yeah.'

Patrick put his phone down and walked over to where Angie and I were sitting (OK, Angie was stretching but that meant her workout was over and she was stretching on the floor). 'The contracts will all be signed on Monday,' he said. 'I'm going to do the play.' And suddenly he looked upset about it.

I stood up and gave him a hug. 'Congratulations?' I said.

Patrick knew what I meant and straightened up, smiling #72, the actor's smile that he used when trying to prove how happy he was, especially when he wasn't. 'I always get this way with a new project,' he said, 'and this one is very different. I have to convince myself I can do it.'

'Don't be crazy,' Angie said from the floor. 'You can do anything.' Angie was a huge Patrick McNabb fan long before she became his right-hand person, and when I had still never heard of him.

I was about to offer similar words of encouragement, but my phone buzzed and there were texts from my mother and Jessica Berliner. Because my mother is my mother, I read Jess's first.

This doesn't happen on weekends, but I just got word that the prosecutor has subpoenaed your mother.

Mom's was more direct than that even: *What does this mean?* She sent it with a picture of a man dressed casually, holding a cardboard placard that read, *You have been served.*

Richard wasn't prosecuting Skinny. He was prosecuting me.

TWENTY-FOUR

'The plea is not guilty, Your Honor.'

'I hope you won't be offended, Ms Moss, but I'd like to hear it from the defendant.' Judge Martinez motioned for Stephanie to stand up. 'Ms Silverstone?'

I will admit to a feeling of trepidation. Skinny had insisted she would do the right thing, meaning what I wanted her to do, at this hearing, but I had more or less promised that she wouldn't have to do any talking. Martinez was right, of course, but I hadn't expected him to insist upon it.

Stephanie stood up, glanced nervously at Richard, who was in yet another impeccable suit at the prosecutor's table, and then looked at Martinez. 'Yes, Your Honor?' Her voice sounded like it had when she was nine.

'How do you plead?'

Richard didn't even look in her direction. He stared forward at the judge. I, on the other hand, was staring directly at my client, who took a deep breath, let it out, and said, 'Not guilty, Your Honor.'

That was when I realized that I too had been holding my breath. Throughout the courtroom, I believed I felt a breeze from all the sighs of relief. My mother, Aunt Fern, Michael the fiancé, even Sarah Panico, who had probably shown up just to unnerve me (it hadn't worked). My client had made me nervous enough all by herself, but now she'd done what was actually in her best interest.

'Mr Prosecutor?' Martinez looked over at Richard, who could have insisted on some more legal maneuvering over the ridiculous plea deal he'd thought he had brilliantly convinced Skinny to sign.

But not this time. 'No objection, Judge,' he said.

Martinez looked relieved, but he didn't know 'relieved.' I hadn't eaten a bite all day and it was two in the afternoon. My stomach just hadn't been in the mood before the hearing and that, I had decided, was Richard's fault. (Granted, Stephanie was a contributor to my condition but only while Richard had manipulated her.)

Patrick, who had completed his preliminary business with the Turned Over Theater Company, was waiting to return to Los Angeles until I was finished with my business in the court, which had now been completed for the time being. We'd spend one last night in the New York suite and leave from Newark the next morning. Angie had flown back already to prepare Patrick's business a day early.

You're wondering why I haven't mentioned talking to my mother about her subpoena yet. You're very astute; it's because I'd been putting it off. Other than telling her that it didn't mean she was in any trouble with the law, I'd said we'd talk about it after the hearing.

Well, now was after the hearing.

Mom, never one to be put off, had been chomping at the bit and caught me even before I could make it all the way up the aisle to the courtroom door. And it was a small courtroom.

'Why did I get subpoenaed?' she demanded.

Stephanie, who had just agreed that she wasn't guilty of murdering a man, might have thought this proceeding was about her. Mom had a different perspective. Stephanie just walked up and out of the room, telling me she'd talk to me later.

'Come with me,' I told my mother, as Judge Martinez was trying to begin his next case. The two of us clogging up the aisle was not helping, and I didn't want the judge to remember this when I filed any motions regarding the upcoming trial. I led her by taking her arm and we left the courtroom, no doubt to Martinez's relief. I maneuvered Mom into a corner in the corridor and sat her down on a bench.

'I understand you're upset about the subpoena,' I told her. 'But this is my place of business, and you can't make me look foolish among my peers.'

She looked at me with wide eyes. 'Who made you look foolish?'

Sometimes there's just no point. I dove in. 'The subpoena just means that the prosecutor wants to ask you questions about what happened at Stephanie's rehearsal party.'

Mom frowned. 'That sounds like I'm a suspect.'

If there's such a thing as an inner eye roll, I am certain I did one. But you wouldn't have known it by looking at me. 'You're not a suspect, Mom. Nobody on this planet believes that you could have gone into that kitchen and stabbed Brandon Starkey multiple times, then walked back out and had a diet ginger ale while you waited to frame Stephanie. *Nobody* thinks that.'

'Then why am I getting a subpoena? Will I have to be arrested?'

'No! Nobody is charging you with anything, Mom. The trial won't even start for six months at least. He'll ask you some quick questions about what you saw, you'll tell him the truth and that will be that. I'll even get on Zoom and listen in as your attorney if you want me to.'

'You won't be here?' Mom was probably already planning the *hors d'oeuvres* for the pre-questioning luncheon.

'No. I live in Los Angeles. And I can't fly in for every motion that takes place in this case. You knew that. If you want, I'll ask my associate Jessica Berliner to sit in with you. She's very good.'

Mom just *humph-ed*. 'Does this go on my record?'

'*What* record?'

This might have gone on until the end of time as we know it, but I got a text from Richard. I should have removed him from my contacts years ago but thought I'd never have to talk to him again. A text from Richard couldn't ever, in any form of reality, be considered good news.

It wasn't.

I've asked the court to put the Silverstone trial on a fast track. Just got word that the trial will begin in eight weeks.

He had to be kidding. This was the kind of sick joke Richard would play just to get my stomach back into non-eating mode. Because he was a sadistic, slimy, evil . . .

I'm sorry – what was I talking about?

'Stop looking at your phone,' Mom was saying. 'I've been subpoenaed!'

'Yeah, and the guy who did that to you is trying to do something else to me,' I told her.

I decided to text Jessica and see if she'd had any notice of a trial date before I texted back to Richard to tell him his joke hadn't landed because he was a disgusting, lying, revolting . . .

But before I did that, I checked my email and yes, there was a notice from the Administrative Office of the Courts. Sure enough, it indicated that *The County of Middlesex v. Stephanie Silverstone* would be heard exactly seven weeks and four days from this very moment.

I texted back to Richard, and I'd like to tell you what I said but my mother was sitting just three feet away.

PART TWO
Marriage?

TWENTY-FIVE

The truth about what I did is that I retreated to Los Angeles. I had a home there, I had work there that needed to be done, and Patrick was going to be there for the first month, anyway, which meant Angie would also be around. And let's face it, technology has made being in person passé. So for weeks while Jessica and I were preparing the trial in separate time zones, I was lining up witnesses and asking Mae to look into the answers to questions I would need.

Spending a regular work day mostly on my cases for Seaton, Taylor (the ones not based in New Jersey, since Skinny's case was also being billed to the firm), I would go home to my apartment or Patrick's house and grab a quick dinner before diving right into the evidence Mae had uncovered or an expert witness on the amount of upper-body strength it might take to stab a man that fatally and that deeply with that kind of a knife.

The time started to blur just a bit as I went through that routine and that's why it was something of a surprise to find Holiday Wentworth in my office when I arrived one morning. I was a little blurry-eyed, I'll admit, but it was the first time I'd been in my office when Holly had gotten there first.

'Glad to see you,' she said. 'On how many ends have you been burning that candle?'

I sat down heavily and put my laptop case on my desk just as heavily. 'If you're planning on firing me, I'd appreciate it if you'd do so as quickly as possible,' I said. 'I might not be able to stay awake too long, and you'd only have to send me packing again.'

Luckily, Holly understands my native language of Jersey sarcasm without quite being able to speak it. Truly, Duolingo is a technological miracle. 'You look tired,' she said.

'Thanks. It's these little boosters that keep me going.' I started to unload the laptop and boot it up, but I didn't want to start shoveling some of my actual hard-copy files on to the desk,

because for a reason I couldn't quite identify, I didn't want
Holly to see how many of them were related to Skinny's case
as opposed to the work I had here in LA.

'Sandy, have you been thinking about what I told you?'
Holly's voice, as always, was warm but now had a bit of an
edge. Whatever she was saying was clearly a high priority for
her. I just wished I knew what it was.

'You haven't told me anything,' I said honestly. 'You said
that you were concerned about me commuting back East
and that there was a reason for your concern, but you didn't
clue me in on what that might be. You said if you told me,
you'd have to kill me and I'd like to avoid that if possible. I
understand you'd prefer if I didn't have this trial coming up in
Jersey, but I really can't quit it now and it's only another few
weeks before the prosecutor is forcing me to start.'

Holly hadn't asked me much about Skinny's case and didn't
now either. She was interested enough, but it didn't have a
bearing on my employment at Seaton, Taylor and she saw no
reason to find out more. She's a very efficient administrator. So
it was a little unnerving for me to watch her dancing around
the issue rather than confronting it head on as she usually did.

'I'm not suggesting you resign the case,' she said. 'We've
had no complaints from any of your LA clients yet, so it's not
an issue.'

'Yet?'

She ignored that. 'Tell me again how long you think the trial
will last.'

'I'd say two weeks – if that – and then however long it takes
a jury to deliberate.' I was adding in a few days for safety.
Holly seemed concerned about my time away, so if I padded
the estimate and got back to California on a full-time basis
sooner, I'd look better as an employee.

Holly nodded, as if having decided. She rubbed her hands
together as if pretending it was cold in the room, but this was
Los Angeles in the summer and even air conditioning only goes
so far. 'All right, then.' She turned to leave, and then, seemingly
remembering something, turned back and pointed at me. 'But
when you're back, you're back, OK? No more taking outside
cases without telling me.'

'She's my cousin, Holly.'

'I know. That's why it's OK.'

And she was gone, leaving me once again to wonder what the hell that was about.

My mother's questioning would have to wait because Richard had even more excruciating plans, which included a subpoena of my very own, which was a low blow no matter how you looked at it. All a prosecutor has to do is invite someone in to answer questions. A subpoena is meant to convince those who refuse to cooperate and to threaten them with jail time if they don't comply. Neither Mom nor I (nor Delia, who I assumed had been contacted but had not gotten in touch with me regarding any possible questioning because, I guess, I had been rude to her at Catherine Lombardi) had refused to do anything, but Richard was the prosecutor and just in case you haven't figured it out by now, you don't want to get a prosecutor mad at you. Particularly when it's his fault.

I had called him when served in my Burbank apartment and awakened him, which was only fair. Then I proceeded to ream him out for sending subpoenas when he could have simply asked the questions. Then I hung up. So the Zoom meeting we were having now, timed badly at one in the afternoon in my office, was something of a compromise, I guessed. I would answer and Richard would, as we had agreed during the phone call, withdraw the subpoena for my mother and simply request she comply with the investigation.

The fact that she was already on his witness list for the trial seemed somehow irrelevant. He wanted to prep witnesses for his case (including me!) against which I would have to defend whatever he decided to use. It was as bizarre a circumstance as I could remember facing in a criminal trial, and I had once asked Patrick on the stand whether he was in love with me, so I know bizarre.

'What do you need to know, Richard?' I started. I saw no reason to be civil, or for that matter at all respectful of his office. My office had a view of Sunset Boulevard, which isn't as good as it sounds.

'Ms Moss,' he started. OK, so we were going that way. 'I'm

informing you that this conversation is being recorded and can be used as evidence at trial.'

'No kidding.' As if I'd graduated law school yesterday.

But Richard wasn't playing along. For the record (so to speak), I hadn't expected him to; the idea was to get under his skin. This wasn't simply a way to express my ongoing contempt for the man; it was also a way to get the prosecutor in my case irritated enough to say or do something that might give me an advantage when we went to trial way too soon because he was being a flaming idiot.

'To begin with, can we establish from where you are offering evidence?' Most people would be questioned in person. I was clearly not doing that.

'In my office.'

Richard was too professional to sigh. 'And where is that, Ms Moss?'

'In Los Angeles, California.'

'But you lived in New Jersey until a few years ago, isn't that true?'

Were we going to get personal? 'I don't see how that is relevant, Mr Prosecutor,' I said.

'I'm establishing your knowledge of the situation and the surroundings. Were you present at a gathering at the Elks Lodge in Woodbridge, New Jersey, on the date in question?'

'I wasn't lying on the beach at Seaside Heights eating salt water taffy,' I told him.

'Ms Moss,' said the prosecutor.

'Yes, I was there. You know I was there. You know what I saw when I was there. It's really something of a mystery as to what you might think you'll be able to learn about what happened when I was there because you already know all the things that happened when I was there except you think you've found the killer and you haven't.'

'Ms Moss . . .'

'When I was there.' It felt like it needed a little punctuation.

'Ms *Moss*,' Richard continued. Zoom meant I could see his face and it was a little red. Good. 'Did you see Stephanie Silverstone enter the kitchen from the main ballroom?'

'That was a ballroom? It looked like the kind of place where you'd hold a school board meeting.'

Richard's eyelids dropped a bit. He spoke more slowly. 'Did you see *your cousin* Stephanie Silverstone walk from the main room into the kitchen?'

'Yes, I did. I also saw at the very least two other people do the same in rapid succession immediately after. What do you suppose they were doing in there?' I'd asked Skinny and had Mae talk to Stephen and Sarah Panico, but they all insisted nothing untoward was going on in the kitchen; they'd gathered there for a quick toast. (It was a very odd gathering for that, but they were sticking to their stories, although I wanted to talk to Stephen again.)

'I'm not interested in the others,' Richard said.

'Oh, but you should be, because my client didn't kill Brandon Starkey. It would serve you well to look into other suspects.' Not that I'd give him any names, but just having that on the record made me feel better.

'Were you there when Ms Silverstone exited the kitchen?' he asked. This was probably his favorite part.

'Yes, I was.' Time to start acting like a witness. Say as little as possible. The 'I was' had probably been too much.

'How did she look?'

How did she *look*? That was a weird way to phrase the question. 'She didn't look her best,' I answered. Counter weird with weird, I always say. OK, that's the first time I said it, but you know what I mean, don't you?

'Can you describe the state of her clothing?'

Now, I'm not an idiot. Richard wanted to get Skinny's lawyer on the record saying she was covered in blood. And she *was* covered in blood, which made not saying that something of a problem. But I was not going to put a nail into the coffin of my own client. 'She had obviously been through a very difficult experience, and her dress certainly did show that.'

Richard knew what I was doing and why I was doing it. 'In what way?' he asked.

'My client tells me that she had discovered Mr Starkey in the kitchen and he had been very badly hurt, so she tried her best to revive him. He was bleeding quite profusely and some of that blood naturally got on to her dress.'

He considered his next move and raised an eyebrow. 'How much blood?' he asked.

I'm sure my eyes were reacting as well. In fact, they were shooting poison darts through my webcam and into Richard's face, but alas, the technology was not everything we'd been promised. 'I am not a medical professional,' I told him.

'No, but you saw what it looked like.' I know when I'm being set up and Richard was setting me up. 'Was it a little blood or a lot?'

Truth be told, I could have ended the interview right there. I was under no legal obligation to answer every question. I wasn't on Richard's witness list for the trial and would not be testifying under oath. So what I had to do here came down to a choice, either one of which was OK but not great: answer the question in the best possible light for Stephanie or end the Zoom session, footage of which Richard would undoubtedly like to show in court if the judge, whoever might be assigned the case, allowed it.

'In my uneducated opinion, it was the amount of blood you would expect to see if a woman had just tried to perform CPR on a man with multiple stab wounds in his chest,' I said. 'But as I said, I am not a medical professional. And I'm afraid I'll be ending this interview now, Mr Chapman, because I have to get back to work here in Los Angeles.'

'I'm afraid I have more questions,' Richard said.

'I have no doubt, but I am not free to answer them right now. I am Ms Silverstone's attorney and not in a position to offer any opinions that can be used in a courtroom.'

'I'm afraid I can't accept that answer.' Richard was trying to play hardball and he didn't realize I was a major-league softball player (not really; it's a metaphor).

'I'm not your witness, Richard.' I sat back in my comfortable chair in my very nice office overlooking some decent scenery if you didn't look down too far. But there was a window behind me, which I sincerely hoped was backlighting me to the point that I looked like a dark shadow staring at Richard. 'If you need more answers from me, subpoena me to testify at trial.

I'll file a motion with the judge indicating that as the defense attorney, it would be a severe breach of my client's rights to have me testify against her and the judge will agree. So unless you want to offer me a sincere apology, something I don't think you're capable of offering, this will be the last time we communicate in person until I see you in the courtroom. Have a nice day.' And I disconnected the Zoom call because I didn't want to give Richard the opportunity to do it first.

'Best talk we ever had,' I said to myself. Then I opened the file on *Casey v. Casey* and took a deep breath.

After all, Holly didn't want any complaints from my clients.

TWENTY-SIX

'This is it,' Patrick said.

I was standing in the front room of Patrick's soon-to-be-former house, the one he'd move out of when I moved out of the Burbank apartment as soon as our new place, which I'd bought from Riley Schoenberg (technically), now living with her father in Visalia, was ready. And I could hear Patrick's voice echo through the halls. The place was almost devoid of furniture.

Patrick had packed up much of his clothing, all of his personal belongings and a few of his movie mementos – the ones he couldn't bear to part with for an extended period of time – and shipped them off to the apartment *The Scottish Play* company had rented for him on the Lower East Side of Manhattan for the duration of the play's run. The car that would take him to the airport was not yet idling in front of his entrance door, but it was reportedly on its way. Patrick was flying to New York to prepare, rehearse and open the play, a process that would take a minimum of three months.

This was, in fact, it. I wouldn't be seeing him for three weeks until I arrived at the apartment to stay with Patrick while the trial was going on, and then to leave within a couple of weeks and stay in the Burbank apartment without Angie until the

opening night of *The Scottish Play*. It was, I think it's obvious,
the longest separation we'd had since we started dating and I
was doing my best to be supportive while wanting to grab on
to his pants leg and beg him not to leave.

'I guess so,' I said. 'Will Angie meet you at the airport?'
She'd left two days earlier to get all the details properly prepared,
like having all of Patrick's belongings placed correctly in the
apartment so he'd walk in and believe everything had magically
appeared there as though Captain Kirk's transporter had simply
sent them there digitally.

'Yes. She's already hard at work. But I'm more concerned
about you. Is your cousin's trial ready yet?' Patrick doesn't
really get the law jargon and I don't speak showbusiness, so
we're even.

'I don't know,' I told him. 'I'm not thinking about that right
now.' What was that moist feeling on my left cheek? It wasn't
that humid today. Especially in an air-conditioned house.

He pulled me toward him gently and kissed me and that was
exactly what I wanted but didn't want because it kept reminding
me he was leaving. I'd never been this way about a boyfriend
before (largely because I usually left them) but this was Patrick,
and Patrick was special.

When we separated, I must have sniffled a bit, but Patrick's
eyes weren't exactly bone dry either. 'We're going to get through
this, love,' he said softly.

'I know. But that doesn't make it easier.'

The damned car pulled up in front of the house as if some
director Patrick had worked with had cued it from off-camera.
'There it is,' I said. Because if you were expecting witty banter
right now, you should brace yourself to be disappointed.

Patrick had one suitcase on wheels that he rolled to the door
with his left hand while holding my hand with his right. 'It's
a good role, Sandra,' he said. 'I had to take it.'

'Don't be ridiculous. Of course you did. I don't want you to
turn down work you want to do because of me. I'm a strong
woman, Patrick. I'll survive and I'll see you in three weeks.'

'I imagine you'll be a tad busy then,' he said with a wry
smile.

'I'll fit you in.'

We kissed again and then he got into the car. I'd offered to drive him to the airport, but he said that he'd prefer to get the sloppy clichés out of the way before that. And to be honest, I had to get back to the office to get my divorces off my desk and confer with Mae and Jess as soon as I could, given they were three hours ahead of me.

I held on to Patrick just too long enough so we'd both be sad and then he left for New York and I left for Seaton, Taylor. And then we could both start acting like adults again. Patrick would be better at it because it involved acting.

Jessica got to me first, texting and then FaceTiming so we could see each other. 'I've been prepping some of our witnesses,' she said, 'but your cousin Stephen refuses to take my calls or open his door, so I have nothing from him. And your sister is answering basically in single syllables.'

I was taking notes on my iPad. 'OK. I'll get to them.' Talking to Stephen was always an enlightening experience (I'm being sarcastic) and talking to my sister quite often made me break out in a rash. 'Let's discuss the most likely suspects in my mind – this Lucia person who dumped or was dumped by the victim recently, and everyone's favorite giant redwood, the bridegroom Michael. If indeed there was something, let's say, untoward going on in the kitchen that day, they would be the ones most likely to be a little miffed by the whole thing. Have you talked to them?'

'Mae is still trying to locate Lucia D'Alessandro,' Jess answered. 'Oddly, she seems to have vanished right around the time her ex found a knife in his chest.'

OK, that was interesting. 'Imagine,' I said. 'Have the cops been on the lookout for her?'

'The county investigator is Randall O'Malley,' she said, and my heart didn't so much sink as it jumped off a bridge.

I knew Randy from my time in the prosecutor's office. If given a map, it would be an even chance as to whether he could find his own apartment at night. With GPS, maybe sixty percent, but I wouldn't bet the farm on it. Randy was hired from the Edison police department when he 'retired,' which meant the chief told him to go away and not come back. Randy knew a couple of people who worked for the prosecutor, including, dare I say it, the prosecutor. He was hired on his merits, most of which were juicy pieces of information he'd gathered about county and state officials. And it wasn't his keen investigative skills that had won him those prizes; he'd just been in the room when stupid things were said and done.

In short, Randy wasn't going to find anybody he was told to find. And who knew if Richard had even suggested he look? He wanted Stephanie to be guilty whether she was or not.

'Oy,' I said.

'Yeah. So Mae is on her own on that one, but she has one of her better people following whatever trail there might be. The current best guess is that Lucia is somewhere in Ohio.'

'So is the Rock and Roll Hall of Fame, but I'll bet it's easier to locate,' I said.

'Considerably. They have signs and everything.'

'What about Michael the Groom? Last I saw of him, he was being unpleasantly grumpy around our client.'

Jess nodded in recognition. 'Yeah, he's a charmer. You can see why she'd be desperate to marry this guy. He has the personality of linoleum except that he snarls a lot. And his story is virtually impossible to check out. He says he was walking around outside the Elks Lodge when it all happened, trying to decide whether he really wanted to get married.'

I grunted involuntarily. 'Don't tell me; let me guess. He said that with Stephanie close enough to hear him.'

She pointed at me to say I'd been correct. 'Give the girl a cigar. And when I asked if that wasn't kind of late in the game to be making such a decision, he shrugged. That was his answer.' She shrugged to illustrate as if I didn't know that shoulders could do that. 'Yup, a shame she got to him first or I'd be all over the guy.'

'You have a husband and children,' I reminded her.

'Some men are worth it.'

'And then there's Michael. Nobody else was outside who could have seen him? He wasn't discussing this inner turmoil with, say, his best friend?'

Jess gave me the look I deserved. 'His best friend was busy getting stabbed,' she said.

I closed my eyes for a second to gather what few thoughts I had. They could have fit in a small salad dressing container from a diner takeout order. But I was the first chair in this case even if I was three time zones away. 'OK, here's what we're going to do,' I said. 'I'll talk to Delia, again, and Stephen, and we'll decide if we want them to testify. But I think we definitely want to prioritize finding Lucia and questioning Michael just a little more adamantly. Let's make sure we put Detective Schultz on our witness list because he didn't seem all that convinced when he was questioning Stephanie. Beyond that, the thing to do is hope that Richard *doesn't* include people like my mother and my sister on his witness list. And if he puts me on it, he'll be in for a battle in court that he'll lose. Do we know who the judge is going to be yet?'

'You didn't get the email?'

I hadn't checked my email in a couple of hours. 'Maybe but I didn't see it.' I started to scroll through the avalanche of divorce emails, spam and a picture that Angie sent me from Patrick's new apartment that just made me sad.

'It's Judge Grossman,' Jess said.

That wasn't groanworthy but it also wasn't exactly the best news I could have gotten. Barnard S. Grossman was old school. Like, one-room-schoolhouse school. He'd be fair as long as I followed every single rule in the book, even the ones I didn't know. And he'd expect precedents for *everything*, which in this case was going to be slightly tricky, seeing as how I had so far been unable to find the case that would stand up as a model for yeah-she-was-covered-in-blood-but-that-doesn't-prove-any-thing. I mean, it was *true* that the sight of Stephanie doing her Vampira impression wasn't proof that she'd killed Brandon, but a jury wasn't going to care.

Sure enough, there was the email from the office of the courts. Grossman it would be. 'I'll start drawing up motions and sending them to his office today and tomorrow,' I told Jess. 'Let me know if there are any you think I might be missing.'

'I'm in New Jersey,' she said. 'I can do some of that.'

That was actually a welcome statement; I was backed up against some of my work in LA and Holly was being mysteri-ously insistent on my having a local presence. 'Thanks, Jess,' I said. 'If you can take care of the request for a later court date, which he'll deny, and for dismissal of any photographs taken of Stephanie when she came out of the kitchen . . .'

'. . . which he'll also deny,' Jess said.

'Maybe, maybe not, but yeah, probably,' I admitted. 'You do those two and I'll do the rest. And thanks again.'

We hung up and I made two calls on a ridiculous custody hearing (neither parent needed sole custody and they both knew it) before I conferred again with Mae, who gave me roughly the same status report and expressed some consternation at her inability to locate Lucia D'Alessandro, noting that 'she shouldn't be this hard to find. I mean, the best we can hope is that she's a Jersey girl running away after she killed her cheating ex-boyfriend. You'd think *that* would leave a trail. It would help if the cops were cooperating with us, but I think you're aware that the prosecutor would prefer that we don't succeed, even more than usual.'

That was unfortunately a given. I could have kicked myself for getting into a position where Richard could try to exact revenge.

'Let me handle it,' I told her. 'I know a guy.'

TWENTY-SEVEN

Detective Lieutenant K.C. Trench of the Los Angeles Police Department is one of the most contained people I have ever met. I don't know whether he is trying to suppress an emotional stockpile that would lay waste to the planet or whether he actually doesn't feel very much and wonders why the rest of us humans expend so much energy on things that science can't quantify. Either way, he doesn't show much and a lot of what he does show seems to be manufactured, as if he were merely *pretending* to have some mild emotions just to keep the rest of us from guessing his hidden superpower.

However you choose to look at it, he's not an easy person to approach, particularly with a request for a favor. I have found that one way to disarm Trench is to make him just a tiny bit uncomfortable so that he'll do almost anything to get you to leave his office and let him return to his work, which appears to be all there is in his life. There are no family photos on his desk and no ring on his left third finger. He exhibits no merch from any sports team. He has, trust me, *nothing* on the walls of his office except certificates that prove he is indeed Detective Lieutenant K.C. Trench of the Los Angeles Police Department.

I went so far as to call Trench this time and ask if I might visit him in his lair. Often, I'll barge in and irritate him until he looks something up or answers a question in an effort to ward me off. But on this occasion, I was asking for something outside the realm of his own police work and thought I might as well not catch him unawares. It makes him testy.

'Lieutenant!' I walked in smiling as if we were old friends. We are somewhat respectful colleagues, in that I respect the hell out of Trench and he doesn't despise me as much as he pretends to, which is something coming from Trench. I had also considered calling him 'Trenchy,' but that wasn't going to help my cause much. I'd call him by his first name, but I have no idea what it might be.

'Ms Moss.' That's the equivalent of a warm hug and a kiss on the cheek coming from Trench.

'How've you been? I haven't seen you in a dog's age.' No, I don't know what that means, either.

'I have been right here working. Is there something I can do for you that actually falls within the definition of police work, Ms Moss? I haven't seen your name on any case that I am currently working.' The man exudes charm. And I like him anyway.

I sat down, uninvited, in the chair in front of his desk. He didn't scream at me to remain standing, so I assumed that was OK with the lieutenant, and it reaffirmed that I wasn't actually in the army. 'I have a situation that is not related to any crime in Los Angeles and I'm hoping that you might be able to offer some advice,' I said.

'Advice?' The right corner of Trench's mouth moved a centimeter, which I thought indicated he would be smiling broadly if he were a normal human. 'Am I now your mentor?'

'No.' With Trench, you have to appeal to his cop-ness or you are lost. 'I am working on a homicide case in New Jersey, and

the police department there has been less than cooperative with
me, particularly in locating one witness who might very well
be the key to exonerating my client.'

That tiny move on his lower lip vanished. Trench has a strong
sense of fairness and, more than anything else, is bound to the
principle that the police have to be above petty grievances and
actually protect and serve the public. If every cop were like
Trench, there would be a lot less crime. It doesn't sound logical
but it is. 'Less than cooperative in what way?' he asked.

'The county prosecutor – we don't have district attorneys in
New Jersey – is not so much withholding information as he is
volunteering none and won't answer phone calls from me, my
associate or my investigator.'

'I am aware that there are no district attorneys in New Jersey,'
Trench said. He is an ardent student of the criminal justice
system, and because he is Trench, he knows everything. 'Why
would this prosecutor treat your case differently from any other?'

'He has personal reasons.' You could say that. I just did.

But Trench looked – for him – as if he'd just been punched
in the gut. '*Personal* reasons?' he repeated. Incredulously. To
Trench, the idea that a cop (or any law enforcement official)
would allow something *personal* to get in the way of doing his
job properly was akin to blasphemy.

Still, he did not ask me what the personal reasons might be,
which should give you an indication of how fervently Trench
considers personal things (I'll stop saying *personal* now) to be
inappropriate to any aspect of the job, and he didn't even know
what the job was yet.

'I'm afraid so, and he's making it a vendetta against me in
particular.' That, I thought, would appeal to the lieutenant's
sense of protectiveness and loyalty.

'That is not relevant.' OK, so maybe not, but he was still on
my side of the argument, at least for now. 'How is this prosecutor withholding information, and what information are we
discussing?'

I gave him a very truncated version of Stephanie's case, and
I'll give this to Trench: he did not comment on the fact that
she was my cousin or how completely guilty she would seem
to any cop who might have wandered into the scene. He just

listened. When I explained about Lucia D'Alessandro and how completely she seemed to have vanished, he nodded.

'You are hoping I might be able to use the resources at my disposal as a member of the Los Angeles Police Department to help track down your missing witness,' he said by way of clarification.

'That's exactly right,' I told him.

'I will not do that.'

I'm sure it wasn't *really* half an hour that I stared at him. It was likely just a few seconds. But life is funny in that the things you enjoy seem to whiz by at the speed of light while watching Trench not only play by the book but drag a copy of it out to read to you can slow time down to the pace of an arthritic snail.

'You won't?' I said. Do you have a snappier retort at the ready? I didn't think so.

Trench stood up because sitting is too passive an action for a dedicated officer of the law. He didn't walk around or pace or even crack his knuckles in preparation for the simple recitation of rules and facts he was undoubtedly about to deliver. He just stood there like a statue of a homicide detective erected to inspire other homicide detectives to live up to the ideal.

'No, I will not,' he began. 'Without a court order or a directive from the chief of detectives, I am not authorized to disseminate such information. It would be a violation of my position and my duty to the people of Los Angeles County.'

It wasn't that I would have expected anything else from Trench, believe me. It was more that he had led me to believe his sense of justice would be offended if I were kept from getting vital information because Richard is such a total . . . Richard. His initial reaction to my story had been so encouraging that I thought I'd appealed to his better nature, but it turned out he was just a police robot and not a sensitive human being. I should have known that going in. But the realization sort of froze me and I stood there again just gaping at Trench in disbelief.

'However,' he continued, making me happy I hadn't been able to verbalize my outrage, 'you should be permitted necessary information under the rule of the criminal justice system.

The fact that it is being denied you is counterproductive to an efficient resolution of the homicide.'

Yes, he really talks like that. Mr Spock would be in awe.

'So what should I do?' I asked. A little prodding didn't seem unreasonable.

Trench reached over, still standing, to his computer keyboard and clacked away at the keys for a few moments without answering me at all. Then he looked at me carefully and said, 'I am going to leave my office for a moment to buy a bottle of water. Under no circumstances should you leave your seat. I will return in precisely four minutes.' And without so much as a glance, he walked out from behind his desk and strode – there is no other word for it – to his office door. He stopped, closed the blinds on the glass door so the interior of his office could not be seen from the hallway, then walked through the door and vanished down the corridor.

Anyone else (and I mean *anyone* else) would have given me five minutes.

Naturally, my first move was to leap up and jump behind Trench's desk to look at his computer screen. What struck me first was how accurate and complete his memory of a case was, because I'd only told him the basic facts and he'd taken no notes, but there on the screen was the information available to police officers given out by the Middlesex County Prosecutor's Office regarding the state of *County of Middlesex v. Stephanie Silverstone*. This was the stuff that Richard should have given me in discovery, which was going to be the subject of a motion that Judge Grossman would be receiving the following day.

In particular, this page was devoted to the interrogation of Lucia D'Alessandro and noted mostly that there hadn't been any such event because the witness had been 'unaccounted for' since the day of the crime. Why this might not have seemed suspicious to a criminal investigator was a subject not broached in the document. What *was* mentioned was the fact that the search for Lucia, halfhearted though it surely was, had been focused mostly on the Cumberland County town of Millville. But so far, the witness herself had not been located, and this document was dated two days earlier.

The name Anthony D'Alessandro was mentioned as the

witness's father but it was seemingly connected to an address in Linden, not Millville. I took a picture of the screen with my phone and sat down just in time for Trench to return to his office, carrying a bottle of water from a vending machine, as promised.

'Good,' he said. He said it briskly, which is the way he said everything. 'You did not leave your seat.'

'Of course not,' I answered. 'You told me not to.'

TWENTY-EIGHT

Sarah Panico had been my arch nemesis since the fourth grade, and if I'm being truthful, she probably never even knew that. My nine-year-old brain had, having jumped the rails of some train of thought, decided I needed an arch nemesis, most likely after watching some cartoon show on TV, and Sarah had fit the bill. She was taller than me, prettier than me and more popular than me. None of those things was her fault, but at that age, they were more than enough.

I'm telling you all this because I was about to get on a Zoom call with Sarah and you need to know why my digestive system was in disarray and my teeth were grinding at a record pace. The things that you decide in childhood might be proven incorrect beyond any reasonable doubt (to employ a legal phrase) but they never actually leave your mind. They lie dormant and wait for the occasion when you have to interrogate Sarah Panico about a murder case.

(If you're waiting for an update on the dragnet pursuit of Lucia D'Alessandro, worry not. I promise you I'll be catching you up soon. Stay patient. Thank you.)

I had sent Sarah the link after she'd agreed by email to do the interview. Mae had offered, but they say you have to face your fears, so I was diving in headfirst. There were only ten days before I'd be packing up to head to New Jersey for the duration of the trial. I had procrastinated as long as I possibly could.

She made me wait for six minutes. I tried to avoid thinking that was a classic Sarah Panico move, but you can only control your mind to a certain extent and then it takes over on its own. When she did show up on my screen, without makeup, she looked terrific. Large eyes, unremarkable nose, lips made for lying.

Don't expect objectivity for the next few pages.

We got the 'pleasantries' out of the way because we were just being pleasant out of some sense of propriety, and I began doing the questioning in earnest. The faster I could get this over with, the sooner I could take off the top of my outfit and put on a grungy tee shirt.

'The day of Stephanie's party, I noticed that you went into the kitchen when she was already there. When we were there, you said that she'd texted you and asked you to come inside. In fact, you said, "Stephanie needs me." What was going on in the kitchen?'

She looked at me blankly for a moment, to the point that I wondered if there was some lag in the transmission. 'Oh, nothing special,' she said.

I waited. Then I waited a little more.

'That's it?' I said. 'You walked out of a party to go into a commercial kitchen because someone said they needed you and when you got there nothing was going on? Why did Stephanie text you about that?'

Sarah didn't want to make eye contact, even if all she was looking at was her webcam. 'She didn't say.'

I wondered if all her answers would be exactly three words long and then realized I wasn't asking the questions in a way that would elicit more detailed responses. This was on me. 'What did you guys talk about once you were in the kitchen?'

'You know, wedding stuff.' Four words. Progress.

'Was Brandon Starkey in the kitchen when you got there?' I figured I'd get only one word this time so my quota would almost even out.

But Sarah surprised me. She started as if awakened and her eyes got even wider. 'Oh, no!' she barked. 'I didn't see Brandon at all in the kitchen! I wasn't there when anything happened!'

Particularly when you're representing the defense in a

criminal trial (although it happens for the prosecution too because people see them as 'the police'), a witness doesn't realize you are questioning them to find ways to help prove your case and not to incriminate them personally. I didn't think Sarah Panico had killed Brandon Starkey because, for one thing, I couldn't think of a reason why she'd want to. But that's how people hear the question, so you have to put that thought to rest as quickly as possible.

'I didn't think you were,' I told her. 'I'm just trying to figure out the timeline because I didn't see Brandon was in the kitchen, and I'm trying to figure out why. So you telling me that you didn't see him says he wasn't there until very late, possibly right before he died.'

'Well, he wasn't there when I was there.' She wanted to be *very* clear about that, and now I actually might have been getting a tiny bit suspicious.

'Right. How well did you know Brandon?' OK, so there was a minuscule part of me that was enjoying making Sarah uncomfortable. I never said I was perfect. Ask my mother.

'I just knew him through Michael. When she started dating him, Brandon just started showing up to stuff.'

Of course. Wait, what? 'Stephanie was dating Brandon? You mean when Stephanie was dating Michael, right?' That was what I'd heard. Surely.

'Oh. Yeah. That's what I meant.' Sure. Yeah, that was it. Have you ever had a conversation with a pathological liar?

'*Did* Stephanie ever date Brandon?' And would the prosecution know about that?

'Um . . . I don't know. I never *saw* them together. Ask Stephanie.' The worst possible response. So there had been something going on between my client and the man she was accused of murdering, who was to be the best man at her wedding to his best friend. I was sure this could get worse, but I was afraid to think how that might happen.

'Sarah. Stephanie's next fifteen years are on the line. Maybe more. So if you know something, I need you to tell me right now so I can defend her against it. What do you know? Did Stephanie have a thing with Brandon Starkey?'

This wasn't a petty thing from grade school anymore and I

think my tone reflected that. Sarah's eyes focused more keenly and looked at her screen (where I was) and not her webcam (where she could dictate how she'd look).

'The fact is, I don't know,' she said. 'But I know Lucia broke up with him over someone else and I know he told Stephanie he was in love with her. So you do the math.'

All my friendly witnesses were lining up to incriminate my client. 'I was a poli sci major,' I said.

Ten more days to go back to Jersey. Twelve days until the trial began.

And I had nothing.

TWENTY-NINE

'I have a break on the back-door key,' Mae told me.

I was driving to the apartment after having had a strange encounter with George Seaton, the Seaton in the name of the law firm that employed me. I think I had met Seaton once before, when I'd flown out from Jersey to interview for the job. I met a number of the partners then, including one who was (thankfully) no longer associated with the firm. I'd shaken his hand and he'd said something noncommittal and that had been it.

Today, however, Seaton had walked into my office only seconds after our receptionist had informed me he'd be coming in. There had been no explanation and no previous warning. So let's assume I was a little flustered.

'Ms Moss.' I assumed he was addressing me and not reading the name off my office door, but it was a close call, seeing as how he didn't say anything immediately after that.

'Hello, Mr Seaton.' At least I'd added 'hello.' It's the personal touch. Why the hell was he here, again?

'Please sit down.' I hadn't realized I'd stood when he'd walked in. Who did I think he was, the king? I hadn't checked recently but I was fairly sure we didn't have one of those in America, at least not since the late 1700s. So I sat down, both because it made sense and because Seaton, the controlling partner in the firm, had told me to.

'Ms Moss, I have been hearing good things about you.' Seaton had lowered himself into the chair in front of my desk without an invitation, which had not been offered because I am inconsiderate and was still reeling a bit at his unexpected visit. But he wasn't here to fire me, it seemed, so that was something.

'I'm glad to hear that, Mr Seaton.' The only place he would have heard anything about me here would have been from Holly. So this had to have something to do with whatever oddball situation she'd been telling me about.

'Feel free to call me George,' he said. Apparently, that was a special privilege reserved for the favored few, of whom I seemed to be one, at least for today.

'I'm Sandy, George.' Not that he didn't already know that, but I was still waiting to hear what had brought my old pal George down from his office on the twenty-second floor. I'd heard tales of that office but had never visited it myself. I hear there's a kitchen. A full kitchen.

'Indeed.' Who knew what that meant? I had to get on a plane to New Jersey in three days, so I was hoping he'd come to the point before my Uber showed up. 'As I was saying, your work has been attracting some positive attention from clients and partners.'

The chances that I was getting fired were seeming considerably more remote, but some executives like to lull you into a false sense of security before lowering the boom. I had quit the only other legal job I'd ever had and so was spared the thrill of finding out what Richard's method of axing someone might have been.

'Thank you.' I mean, what do you say to that?

Then Seaton did the absolute last thing I would have expected: he stood up. 'Keep up the good work,' he said, and walked briskly (for a man of eighty, which he was, or even fifty, which I had to assume he had once been) out of my office. I was sitting there alone as I'd been before he'd arrived, but now it seemed weird to be alone in my own office.

'What was *that* about?' I asked the walls, but they didn't know either.

So now in my car, Mae's call was interesting, but my mind was torn between trying to decipher Seaton's bizarre visit and listening to the investigator who might help me keep my cousin out of state prison.

'The back-door key?' I asked. Was it code for something?

'Yeah, but now that I have your attention, I found out something about the victim, Starkey.'

'Brandon Starkey,' I said.

'Yeah. Seems that a few months ago, good old Brandon was working at a gas station on Route 9 in Old Bridge and he was the victim of an armed robbery. He got bonked on the head with the gun.'

OK, that *was* news, but I didn't see how it fit into our case. 'OK, that's bad, but what does it have to do with him being murdered?'

'The gas station was owned by some guys who might not be exactly as legit as they'd like you to believe,' Mae told me.

Interesting. More interesting than the seventh Tesla I'd seen in this short trip, each driven by a guy looking a little more bro-ey than the last. I ignored the latest one. 'So he was working for the mob? Did Brandon know that?'

Mae took a minute, I assumed to consult notes. 'There's no way of knowing, but he did have a couple of misdemeanors on his records. Nothing serious. One breaking and entering but it was never prosecuted. Think maybe there was some pressure from his bosses?'

This was definitely something, but as usual in this case, I didn't know what. 'Do me a favor and send me the whole file on him if you have it.'

'I have it. Now. The back-door key. The one to the Elks hall. For the door that could have let someone into the kitchen without you seeing them walk in.' Mae was clearly wondering if I'd bet some IQ points and lost.

'Oh! Yeah. You know who had it?' She'd said something about a break. Had a person we hadn't considered yet broken into the Elks kitchen and killed Brandon? To be honest, I'd forgotten about the key because it seemed like everyone who could have supplied one had an airtight alibi.

'We know who had three copies. Tony Angelino, the Elks

chef, the grand exalted whatever, Sylvia Keene, and Larry Mandrake, the building superintendent.'

'And as I recall, each and every one of them checked out as not being at the Elks the day Brandon Starkey was killed,' I said. There was a guy driving a Hyundai Ioniq, the latest trendy electric-ish car (less expensive than most) in the lane to the right of me and my ancient ancestor to his car, and he was grinning at me in a mean way.

'That's right.' I hit the gas a bit just to pass the guy in the Ioniq, because I was pretty sure he was dissing his predecessor and I won't put up with someone mocking my car. I'm from Jersey. 'But I now believe there was a fourth key.' Mae sounded certain, but then she always did.

I forgot about the Ioniq. 'Really! What makes you think so?'

'Because someone found it next to a Dumpster in the parking lot the same day as the murder,' Mae said. 'Believe it or not, they actually brought the key to the nearest police station because they couldn't get into the Elks when it was blocked off for the crime scene investigation.'

So someone walking through the parking lot of a crime scene, with a squadron of cops around, found a key nobody from the investigation team managed to locate, and either tried to bring it inside the building or maybe even hand it off to one of the officers there and was rebuked. So this civic-minded citizen took the key, probably thinking someone had lost it and would need it back, to the closest police station. The situation just kept getting weirder.

'Don't keep me in suspense, Mae. There had to have been video surveillance running.'

'There was.' She almost sounded amused.

'So who do we see picking up a small object near the dumpster and then . . . I'm not even going to speculate. Who found the key?'

She let a small rasp escape from her throat, a sign of disgust. 'The county prosecutor's office won't release the footage,' she said. 'They say it's not relevant to the case.'

'Not . . .' I didn't want to, but I had to. 'OK. I'll be on a plane tonight.'

'What are you going to do that I can't?' Mae asked.

'I'm going to my old office to raise some hell,' I said.

As it turned out, I needed that Uber three days early.

THIRTY

It's not that you become immune to the drudgery of air travel when you do it frequently. It's more that you become resigned to it, like the twice-a-year visit to the dentist you know will be awful but is the only alternative to a worse reality.

I arrived at Newark after a flight accurately referred to as a 'red-eye.' It flies through the night and arrives three hours later than it should, meaning you get to your destination (assuming you are, like me, traveling from Los Angeles to New Jersey) at seven a.m., but your body knows for a fact it's four in the morning.

One of the things I did when not sleeping was read over the file on Brandon Starkey that Mae had supplied, which included the reports on his three arrests, two for disorderly conduct, which hadn't amounted to much of anything, and the third for breaking into a paint store in Iselin but getting caught before he could steal anything from the cash register or the safe. Maybe Brandon just wanted to brighten up his living room. Either way, the charges were dropped and there was no trial. Maybe someone was covering for him and maybe not. But by then we were landing.

This time, I didn't stop at Patrick's apartment first. I hadn't even told Patrick, Angie or anyone other than Holly Wentworth and my neighbor who waters our plants when we're away that I was going back to New Jersey three days early. I didn't know where there were moles giving out information and I didn't want to be expected at my former office ahead of my arrival. I took a Lyft from the airport to Highland Park, where I had breakfast at a little diner called the Dish Café ('Food for the Palette') because there wouldn't be anyone working in the county building in New Brunswick until at least eight thirty.

Figuring I was on Skinny's dime (and because it was too hot to walk), I took an actual taxi to the courthouse (where all the offices are kept) as soon as I could be sure the doors would be opened. I couldn't barge right through the metal detectors at the entrance because I was no longer an employee, but barging was definitely on my mind. As soon as I cleared security, I did some.

Ron Barkley was the first of my former colleagues to recognize me once I pushed through the office door. 'Sandy!' I wasn't sure if it was a warm welcome or a warning to all others in the room.

'Ronnie,' I said, but I didn't stop walking. I knew where Richard's office was, and I wasn't going there. With any luck at all, he wouldn't know I was there until after I'd left. But that meant working fast and not stopping to catch up with the 'old gang.'

'Hey, I heard you moved to LA.' Was Ron going to ask me if I'd met any movie stars? Because I could really blow his mind if I answered in detail.

'Yup,' I said and kept going. The evidence room was upstairs and only Randy O'Malley, the investigator in charge of the case, would be able to open the door to that room. But I didn't need to get into the room. I just needed to get into the computer files.

And believe me, I had tried to do so before leaving California. Discovery is kept online in specific files that are supposed to be made available to all attorneys listed as attached to the case in question. But Richard had managed somehow to, um, forget about the existence of the parking-lot video footage from the Elks. Confronting him would have been pointless. Confronting Randy O'Malley would have been excruciating because the man is dumber than a bag of hammers and considerably less useful.

But confronting Robert Conforto, on the other hand, could be fruitful, if less satisfying than telling Richard to his face that I was going to try to have him removed from his office at my earliest opportunity. That could wait, and Bob Conforto, the chief of county detectives, could not. But he didn't even know that yet.

I didn't knock on Bob's door, even as Ronnie, behind me and trying to keep pace, was asking about the weather in

Southern California. I muttered something about it being nicer than here and pushed Bob's door open.

He was standing at his window when I walked in and, not surprisingly, looked sharply in my direction, not expecting the interruption and certainly not anticipating that the interruption might be me. 'Sandy!' This time, it was not warm or warning but puzzled.

'Hi, Bob.' I closed the door behind me. I don't generally do that when I'm in a room with a man by myself, but I knew Bob and didn't think he'd appreciate the rest of the office hearing what I was about to say. 'I need some discovery that Richard doesn't want me to have, and if you don't allow me to have it, I'll file a complaint with the courts and it's entirely possible you could get fired, and possibly indicted.'

Bob is one of those older guys who gets all paternal when he's talking to a younger woman. He smiled. 'Nice to see you too, Sandy,' he said. 'How is LA treating you?'

He is generally a sweet guy, but he's a cop and cops tend to do what prosecutors tell them to, which in this case was the opposite of what I wanted. I had to maintain my take-no-prisoners approach or he'd soon be ushering me out the door without the video footage I needed.

And it's possible I mentioned the trial was starting in four days?

'It's fine, Bob,' I told him. 'The weather's great, I have a gorgeous office overlooking Hollywood and I have a boyfriend who's a movie star. So you can imagine how thrilled I am to have taken the red-eye here this morning just to get a piece of evidence that you should have sent to me by secure email in the first place. So how about you find the file of security footage from the Stephanie Silverstone case that shows someone picking up a spare key to the Elks Lodge after a man had been knifed to death in the kitchen of that building.'

(My office hardly qualified as 'gorgeous.' I used the word for effect. And Hollywood, as any resident of Los Angeles will tell you, ain't exactly what you think it is.)

'Wow! What movie star?' Bob was being cute and showing me that I hadn't managed to intimidate him. Which, to be fair, I hadn't expected to do.

'The footage, Bob. Open up your files and give me the footage. I have a very handy little thumb drive right here in my purse if the file's too big to email.'

Bob indicated a chair in front of his very basic desk. 'You want a water or something?'

'I just ate, thanks. The footage.'

He sat down as I did and made a show of firing up his desktop computer. It was, as might be expected from a county budget, not the flashiest on the market. It was also probably from 2004. 'Now, what footage is it you're talking about?'

That was just patronizing enough to stoke the fire of outrage (and possibly jet lag) in my belly. 'Let's not be adorable, Bob,' I said. 'You know exactly what I'm talking about. There's footage of the Elks parking lot and someone walks by, notices a key on the asphalt near the dumpster and picks it up. It's not clear if they try to give it to the platoon of cops you had there or not, but it ended up in the nearest police station and I need to know who it was that picked it up. So stick a shovel into your hard drive and get out that footage before I take an elevator to a judge who can force you to do it, OK?'

Being the chief of county detectives did not require Bob Conforto to wear his uniform, and he wasn't today, dressed in a gray suit that was probably issued to every detective working for a government agency until you got to the FBI, where the suits became blue. So he didn't have quite the same authority as a man in blue who might be packing heat. I didn't for a second think Bob would shoot me rather than hand over the evidence, but it was just good policy not to take the chance.

'I don't believe there's any relevant information on that footage,' Bob said. 'You won't want to use any of it in court.'

'You don't get to decide that and you know it,' I told him. 'I could have simply filed to have the case dismissed, but I figured I'd give you a chance to hand it over before I took it upstairs and got someone to fire you, because I like you. So this is the last time I'll ask, and then I'm heading for the elevator. Where is that footage?'

Bob's avuncular face hardened and his eyes narrowed. 'You don't have to threaten me, Sandy. You're legally entitled to this file and you're going to get it. But I remember when you were a prosecutor and you would have done anything to get a woman who stabbed the best man at her wedding seventeen times to go to jail for the rest of her life, and you know *that*. You would have done anything.' He had been copying a file on his computer to a thumb drive, which he handed to me.

I took it and stood up. 'Anything *legal*,' I said and walked out of the office. 'Nice seeing you, Bob.'

THIRTY-ONE

' I have missed this,' Patrick said. And no, he wasn't talking about me.

We were standing on the empty stage at the Public Theater on Lafayette Street, far downtown in Manhattan, where *The Scottish Play* was now in full rehearsal mode. The rest of the company, including the director, were on a lunch break of one hour, and Patrick was taking the opportunity to show me around the set. Which was to say, around an empty stage because the sets had not been completed yet.

'Live theater?' I asked, largely because he hadn't said what he missed and I needed to prod the conversation along a bit. I had to be back in New Brunswick to gather some of my more reluctant witnesses in one place and browbeat them into saying what I wanted them to say on the witness stand. I mean, not really, but I at least had to know what to expect from them. And that was on the schedule for four p.m., a little under three hours from now.

Patrick nodded. 'I hadn't even realized how much I'd missed it,' he said. 'I'd gotten so used to film sets.'

I wanted Patrick to love his work in New York; believe me, I did. He'd sounded so happy when I'd called to tell him I was in the same time zone again. But a play isn't like a movie or a TV series. (Series are the best. They rarely leave their base, be it LA or Vancouver, and you get to see the person you're with pretty much every day.) Plays at theatrical companies like the Public will have a limited run of however many weeks, but if it's a big hit (with, let's say a very recognizable TV star in the cast), it might transfer to Broadway and have an open-ended run that could monopolize that TV star – whoever it might be – for as long as they want to stay. If Patrick loved doing the play *too* much, he could be here for years, and I was going back to Los Angeles at the end of this trial no matter what. Because law firms, oddly, expect you to stay in one place as long as you work for them.

'But you love acting on film,' I reminded him because that was exactly as possessive and constricting as I was feeling that day. I hadn't gotten to see the footage I'd just extorted from Bob Conforto yet because I hadn't been near a computer, just my phone. But I guessed that it was going to be yet another roadblock in the two-lane highway that was Stephanie's case. Everything I'd done so far had led to virtually nothing, and time was rapidly running out.

'Of course I do,' Patrick said. He stopped himself and looked at me. 'I'm not moving out here permanently, Sandy. For one thing, it gets cold here in February.'

'It gets cold here in October.' (OK, actually November, but I was making a point.)

'I'm just saying that this kind of work has been out of my life for too long and I'm glad to be back.' He gave me a significant look. 'They have theater in Los Angeles too, you know.' That was true, but this might become Broadway, and if you're not performing in the West End in London, Broadway is what theater is about in Patrick's business.

I sat down on the lip of the stage as if I were trying to ingratiate myself with an invisible audience. Pretty soon, I'd be asking empty seats where they were from. 'I'm sorry, Patrick. I don't mean to dampen your fun. You're so happy doing this, and I'm a bundle of nerves over Skinny's trial.'

Patrick looked down at me for a moment and then joined me, dangling his legs off the stage, too. But somehow he looked more professional doing that. Never tell me anything an actor does is 'effortless.' 'Is it going that badly?' he asked.

'Honestly, if I were a juror in that box, I'm not sure that I wouldn't vote to convict her. My evidence is all circumstantial and the prosecution's is, too, but they have countless iPhone pictures of the defendant holding the murder weapon and covered in blood. That's not so easy to erase from their heads.'

Patrick pursed his lips a bit because he was thinking. 'In my business,' he said finally, 'I have to convince people of a lot of things that are crazier than that.' It was true: he'd once played a two-fisted anthropologist and nobody blinked, even if the movie was . . . disappointing.

'So how would you go about it?' I asked him. It was an honest question. Any piece of advice I could pick up here would be more than I had now.

'It's not the same thing as what you do,' he admitted. 'But most of my job is made up of me trying to convince the audience that *I* believe in what I'm saying and doing. I find that if I can make myself believe in it, I can make them believe in it.'

I wanted to kiss him for clarifying the situation so well. But his words had hit me in a way for which I hadn't prepared. 'That's the problem, Patrick,' I said. 'I'm not sure I believe it.'

That was when he kissed me on the forehead, a gesture of comfort. 'Well, then,' he said. 'I shall have to give you acting lessons.'

'I suppose you're all wondering why I asked you here today,' I said.

My cousin Stephen, my Aunt Fern, a woman named Diana Bancroft whom I had not met before (but who had been at the party and seen, you know, everything) and Michael the Groom, whose last name turned out to be Fortunato, stared at me blankly. Apparently, not one of them had ever read a mystery novel or seen a detective movie. It happens. I personally have only read the classics – Agatha Christie, Raymond Chandler and Dashiell Hammett.

'I figured it was because you wanted to talk to us about the trial,' Diana said.

'Yeah, what was the deal sending me a subpoena,' Michael said. 'Did you think I wouldn't show up?'

'Subpoenas are issued to everyone who will be called as a witness,' I explained. 'You may consider it a courtesy, so you know the date, time and place you need to appear ahead of time.' And I wanted to be able to have a bench warrant issued if he didn't show up. You don't have to tell people *everything*.

'Huh,' Michael said. I decided to question him last just to make him wait as long as possible.

Jessica had lent me a spare office in her suite and right now we were in the waiting area. 'I'm going to call each of you in separately,' I said. 'That's so I get to hear your answers without anyone else listening or trying to help. You're going to be testifying in a murder trial, probably next week, and I want to be sure that you are prepared.'

'Are you going to tell us what to say?' Stephen asked. He didn't look up from his phone as he spoke.

'No,' I answered. 'I want you to answer truthfully no matter what the truth is. If there are things I think won't be helpful to Stephanie's defense, I probably won't ask you about it on the stand, but the prosecutor might.'

Stephen actually looked disappointed that he was not going to be scripted. I decided to brighten his day. 'Why don't you come in first?' I said.

My cousin, whom I've known all his life, looked at me as if I had just transformed into a werewolf before his eyes. 'Me?' He had actually taken his eyes off his screen, a sign of absolute panic.

I smiled a friendly cousin smile at him and held out a hand. 'Sure, come on,' I said. 'Get it over with right away.'

Stephen was not the type to object strenuously, but I did see him sneak a frantic peek at the office door as if he might decide to bolt rather than face a conversation with me. I knew he was a little odd. Now I was starting to wonder if he might also be homicidal. But it was too late to ask Jess if there was security available in the building. I had a phone and knew the number for 911.

I ushered my cousin into the waiting office, which was small but perfectly functional for what I needed. He watched his feet as he walked inside, as if each step was something of a surprise for him. The other witnesses-to-be couldn't have been terribly encouraged watching Stephen slink off as if he were attending his own execution.

He stood across from me as I sat down at the desk. It was a pretty spare room, but it had touches that I attributed to Jessica. There was a well-tended plant on the desk, to one side and not so big that it blocked my view. Stephen's client chair was cushioned, but he wasn't using it. The walls had been painted fairly recently, and the rug on the floor complimented them nicely. 'Sit down,' I said to my cousin.

Stephen's head snapped to attention. He had pocketed his smartphone, which was a signal in itself that he was on edge. 'Sit?' He pointed to the chair, which was, to be honest, the only place other than the floor where he could sit.

'Yes. Don't worry, Stephen. This isn't going to hurt at all.'

He stopped in mid-sit and considered. 'I hadn't thought it was going to hurt,' he said.

'Good, because it won't. Now, please tell me how well you knew Brandon Starkey.'

Stephen's responses came with a pause each time as if he was translating from another language in his head. 'How well?' His first line of defense, it seemed, was going to be repeating what I'd said. I didn't respond because I figured it was just Stephen's timing device, and I turned out to be right. 'I just knew him from when Michael started bringing him around.'

'I didn't ask how you met him. Remember this for the trial – just answer the question that's asked and don't volunteer anything that's not, OK?'

Stephen looked at his shoes again. 'Sorry.'

'You don't have to be sorry because you didn't do anything wrong. You couldn't have known that. But please tell me, were you and Brandon friends?'

Stephen nodded slowly, but that was more or less to himself, absorbing what I had said. 'Friends?' I sat and waited. 'I don't know. We didn't do anything together. He was the guy that Steph's guy hung around with. He was nice enough.' A small private grin showed up on Stephen's face for a moment and then vanished.

'Now, the prosecutor is going to ask you how you're related to Stephanie. What will you say?'

He looked surprised in a totally predictable way. His eyes got slitty. (And I will from this point omit the times he repeated the question back to me, for your reading pleasure.) 'I'm her brother.'

'Good.' It was best to make him feel as though he'd succeeded. I didn't expect grandiloquence from Stephen, but an answer beyond one word – at least before he got on the witness stand – wouldn't be an awful idea. 'Now. Let's get to the day of the rehearsal party.' I didn't give him time to explain to me that time travel was not possible, at least not yet. 'Right after you and I talked, I saw you walk into the kitchen. Why did you go in there?'

Actual sweat appeared on Stephen's forehead despite the efficient air conditioning in the office building. 'I didn't kill Brandon,' he said.

'I'm not suggesting you did. Take it easy. I'm more interested in what you saw when you were in there. What was going on?'

I had tried to make the question sound almost casual, like I was just shooting the breeze and hoping for some good gossip from my cousin. But because Stephen and I had never had that kind of relationship in our lives, he was naturally cautious in his response.

'Nothing.'

Maybe *cautious* was understating it. I was going to have to take it step by step. 'Who was in there when you arrived?' I asked.

'Well, Steph was in there.' Sometimes a witness will repeat a phrase you use in an effort to be especially specific in the answer to the question. I didn't think that was the case here. 'And Brandon was there. Maybe Sarah; I don't remember.'

It was significant that he'd mentioned Sarah Panico at all, but I didn't want to scare him off by making a big deal out of it. I pivoted. 'Was Michael there? In the kitchen?'

The quickest answer I'd gotten yet. 'No! Michael wasn't there.'

Michael was totally there.

'One last question. What were the bunch of you doing in the kitchen?'

Stephen looked me straight in the face for that one.

'I got myself a steak sandwich,' he said.

THIRTY-TWO

lied. I got Michael Fortunato in the room next. I was annoyed enough to face him now, so why wait?

Sitting down, he looked more like a potted plant, but the effect was still there. He was not fat, but thick pretty much everywhere. His neck especially looked as if it could hold up a small building. Leaves would not have been incongruous on his head and arms.

I wasn't trying to make nice with this guy, partially because I'd seen how he treated my cousin, the woman he supposedly loved. 'So what were you doing in the kitchen of the Elks Lodge before Brandon got stabbed?' That was my opener.

'What?' Clearly, Skinny had fallen for this man's witty banter.

'You heard me. I know for a fact that you were in there right before the murder.' I knew nothing of the sort; I was going on a hunch. Cops do this all the time. 'So tell me why you were there if it wasn't to stab your best friend multiple times.'

'I wasn't there.' In the way he said it, I was immediately sure he was lying.

'Yeah, you were. Multiple people saw you there.' None of them had said so, but if you don't tell him that, I won't either.

'I was just checking in on Steph.'

'That was a quick segue there, Mikey.' I didn't wait for him to ask what *segue* meant. 'OK, so you were there to check on Stephanie. Why? Were you worried about her? And why didn't you go in through the front door?' Had he been the guy with the spare key to the back? Why not see if I could get him to admit that, too?

'We were gonna get married,' he said. 'You get nervous.'

'The back door, Mike. Why'd you use the back door?'

'I don't know what you're talking about.' Maybe a couple of leaves fell off his left bicep.

'You forget that I was there, too,' I told him. 'I saw everyone who went into the kitchen before the murder. You weren't any of them. The only other way was through the back door. Why'd you go in that way?'

'I was out walking around, thinking things over. The back door was open, so I went in that way.'

This guy was going to be the worst witness in history. He couldn't validate any of what he was saying.

'The back door was just open?'

'Yeah.' Franklin Delano Roosevelt in his prime wished he could be so eloquent.

'You were thinking what over?' I asked. 'Getting cold feet about the wedding?'

His face took on a little swagger, a little combative spunk. (I hate combative spunk.) 'Yeah, maybe. You know, your cousin's not necessarily the best possible wife in the world.'

I had to ask. 'What makes you say that? What did you see when you walked into the kitchen?' Because from what I'd been told, there had been quite the sight to see.

But Michael squinted at me as if the sun was in his eyes. 'You want to know what I saw? I saw your cousin and her wimpy brother. I saw Sarah Panico, the biggest pain in the ass this side of the Rocky Mountains.' (OK, on that we were agreed.) 'And I saw my closest friend, but I didn't know it was for the last time. And they were all drinking champagne without me.'

Was that the issue? He was feeling left out?

'How did you react?' I asked.

He shrugged. 'I poured myself a glass, drank it and went out the way I came. Because now I didn't want to get married anymore.'

OK, that was news.

Diana Bancroft was the person I knew the least about (aside from a brief document Mae had provided, which was helpful) so I brought her in next. Admittedly, I was trying to avoid any member of my family and Michael, who had jumped to the top of my suspect list, at that moment.

Diana sat down with an air of professionalism. She was tall in the chair, back straight and clothing unwrinkled in any spot. She was my Bizarro World self. I tried not to hold that against her.

'So how do you know Stephanie and Michael?' I asked as a kickoff. I was already scanning the notes Jessica had given me to determine why I was talking to Diana. Because I'd read them on the plane and go remember anything you read on a plane.

'I don't,' Diana answered. 'I was a plus-one for Ben Canowicz, a guy who works with Michael. I'd never met them before the rehearsal party.'

'That was quite an introduction,' I said without really considering it.

Luckily, Diana just nodded in a professional manner. 'I know, right?'

'You didn't go into the kitchen at any point that day, did you?' I asked. Jess's notes indicated Diana had been close enough to hear something relevant to our case, but they weren't specific, at least not on this page.

'No! Thank goodness!' Diana mimed wiping sweat from her forehead. Seriously. 'No. I didn't even see what happened after until the police were already there.'

She didn't? 'So what *did* you see?' I asked. Which page was that on, again? I rifled through the hard copy again.

'I didn't see anything,' Diana answered. Before I could ask why the hell she was in my office, she said, 'But I did hear something.'

OK. Yes. On page four. 'You heard Stephanie walking into the restroom next to the kitchen, right?' Thank you, Mae.

Diana looked pleased like the good little girl who had done the extra credit assignment for social studies and didn't realize the rest of the kids hated her for that. 'Yes, that's right. I was in the restroom in the main hall, but it shared a wall with the one for the kitchen employees. And I could hear Stephanie in there.'

Well, that was disturbing. I made a mental vow never to use a public restroom again.

'You sure it was Stephanie?' I was trying to head off any balloon-busting arguments Richard was going to try to mount. 'Anyone could have been in there.'

'It was her. I didn't know it was her then because I hadn't heard her voice more than maybe once. But I've heard her voice on the news over and over, now. She was singing along with Taylor Swift and she was pretty loud.'

Well, that certainly brought up a lot of new questions. If Skinny was singing her brains out in the bathroom, how did whoever killed Brandon not hear her? How come Brandon didn't hear her? On the other hand, maybe he did, because I wouldn't be able to ask him now.

'Could she have been in there before Brandon was killed?' Richard would be sure to ask that one, too.

Diana's face took on an expression of dismay. She seemed to be mortified that she couldn't necessarily give me the answer I wanted. 'I can't be sure,' she said. 'I didn't hear a struggle or anything, but I did hear the commotion outside when, I guess, she walked out with the knife.' This was a witness who had been following the case closely. That's not bad in the way it would be with a potential juror, but it wasn't great. People get into strange fan-like situations with people involved in sensational crimes. I can't tell you how many women I've tried to talk out of marrying a man in prison for killing his wife. OK, I *can* tell you. One. And she married him anyway. Let's say it didn't end well and leave it at that.

I established that Diana had not taken accurate notes of the time she entered and left the ladies' room (imagine) and thanked her for her time. She wouldn't be a bad witness, but she wasn't a slam dunk by any stretch of the imagination. She got up and left the office. I asked her to close the door so I could regroup before calling in my Aunt Fern, who *would* be a bad witness in that she'd clearly say anything necessary to clear her daughter and the truth might not be her top priority.

Aunt Fern was the kind of woman who appeared to outside observers to be almost unbearably meek. She rarely spoke at length, and even when she did, it was in such a subdued tone that you weren't sure even *she* wanted to hear what she had to say. But that was all an image she'd decided to project. Behind the scenes, she has raised two children pretty much on her own and had pummeled at least one of them (Stephen, let's be real) into being as timid as she wanted you to believe she was. The woman was made of steel, but in cables that could bend to whatever shape she decided they should be.

I gave myself a good cleansing breath and then walked to the door to bring her into my office. Aunt Fern rose, straightened

her skirt and walked formally into the room. But she did it
meekly. It's not easy to pull off.

'Stephanie did not kill that boy,' she said before I had asked
her a question.

'I tend to agree with you, Aunt Fern, but you're here as a
witness to an incident and I don't want you offering opinions,
just facts. OK?' Dealing with my family was without question
the trickiest part of this whole deal. At dinner, I'd see Angie
and could unload all the stories from today. She'd get it.

'Well, she didn't.' One other thing about Aunt Fern is that
it's impossible to get her to say anything other than what she'd
rehearsed for herself. She was going to be a nightmare on the
witness stand.

The only option was to dive right into questions. 'What kind
of mood was Stephanie in before the party?'

She raised an eyebrow. 'What do you mean by that?'

'Aunt Fern . . . no, Mrs Silverstone, because that's what I'm
calling you at the trial. Keep that in mind. You're a witness,
and even if I don't call you at the trial, you know the prosecution will. So I am going to tell you the rules for testifying. You
answer the questions directly, and you don't add *anything* that
doesn't respond exactly to what was asked. OK?'

My Aunt Fern is my mother's sister and that should be all
you need to know. 'Well, there's no need to be rude about it,'
she said.

Mentally, I took a deep breath. Mentally, I rolled my eyes
heavenward. Mentally, I resigned from this case and booked a
flight back to LA. Mentally, I hoped Patrick's play would bomb
so he could come home sooner.

Outwardly, I showed nothing. 'What kind of mood was
Stephanie in before the party?' I repeated. It was a test of my
witness.

Surprisingly, she passed. 'She was excited and happy. She was
getting married the next day, after all. She was anxious about the
party going well, but other than that, she was just fine.'

'Very good, but leave out the part about being anxious,' I
told her. 'Don't let the jury think it could have been something
more than just regular pre-wedding jitters, OK?'

Aunt Fern nodded. She was on the defense team now. She

stopped just short of making a come-get-me gesture with her fingertips and saying, 'Bring it on.'

'Great.' I wanted to keep giving her positive feedback. Prepping my mother for the stand was going to be an even bigger headache, so this would prove to be useful practice. Patrick was rehearsing for his performance and I was rehearsing for mine. Maybe I could, after all, convince myself I believed it. 'Did she ever mention Brandon Starkey that day before the party?'

This time, Aunt Fern made a show of thinking. Maybe she was rehearsing, too. 'I don't recall his name coming up.'

A direct answer with nothing attached. 'Excellent,' I said. 'You're a born witness.'

'What do you mean by that?'

Thank goodness I never had to answer that one because my phone rang. Under normal circumstances, I never would have answered it while in a pre-trial conference with a witness, but I hadn't been under normal circumstances in years, and this time the screen showed that Mae Tennyson was calling. Mae usually texts. This had to be something.

'Excuse me,' I said to Aunt Fern. 'I absolutely have to take this call.'

She sniffed at my appalling manners. No doubt she would confer with my mother on the subject at her earliest convenience.

I stood and walked to the far corner of the room, which wasn't that far, just to have some semblance of privacy. 'What's up, Mae?'

Mae sounded positively breathless. 'You're not going to believe it.'

'Probably not. What?'

'I uploaded that video file you sent me on the thumb drive,' she said. 'Quaint, that.'

'Thank goodness you could get it to open. I had no luck at all. But let's not have a technology critique, Mae. What does it show?'

Aunt Fern got out *her* phone just to show me she could do it, too. She was probably texting my mother about the manners thing.

'Exactly what you thought. Someone is walking over by the dumpster outside the Elks Lodge and picking something up off the ground.'

I brushed my hair back with my hand for no reason other than to give my hand something to do. 'So far, I'm not not believing anything,' I said. 'Do we know the person who's picking up the spare key to the Elks kitchen?'

I could actually hear Mae grinning. 'We certainly do,' she said. 'It's the Middlesex County Prosecutor himself.'

You know when someone in the movies says something nuts on their phone and they cut to the person they're talking to, who just stares at the phone as if it were a crazy person? I completely did that.

'Richard Chapman is the guy by the dumpster?' I said.

'I told you that you wouldn't believe it.'

THIRTY-THREE

It had never in my most demented dream occurred to me that I'd be back at Richard's office that day, but here I was. The offices were mostly closed already, but the guy at security remembered me from the morning and acted as if he recognized me, and he wasn't even working there when I was an employee. I got my stuff through the metal detector, pretty much ran to the elevator and tried to still my pounding heart as I made it to the floor where I had once worked.

The receptionist had gone home so I sprinted to Richard's office and pushed the door open.

Richard was standing behind his desk with an assistant prosecutor (male), both in dark gray suits. The assistant was a fair amount younger than Richard, and Richard was pointing at a document on his desktop. He looked like he was instructing his son in the ways of prosecution.

He looked up and took a moment to decide if he should be Avuncular Richard or Viper Richard. He made the wrong choice, as he often did. He grinned in what he thought (and to be fair

what I once would have also thought) was a warm smile and
said, 'Sandy! Can you give us a minute, please? We're just—'

'I don't care what you're just, Richard,' I said. 'You're going
to want to talk to me *right now* and you're going to want to do
so in private. I'm telling you that for your own benefit.' Then
I looked over at the assistant to challenge the prosecutor's
instinct to tell me to go away.

Without so much as missing a beat, he said, 'Would you
excuse us please, Peter?' The assistant, no doubt hoping to
reach the next level soon, nodded, wisely said nothing and left
the office taking the file with the document in question (which
for all I knew was relevant to my case) with him.

The last thing you want to do when trying to get me out
of an angry mood is condescend or patronize. OK, the two
last things. Patrick was an expert at not doing either of those,
and that was part of why I loved him. Richard tried at this
moment to do both and that's only a tiny part of why I despised
him.

'Now, what's gotten you all upset?' he said. I looked around
the room for the five-year-old he was clearly addressing, but it
turned out to be me.

I stared at him and then blinked to get the red out of my
vision. 'What's gotten me so *upset*?' I came close to shrieking.
'Richard. I saw the video from the Elks Lodge security cam. I
saw you picking up the spare key to the kitchen door next to
the dumpster. That's withholding evidence even more than when
you tried to keep me from getting that video. You want to know
why I'm upset? You'll be lucky to stay out of jail after I get
done filing grievances.'

The bluster and superior attitude he'd had a few moments
ago weren't immediately gone but they were fading. Richard's
voice became softer in volume and tone. He sat on the front
edge of his desk and looked up into my eyes.

'Sandy, you need to understand,' he said. Uncle Prosecutor
was going to hold court. He thought.

'I understand. Trust me, I understand. I ratted on you to your
wife and moved away to a better job and a *much* better boyfriend,
so you want revenge by putting my cousin away on charges
you can't even hope to prove. I get all that. But if you're doing

all this just to get back at me, I sincerely believe you need to seek psychiatric help.'

'No. I didn't – no! You think this is all about *you*?'

'It sure as hell isn't about Stephanie Silverstone. I can tell you that for sure. You know you don't have any concrete proof, so you're going to try to convince a jury using circumstantial evidence that looks flashy but doesn't prove a thing. But stealing the key to the Elks back door? That's beneath even you, Richard. What I don't understand is why you immediately took it to a police station and handed it over.' I refused to sit in his guest chair. The heels I was wearing were killing me, but I wasn't going to let Richard look down at me ever again.

He was processing; I knew the look. Richard's eyes narrowed and wrinkled a bit at the sides, something I once foolishly thought looked distinguished. But this wasn't processing for show. He was trying to decide what next to do.

'I'm going to say it again,' he finally began. Before I could lash out, he added, 'There are things going on in this case that I can't tell you about, things that change the complexion of the whole thing. I *can't* tell you more than that, but you need to believe me. Everything I've done has been legal and ethical.'

Yeah, and John Wilkes Booth was a swell guy once you got to know him. This line of manure wasn't even the highest quality I'd heard him spread around. 'I *saw* you pick up that key,' I told him. 'I *know* that key is the crux of the murder, and you didn't list it in your discovery so you're not going to introduce it in court. That means you're suppressing it from the defense, and believe me, I will file a motion to retrieve it before the end of business today. So tell me, while you're being all legal and ethical, why shouldn't I write letters to the governor, the bar association and the sheriff of Middlesex County asking for you to be removed? Why shouldn't I file a motion with Judge Grossman to bar you from trying this case due to bias and illegal behavior?'

Richard seemed to age ten years as I watched, but not from fear of exposure or worry about his career. He just looked incredibly tired. 'I am not able to give you any more information, but I guarantee Judge Grossman will not, under any circumstances, remove me from the Silverstone case even if I were to recuse myself, which I won't,' he said. 'But, Sandy, for your own good, for your cousin's good and for the good of everyone involved in this case, I can't urge you strongly enough to accept the revised plea agreement I'm going to send you later today. It has more advantageous terms than the last one, and I assure you it's better than anything you'd have gotten from any other prosecutor in the state. If you advise your client to accept it, I'm certain she will. So please, advise her to accept it. You have to trust me.'

Since I had not sat, I didn't have the advantage of standing to make a point. I turned on one of those lethal heels and headed for the door.

'I'll see you in court, Richard. And just for the record, I was almost convinced until you said I had to trust you.'

And I left.

THIRTY-FOUR

Patrick, Angie and I decided to have dinner in the apartment that night. Angie cooked, which meant we were the only three people in Manhattan not actually at a restaurant or ordering in that evening. It felt homey, in a weird way. None of us actually lived here, and the remaining New Jersey contingent of my family, Mom and Delia, were not part of the group. I should have at least felt guilty about that but I didn't.

The apartment Angie had found and the theater company was renting was just like a regular New York apartment, except better. The rooms weren't enormous but they were more spacious than you'd normally find in this part of town, since the building had been renovated from office space in the early 2000s. The kitchen had enough room for two whole people to maneuver, although Angie had insisted that the chicken cacciatore she was cooking required only her presence. There were actual bookshelves lining the walls of the living room. And that meant there was a living room.

Patrick, having listened to my account of one of the weirdest days I've spent as a lawyer, sat back on the sofa next to me and continued to shake his head. 'I don't understand any of it,' he said. 'But what really fascinates me is his assumption that you'd never find the security tape, especially after you got it from someone who works for him this very morning.'

Angie called from the kitchen, which was just ten feet or so away. 'None of it makes any sense,' she said. Angie absorbs other people's expertise like a sponge by watching and listening. She's hung around me long enough that she has a working knowledge of the law. She understands showbusiness because she works for Patrick. She apprentices with our investigator Nate Garrigan two half-days a week and can already speak intelligently about how to run a stakeout. She can tell you about the ins and outs of soft-serve vending because she used to manage Dairy Queen franchises before she joined me in Los Angeles. 'Richard had to know you'd catch him and that would lead to him probably losing his job. Why walk right into that?'

'And at the end of all that, he wants me to get Skinny to agree to another bogus plea deal,' I told them both. 'Has he not been paying attention?'

'Dinner in ten minutes,' Angie called.

I got up to set the table and then remembered that this was Patrick's rental and I had no idea where anything was. But Patrick had already stood to take care of it, so I just watched. I can absorb like Angie when it's necessary.

That left me alone in the living room when there was a knock on the door. I don't know why it never occurred to me that we hadn't had anyone buzzing the apartment to identify themselves and ask to come in; I was thinking about Stephanie's case. So I got up and looked through the door's peephole to see a man in his thirties wearing a business suit. I figured it had to be a representative of the theater company or Patrick's agent, so I opened the door.

Yeah, I know. You don't have to say it.

Even as I heard Patrick, from inside the main room, say, 'Sandy, why are you—' I realized I'd made a mistake. But the man in the suit, whose name I decided was William because he looked like a William, did not appear threatening. He wasn't exactly smiling but he didn't look angry. He was not holding a weapon of any sort. He just stood there like a businessman contemplating his next tedious piece of work.

'Can I help you?' I asked. Some people might have said, '*May* I help you?' but I wasn't asking for permission. I was trying to find out if it was possible I could do something for this man that he might need doing.

'Are you Sandra Moss?' The voice was flat and uninterested. I could either be or not be Sandra Moss and it would be all the same to him, but it was written on a piece of paper or a pixel somewhere that he had to ask, so he was asking.

'Do you have something for Ms Moss?' I said. I lived with my mother long enough to know when to answer a question with a question.

His dull expression didn't change. 'Are you Sandra Moss?' he repeated.

My instinct was to close the door in his face, and I could sense Patrick coming up behind me for backup, but William wasn't on his first house call, I sensed, and put up his hand to land flatly on the door, extending his arm and holding it open. 'Are you Sandra Moss?' Nothing was going to stand between him and the answer to that question.

After a while, you've just had enough. I'd been pinballed around by Richard, by my own client and by whatever was going on at Seaton, Taylor to the point that something was bound to happen. So I pointed my right index finger at William and poked him in the chest.

'Huh?' he said. It wasn't as eloquent as you might think.

'I'm not interested in what you're selling, but you're not selling anything because you're looking for me and this isn't my apartment,' I started, but I was just building up a head of steam. 'If you're from one of the tabloids, you're way overstepping your bounds and there'll be a harassment suit against your station, website or newspaper in the morning. If this has something to do with the gross misconduct of the Middlesex County Prosecutor regarding a case I'm defending, then you can take a walk right back to where you crawled out of in your nice new suit. I'm done playing. Scram.'

I thought Patrick might applaud. And now that Angie had

joined him right behind me, we had William outnumbered by
two.

'So you *are* Sandra Moss.' Among other things, William was
quick on the uptake.

'Yes! Yes! I'm Sandra Moss! Congratulations, you've worn
me down! Now get out before I call the cops.' The NYPD
would easily be there within three hours once they heard my
complaint. A man had come to my boyfriend's door. They'd
alert the commissioner on that one.

'Then remember this: Take the plea deal. Your client will live
longer if you do.'

What? 'Are you threatening my client?' For some reason,
we weren't saying Stephanie's name.

'No. I'm telling you how to make her life longer and easier.
Take the plea deal.' With that, he turned and headed for the
stairway.

'Wait a minute!' Now I was asking him to stay. 'Who
are you?'

'Call me Bill,' he said.

I was right!

Quickly, I turned both deadlocks on the door and put the
chain on (because that was for sure going to help) to boot. I
turned to see Patrick and Angie staring at me wide-eyed and
puzzled, as if I'd suddenly appeared nude and juggling flaming
chainsaws. 'What?' I said.

Angie broke into a grin and put her hands on my biceps.
'Who was that woman I just saw face down a threatening
enforcer?' she said. 'Wow, Sand, you were amazing!'

Enforcer? Was that who I just sent away from Patrick's door?
I thought those guys all had broken noses and talked like
secondary characters on *The Sopranos*. My pal William had
looked like he just graduated from business school two weeks
ago.

Patrick, for the first time since I'd met him at a loss for
words, just walked over and embraced me (once Angie let go
of my arms). He held me close to him and stroked my hair a
little.

'Hey, get a room, guys,' Angie said from somewhere in the
beyond-Patrick space.

Patrick cleared his throat as if that was what had been stopping him from speaking. 'You were magnificent,' he said in a raspy voice. 'But we have to be ready for the next time.'

Oh, man. The *next time*? I didn't get to just live under the illusion that William – or someone more intimidating – might not be back? I wobbled into the living room and sat heavily on the sofa. 'The next time,' I whimpered.

'Do you think Richard sent him?' Angie asked. Angie's ability to read a room is not quite as strong as her ability to go right to the heart of the subject.

I put my head back and rested – you know, closed – my eyes. It was a metaphor for not facing reality eye to eye. 'I can't think of anyone else, but intimidating a defense attorney, or for that matter anybody, in your trial is just more fodder for a review board and maybe the state attorney general. I can't believe he'd be that stupid.'

We batted that back and forth for a few minutes and then paid attention to Angie's chicken cacciatore, which was perfect, of course. And just when I was starting to feel my shoulders relax again, I got an email. From Richard.

The new plea offer. And before I could even open the file to read it, I got a text from Skinny.

Let's take the deal.

This again.

THIRTY-FIVE

After giving serious consideration to filing a motion with the judge to resign from the case of *County of Middlesex v. Stephanie Silverstone*, and after having a very large glass of the excellent red wine Patrick had bought to go with the cacciatore, I texted back to Skinny and told her I thought it would be a terrible idea to accept the plea offer, especially since I hadn't read it yet.

She said she'd get right in the car and meet us at Patrick's to talk it over. I'd have time to read it while she was driving.

I'll forgo the obvious insanity of choosing to drive into Manhattan when there is public transportation readily available to you and comment only that Stephanie, a woman who had emerged from a public kitchen wearing some bodily fluids from a murdered man, was afraid of the New York City subway system and wouldn't consider the idea of an Uber. My client, innocent or guilty, was a lunatic. (No, I'm not referring to her addiction problem.)

I did retreat into the bedroom to read the plea offer on my laptop. While it was an improvement on the first one, it did not eliminate jail time or declare Stephanie innocent of the crime, which were the only conditions I'd decided I would accept. You don't send a (somewhat wan and thin) enforcer to my door and expect me to cave. I am woman, leave my door.

Actually, Richard had sent a cosmetic rewrite of his first plea deal with five years taken off the recommended sentence (which the judge could ignore at a hearing) and dropping the charge from premeditated murder to aggravated manslaughter. Which only served to aggravate me, and I wasn't sure that hadn't been his objective to begin with.

By the time Skinny showed up at Patrick's apartment door (and don't for a second think we didn't look carefully through that peephole and require her to spin around with her arms out to show there was no one else there), I had worked out my argument. I was bound as an attorney to carry out my client's wishes, and if she was determined to go to jail for a murder she insisted she didn't commit, I had to go along with the plan. But I wasn't going down without a fight.

I had relocated back to the living room at that point. Angie had retreated to the second bedroom, where she'd been staying. Yes. A theatrical star's apartment has a second bedroom even in Manhattan.

But Patrick had chosen to stay in the room with Skinny and me after taking a solemn oath not to offer any opinions. Twice.

'We've had this conversation more than once before,' I began before she could start to weep and tell me how this was her only way out of life imprisonment, because it wasn't. 'What's being offered here is the old plea deal with a new coat of lacquer. I said you shouldn't take the last one and I am telling you now that you shouldn't take the new one.'

Patrick was leaning forward in his overstuffed chair, looking like the most eager land baron ever to grace the halls of a London gentleman's club in 1887. Except he was dressed in a T-shirt and jeans.

'I'm scared, Sandy,' Stephanie said. 'Don't you understand that?'

'Yes, I do, and that's why you need me to be the voice of logic here,' I told her. 'You're thinking with your fear. I'm thinking with my brain. We can win this case, but you have to let me do it.'

Skinny didn't say anything, but she was shaking her head back and forth slowly. *No.*

It was necessary to convince her. The offer Richard had made would guarantee her at least seven years in prison. That wasn't a good deal for anyone who wouldn't otherwise be facing execution. There was always the possibility that we could lose at trial but then there would be appeals during which more evidence could be uncovered and she'd still stay away from incarceration. It was baffling to me that Stephanie would even consider accepting such a fate.

'Why do you want to take the deal?' I finally said. 'Do you think that I won't be able to get you acquitted?' Passive aggression is deep in my DNA. The Force is strong with my family.

Stephanie didn't cry, which I appreciated, but she looked remarkably unhappy and sort of scrunched up her face to make an expression that I think was supposed to communicate contradictory feelings. It looked more like indigestion, but not everyone is as good an actor as Patrick.

I figured I could get personal with the persuasion. 'You know your fiancé told me he's not sure he wants to marry you anymore?' It was cruel but this was for keeps. 'Is he worth going to prison for?' Maybe Michael killed Brandon, maybe not, but a tactic is a tactic.

Her lip curled into a near-sneer. 'Who says I want to marry him? Who says I ever did?' OK, so some tactics work better than others.

The fact that I'd flown in to attend their wedding had been some indication she'd wanted to marry the guy, but then I remembered this wasn't about me. 'Then focus on the years. Seven years is not nothing, Steph. Don't do the time if you didn't do the crime.'

'This seems like a sure thing,' she mumbled after a moment. 'If we go to the trial, I'm not sure what will happen.'

'If you take the deal, you *can* be sure what'll happen,' I reminded her. 'You'll go to county prison for a number of years, and not a small number. That can't be what you want.'

But then her entire demeanor changed. She put on a determined face and stood up in one motion, standing straight and tall like a soldier. 'I'm taking the deal,' she said. 'I've decided.'

I had to give Patrick a 'shoosh' look, which he accepted and sat back in the chair.

'OK,' I said. And I waited a beat.

'Good.' Stephanie felt like she was in control now and she was going to use it. 'I'm glad we're agreed.'

Clearly, she didn't understand who she was dealing with.

'Oh, we're not at all agreed.' I sat back and tried to look confident and relaxed. But I'm not as good an actor as Patrick, either. 'You can take that deal if you want to spend a decade or so behind bars, because you can't believe that seven-year figure he put in there. A judge will probably take a look at the crime scene pictures and give you the maximum, which is fifteen years, unless they decide to charge you with anything they want once you're inside. You can do that. It's your decision.'

I'll admit Stephanie looked less confident after that but stood defiant. 'I need this to be over,' she said. 'If that's what I have to do, then that's what I'll do.'

I head-titled in her direction. 'That's your right. Go to jail. But you're going to do it without me. You sign that agreement and I will file a motion to remove me from your case. I can't let my reputation be ruined by lending my name to a deal like that.'

Patrick – and only a few of us on the planet would have known it – stifled a tiny grin.

'You wouldn't,' Stephanie tried, but she knew it was a losing ploy. The Force wasn't as strong with her.

'Watch me.'

The steel in her backbone turned to cooked fettuccine. She sagged. Her shoulders dropped five inches and her knees gained bends. Her arms dangled at her sides. I'm saying, she didn't look quite so determined anymore.

'Sandy,' she said. It was the same voice and inflection she'd had when she was thirteen and wanted to convince me to shoplift a lipstick for her, which I did not do, officially. 'Don't do this to me.'

I folded my arms. When the person you're talking to folds their arms, you're done. Or they're cold. I was not cold. Stephanie was done. 'I'm not doing it to you,' I said quietly. 'I'm doing it *for* you. This is my job. If you won't let me do it, you can find someone who will.'

Out of the corner of my eye, I could spy Angie watching through a slightly opened bedroom door. Apparently, I was the best form of entertainment available in the place tonight.

'Oh, all right, *fine!*' Stephanie yelled and stomped out of the apartment.

I called over to Angie. 'It's safe! You can come out!' But she just closed the bedroom door again because the show was clearly over.

Patrick looked at me with considerable admiration. 'I'm seeing sides of you I've never seen before, Sandra,' he said. 'Even when you were defending *me*. You were awfully convincing. So you're sure you can win the case?'

He was the dearest man.

'Honestly, Patrick,' I said, 'I have no idea.'

THIRTY-SIX

'All rise.' Judge Barnard Grossman entered and took his place on the bench, after which we were all allowed to sit as well. It's an old tradition and a fairly silly one, but it does project some respect for the person making the decisions in a courtroom, and that has value.

The place was packed with the assembled cast of characters, some of whom actually needed to be there. Patrick was in rehearsals (or would be later; this was too early an hour for theater people to work) and had dispatched Angie to attend as his surrogate, something she absolutely would have done whether he told her to or not. Mom was there, but Delia, who was not on the witness list for today (since it would be mostly jury selection and opening statements), was busy saving people's lives or something. Stephanie, to my right, was pretending she hadn't actually wanted to throw in the towel only two nights earlier. Her maybe-still-fiancé Michael was sitting in the row behind Angie, not wanting to be too close in case Stephanie was found guilty. Aunt Fern, doing her best not to sob, was next to Mom. They had foregone the usual indirect competition over who looked the younger.

Jessica Berliner, having waited so patiently, was my second chair, to Stephanie's right. She was an attractive woman in her forties who didn't surprise me in the least by looking very professional. Jess, I'd learned in the past few weeks, was a godsend, finding precedents for every point I wanted to raise or refute and suggesting strategies, particularly in the area of jury selection. For one thing, we wanted as many young women as we could get, people who could identify with Skinny and sympathize with the ruination of her wedding, not to mention her life.

Stephanie put her hand on mine more to get my attention quietly than to make some emotional connection. She whispered, 'Are you *sure* we shouldn't take the plea offer?'

Some clients inspire you to do your best work and others are from your family. I nodded and focused on Grossman.

'This case has gained some reputation for sensationalism,' he said. Grossman didn't dillydally; he got right to it. 'That ends now. We're going to choose a jury, the prosecution and defense will make their opening statements and then we will begin to hear from witnesses. I want nothing to distract from that. The press is allowed in this courtroom but displays of support for either side or any loud speaking will not be tolerated. *Anyone* who violates that direction will be escorted from the room and not allowed to reenter.'

Clearly, he was going to be a fun judge.

I'd argued in front of Grossman three times before, but as a prosecutor. He was fair and focused on precedent. Give the man a good precedent and he would probably go home happy each night. So Jess had supplied me with a very serious backlog of them. Each of us had an iPad on the table and could access our research whenever necessary. This was something of a change from even five or six years ago, when it all would have been on paper in front of me on the defense table.

'Are there any motions to be made before we begin?' the judge asked.

I had given serious consideration to filing for Richard to be removed from the trial due to both his withholding of pertinent evidence and my suspicion that he had sent an enforcer (might as well use the word) to my (Patrick's) door to intimidate me into taking a bad plea deal. The fact that he'd almost succeeded in convincing my client she should accept a jail term – twice! – was not something I could prove. I had no precedent. So after conferring with Jess, I'd decided to proceed without taking shots at the prosecutor, much as it would have been satisfying. It wouldn't have been good for my client. Who was still asking me to this minute if she should just concede the whole thing and get fitted for an orange jumpsuit.

(The uniforms actually come in different colors depending on the prison and the prisoner, but everyone thinks they're all orange.)

'I move to dismiss the charges based on a lack of evidence,' I said when Grossman acknowledged my motion. 'The prosecution has nothing but circumstantial evidence, no idea of a motive and no witness to the crime.'

Richard stood up, buttoning the jacket of his dark blue suit. 'We have a number of witnesses who saw the defendant leave the scene of the homicide covered in the victim's blood,' he said. 'We have witnesses who will testify to motive and she was carrying the murder weapon in her right hand.'

'Motion denied,' Grossman said. 'Nice try, Ms Moss.'

It had been worth a shot.

We spent most of the morning interviewing potential jurors and objecting to the ones that the other side would have welcomed. I managed to seat two women under forty when I'd have preferred four. Richard got three men about Brandon Starkey's age on the panel, which was at least two more than

I would have wanted. The rest was filled out with the usual members of the jury pool: retired people, unemployed people and people who had tried to convince the judge they couldn't be away from their work for the two weeks it was likely to take to try this case, but failed.

It wasn't the worst jury I'd ever seen or the best. It was an extremely average jury. There were two people of color, which didn't in any way reflect the population of Middlesex County, but race was not a factor in this case as far as I could tell. One person had identified as non-binary and neither Richard nor I had objected to them. Why would we?

The jurors were seated right before Grossman banged his gavel and broke for lunch. The Silverstone contingent (minus Michael, who had gone to get a hamburger) exited together and migrated to a Korean fusion restaurant a few blocks away called Rooster Spin for reasons unclear even when explained. The name, that is. The food was quite lovely.

I was enjoying the bibimbap and awaiting the arrival of the double-fried chicken (which I'd had before in my pre-LA lifetime) eagerly while my family and Angie batted around the events of the morning as if I weren't there, which was just fine with me. The last thing I needed was to explain every choice I'd made and every one I hadn't. Because that chicken was going to be really crunchy.

But I knew my period of immunity was going to be temporary. 'Is the jury the kind of people you wanted, Sandra?' my mother asked. 'Did you want more women or more men?'

'I just wanted jurors who hadn't read all about the case on the internet and didn't walk in with a vision of Stephanie in a dress that hadn't started out red,' I said. 'The makeup of the jury in terms of gender or race is really not as important as that.' I know, I just told you all about how I wanted a jury of young women and lamented the lack of people of color, but what I'd said to Mom was true, too.

She stared at me blankly. 'Oh.' That's my mother when I speak about trying a case. I imagine it's the same reaction Delia gets when she discusses the use of chemotherapy and immunotherapy for the same patient. To be fair, I rarely want to talk shop with an oncologist, either.

Throughout the lunch, Skinny had been silent, which is never a good sign with her or any other client. She sat there not eating the amazing fried chicken and picking at, of all things, rice. I decided she was lost in her own thoughts, and since I didn't need any specific information from her at the moment, I'd leave her to it.

Aunt Fern, however, was rarely if ever the type to leave any thought unexpressed. 'Is the judge Jewish?' she asked. 'I think I might have seen him once at Rosh Hashanah services.'

I had no idea at all what Judge Grossman's religious bent might be and told her so without inquiring as to why that would make any difference at all in Stephanie's murder trial. Largely because I was afraid she'd answer.

'The rest of the day should be fairly simple,' I said, although no one had asked. 'Richard will lay out his case in general terms and then I'll do the same. We just want to get the jurors informed about the basics and why we each think our side is right. I can't imagine the judge will let us start calling witnesses before tomorrow morning.'

'So I didn't actually need to be here?' Aunt Fern said. I think Angie might have stifled an unintentional spit take with the water she was drinking.

'Your daughter is on trial,' I said while trying not to sound like I was judging my mother's sister, which I definitely was doing. 'We appreciate your being here for support, both emotional and visual.'

Aunt Fern's eyes got quizzical. 'Visual?'

'Yes. The jurors seeing that her mother is here and supporting her makes Stephanie more of a human being in their minds and not a defendant. It might make them think about how their mothers would feel if they were in the same position. So you are filling a very important role here today and we are glad you did.'

'Why would you ever think I wouldn't?' Aunt Fern said. With some people, you just can't ever win and it's a silly thing to even try. So I nodded at her as if what she'd said had been very sage and appropriate.

'Do you write out these openings ahead of time?' Angie asked. She had been my best friend since long before I took the bar exam and had been living with me through all four of my previous homicide defense trials, so she knew the answer and hadn't needed to ask. She was trying to boost my professional reputation within my family – a noble but futile goal.

Before I could answer, though, Stephanie dropped her fork loudly on to her plate and ran her hands through her hair in a behavior of anxiety. 'Why didn't you let me take the plea deal?' she said and stared at me as if I'd personally suggested she drink a vial of hemlock with a strychnine chaser.

My mother's head swiveled from Stephanie to me in the amount of time it takes a Formula 1 racer to drive two feet. 'They offered a plea deal and you stopped Stephanie from taking it?' Never accuse my mother of assuming the best about her daughter. Well, her younger daughter.

'I'm not discussing this with anyone but my client,' I answered in as even a tone as I could muster. I looked at Stephanie. 'And she knows precisely why I *advised* her not to take a proposed plea agreement that was offered. She also knows that she could have hired another attorney to represent her and agree to anything she wanted.'

'But I wanted you as my lawyer,' Skinny whined.

'Why?' It was a question that needed asking, but admittedly not in the middle of a Korean lunch with much of our family attending. 'If you don't trust my judgment, what good does it do you to have me representing you in court?'

'Because . . . I can't . . . you're my cousin.' That certainly cleared it up.

'If you like,' I said, knowing I shouldn't, 'I'll text Richard right now and tell him that you want to accept the offer. And then I'll go into court after lunch and resign from the case.' I got my phone out of my pocket. 'Tell me that's what you want and I'll be perfectly happy to do it. But if you really didn't stab that man to death in the Elks Lodge, then you'll be lying in court and they can add perjury to the charges against you. Right now, Skinny. Are you in or out? I'm good either way.'

Mom and Aunt Fern had never heard me talk that way to a family member before, or at least since I was seventeen. They gaped at me, apparently unable to move.

Stephanie looked from me to her mother, then to my mother,

then back at me without answering. 'Well? What'll it be?' I asked her. 'If you want to take the deal, there's paperwork that needs to be filled out.'

'Fine,' she said and got up to walk out. I stood up and got into her path.

'No,' I said. 'You don't get to walk out in a huff this time. You say the words right to my face. For the last time, do you want me to let some other lawyer negotiate your confession or do you want me to defend you in court?'

Stephanie gave me the exact look Robert E. Lee gave Ulysses S. Grant at Appomattox Court House and spoke through clenched teeth. 'I want you to defend me,' she said. 'And then I never want to see you again.'

I got out of her way and she stomped off. Then I turned to the rest of the people at the table, all of whom were looking stunned. 'You're my witnesses,' I said. 'You heard her say it.'

Immediately, Angie said, 'I heard it.' Then there was a long silence during which everyone else at that table stared at me.

Finally, my mother said, 'I can't believe you were so rude to your cousin.' Then she and Aunt Fern made some odd excuses and left me with the bill for everyone's lunch, which I planned on adding to Skinny's bill for the case. Angie and I stood up and then I spotted the last person I expected to see in the restaurant entrance, looking tentatively in my direction.

My sister Delia. And the look on her face was enough to worry me.

'I'll meet you back there, Ang,' I said. Angie looked at me, then where I was looking.

'OK.' She walked right past Delia, nodded at her and left.

I walked out of the restaurant and met my sister on Albany Street. Without discussing it, we started walking in the opposite direction of the courthouse.

'I want to apologize,' Delia said.

'OK, who are you and what have you done with my sister?' An oldie but a goodie.

Delia didn't react. 'I've been acting weird because . . . because—'

'Because your marriage is in trouble,' I said. 'And you're not used to dealing with that or how it looks to people.'

She stopped walking. 'How did you know that?'

'I'm your sister. Did something happen? Mark seeing someone else?'

We began walking again, too slowly for some of our fellow pedestrians, who passed us with looks that indicated we didn't understand how quickly they needed to be somewhere else. Delia shook her head. 'No. It's nobody's fault. We're just not as happy as we should be.'

'Counseling?'

'We did it for six months. What we figured out is that we're not as happy as we should be.'

It was my turn to stop walking, which severely chapped a guy in a business suit who chose not to engage because he was so important he didn't have the time. 'Does Mom know?' I asked.

Delia's voice got small. 'No. We told the kids last night and they actually took it well. They'd heard us bickering for a couple of years.'

That brought back memories. 'I can imagine. But Mom?'

'I'll tell her. I swear. I just . . . I wanted you to know first.'

I stared at her. 'Why?'

She smiled for the first time. 'You're my sister,' she said.

I went back to the courtroom and delivered my opening statement, then headed back to Patrick's apartment and called my father.

THIRTY-SEVEN

'**M**s Danforth, can you describe the defendant's clothing when she emerged from the kitchen?' Richard asked.

Bernice Danforth, who had been on the prosecution's witness list but hardly seemed like a witness to start your case with, was a second cousin of Michael Fortunato (who was turning out to be less of a wonderful fiancé every minute) and had, of course, been present in the rehearsal party. So had eighty-seven other people, but for some reason, Richard had started with Bernice the next morning as he began to build his case. To each one's own.

'Well, she looked just awful.' Bernice was in her forties, if I had to guess, and was dressed like someone who had led something of a sheltered life. Every button was buttoned. Every hem was at its maximum. Sleeves were long. It was ninety-six degrees outside and the air conditioning in the courthouse was doing a yeoman's job but had been installed when Jimmy Carter was president.

Richard waited and didn't get anything more from his witness, who had no doubt been told to answer questions as briefly as possible. 'Can you be a little more specific?' he asked. 'I'm not talking about the fashion she chose to wear and neither were you, is that correct?'

If I'd really wanted to be a jerk about it, I could have made some objection about leading the witness, but there were photographs on their way that were going to do far more damage than Bernice would be able to muster. I sat quietly and waited for my turn.

Skinny sat to my right, pouting. You'd think a person on trial for her long-term freedom might be frightened, or at least tense. No. Stephanie was mad at me for forcing her to go through the trial. Because I was trying to keep her out of jail . . . OK. I'll stop now. There's no point.

'That's right,' Bernice said. She looked very much like she wanted to get all the answers right and be given a gold star at the end of her testimony. 'Her dress was covered in blood.'

Not one of the jurors, who had heard an overview of the case from both the prosecution and the defense, gasped. Bernice looked a little disappointed.

But Richard was not, because it gave him the opening he needed to present the most damning piece of evidence he owned, and that was why Bernice, the visual representation of a schoolmarm, had been chosen to lead off his batting order. He looked up at Judge Grossman.

'Your Honor, I would like to submit the prosecution's exhibit number one, a set of photographs.'

The days when a judge would be handed physical photographs

to review before ruling are long gone. Grossman put on a pair of reading glasses to consult an iPad on his bench, scrolled through a bit and nodded. 'Any objections, Ms Moss?'

I had tons of objections but none of them were legal arguments that could lead to the pictures being deemed inadmissible. It *was* Skinny, she *was* covered in a bodily fluid and she *did* hold a rather nasty-looking knife in her right hand. Having been present at the event itself, there was no way I could object to the pictures. 'No, Your Honor.'

'Admit the exhibit,' Grossman said, as if he had allowed some groundbreaking legal bombshell. Violent crimes often lead to sensational images and they get shown to juries. My job would be to give them an alternate explanation to the prosecution's because theirs would be that Stephanie had stabbed Brandon Starkey over and over again.

The pictures were projected on a screen mounted on either end of the jury box so there was no doubt each juror could see them. All exhibits would be shown that way and these were clearly having the effect Richard wanted them to have. A few jurors put their hands to their mouths. One paled and looked to be in some danger of passing out but recovered after putting his hands over his eyes for a moment.

I couldn't wait until they showed the crime scene pictures of the victim.

'Is this what you saw that day, Ms Danforth?' Richard asked, suppressing (badly) his urge to smirk.

To her credit, Bernice did not sob or dab her eyes. She was still interested in being the best girl in the class. 'Yes,' she said and looked at Richard for his approval.

'What do you think happened that made her dress look like that?' he asked without patting his witness on the head, which I thought was inconsiderate.

I was on my feet before she could respond. 'Objection. He's asking the witness to draw a conclusion that is not within her testimony. She was present outside the kitchen and saw just what the prosecution has made certain the jury would see. Nothing more.'

'Objection sustained,' said Grossman. I don't even think Richard was considering mounting a counterargument. He'd made his point. He just continued on his quest, hero that he was in his own mind.

'What was the defendant, Ms Silverstone, holding in her right hand when she walked out of the kitchen?' he asked.

'A knife,' Bernice answered.

Richard walked over to his table, where his assistant handed him an evidence bag, tagged by the Woodbridge Police Department. To no one's surprise, it held a large, dangerous-looking knife. 'Is this that knife?' he said to his witness.

Again, I was on my feet. 'Objection. How can the witness know if that is the same knife?'

'The weapon' – Richard was painting the evidence as clearly as he could. The defendant was 'Ms Silverstone' and not 'Stephanie.' The knife was a weapon and not a culinary instrument. No doubt soon he'd refer to the defense attorney as a disciple of Satan, which wasn't the least bit true. I'd never met Satan – 'was tagged and labeled by the Woodbridge Police Department,' he said. 'It is clearly the same knife.'

'Then let the prosecution produce the police officer who bagged it and the evidence clerk who labeled it,' I said to Grossman. 'The witness was a bystander and has, to my knowledge, no expertise on the subject of kitchenware. For all she knows, that's the knife that was used to stab Julius Caesar.'

'A little less sarcasm, but I'll sustain the objection, Ms Moss. Mr Chapman, please limit your questions for every witness only to those subjects on which they can speak directly.'

'Yes, Your Honor. Ms Danforth, this is a question that surely you can answer better than anyone else: How did you feel when you saw the defendant Ms Silverstone burst out of the kitchen drenched in blood and holding that knife?'

I was going to get my own chance to talk to Bernice so I didn't object at that obvious and idiotic question. What possible difference did it make how she *felt* when Stephanie walked out of the kitchen? How would her feelings, which I was certain would not be described as jubilant or comfortable, help prove that my cousin had murdered a man with a kitchen knife?

'I was horrified,' Bernice said. No kidding.

'Thank you, Ms Danforth.' Richard walked back to the prosecution table. Bernice started to stand.

'Not just yet,' Grossman told her. 'Ms Moss still gets a crack at you.' The jury (and the people in the gallery who were watching for news organizations or for . . . fun?) chuckled at that one. That Judge Grossman – what a wit.

I stood up and smiled as warmly as I could as I approached the witness box. 'Ms Danforth, did you see Stephanie Silverstone stab Brandon Starkey?'

She looked a little surprised and a little appalled. 'No,' she said.

'Did you hear any sounds coming from anywhere in the Elks Lodge that indicated someone was being stabbed?'

Richard, because he wanted to live up to his nickname, stood up. 'Objection. Is the defense counsel suggesting that Mr Starkey was *not* stabbed in the Elks kitchen?'

Grossman looked at me for a response so I gave him one. 'I'm not suggesting that he was or wasn't. We will hear testimony later indicating that it's unclear whether the kitchen was the place or if the body was merely found there, but the defense does not offer either option as the definitive truth at this point. I'm asking the witness for her experience and I think the answer to this question is important. Ms Danforth has not testified that she heard sounds of a struggle or any violence coming from the kitchen. I'd like to know if that was because she wasn't asked or because she didn't hear anything.'

The judge nodded. 'I'll overrule the objection. The witness may answer the question.' Richard sat down, and Bernice had the class not to ask for the question to be read back to her. She knew what had been asked.

'No,' she said. That was it. She was the kind of witness I wished was on my side.

'So you didn't see the murder and you didn't hear it. Is it your opinion that Stephanie Silverstone killed Brandon Starkey?'

'Yes.' There was an air of defiance in Bernice's voice. That was fine with me; I'd expected that answer. Stephanie, on the other hand, looked at me with something approaching disgust because, she told me later, she thought I'd just said she was guilty.

'Why?' I asked.

For once, Bernice was not coached in an answer. 'Why?' she repeated with a tone of confusion.

'Yes. What led you to believe that my client is guilty of the murder of Brandon Starkey when you didn't see the act happen and you didn't hear any indication of violence?'

Bernice opened and closed her mouth lightly a couple of times. 'Because . . . her dress . . .'

'So judging from the way Stephanie looked when she left the kitchen, without any previous information of the crime, you decided she had stabbed Brandon Starkey to death?'

'There was all that blood,' Bernice said.

'If Stephanie were dressed in the uniform of an EMT, an emergency medical technician, instead of a party dress, but was still covered the way she was, would you have assumed that EMT had killed Brandon?' I asked.

'Yes, I think so,' Bernice answered.

I looked up at the bench. 'Your Honor, may I submit defense exhibit one, a photograph?'

Grossman looked at his iPad again. 'Any objection, Mr Chapman?' he asked Richard.

'I question its relevance,' Richard said.

'In light of the question I just asked?' I said to the judge.

'I'll allow it.' Grossman was presiding over a fair trial. I'd expected it, but it's always reassuring when it happens.

I nodded to the video technician, who produced the picture on the jurors' monitors. It showed one of the EMTs who had answered the 911 call to the Elks Lodge when Brandon was killed.

'I'd like to direct the witness's attention to the screen in front of her. Ms Danforth, that is a photograph of Henderson Coltrane, a member of the Rapid Rescue Ambulance Service. Mr Coltrane was among the first responders to the calls for help when Brandon was killed. Can you describe his clothing in this photograph for the court, please?'

Bernice, knowing exactly what I was doing, was still bound to answer truthfully or to face charges of perjury. 'He is wearing a rescue responder's uniform,' she said.

Clever, but I wasn't that easy. 'Is there anything unusual about his uniform in that photograph?'

'It is covered in blood.' She didn't look as pleased with herself as before. That gold star she was expecting might be in jeopardy.

'Mr Coltrane had just attempted, as is standard in such circumstances, to perform CPR on Brandon Starkey and that's why his uniform is quite so splattered,' I said. 'Now, Ms Danforth, do you believe that Henderson Coltrane, who is on the defense's witness list and will testify later in this trial, killed Brandon Starkey?'

Now Bernice's jaw was clenched. 'No,' she said.

'No further questions.'

THIRTY-EIGHT

'From what I hear, you were amazing,' Patrick said through my phone.

We were on a lunch break from the trial, and Angie, Stephanie and I were seated around a table outside Old Man Rafferty's, a popular lunch spot and bar a couple of blocks from the courthouse. (This is the place to point out that we did indeed invite Jessica to join us, but she had a business lunch with a prospective client and had to bow out.) We'd have to be back in ninety minutes and we'd told our server, a Rutgers student named Taylor, of our circumstances, which had seemed to make something of an impression on her. We'd gotten menus without having to wait.

'Amazing isn't the word I'd use,' I told him. 'I appreciate it; thank you. But all I did was make a legal point the jury probably won't take to heart.'

'Don't listen to her,' Angie said. I'd foolishly put Patrick on speaker and told him so (in case he was planning on making any embarrassing remarks). 'She was brilliant.'

'*You* can say that,' Patrick told her. 'I'm not allowed to use that word and I'm not allowed to ask her to, you know . . .'

'Marry you?' That was actually Stephanie, whose spirits weren't exactly buoyed but had rebounded a bit from when she thought I was throwing her to the wolves.

'We don't talk about that,' Patrick told her. Behind him, I could hear the sounds of construction as sets were being built, but I didn't hear any other actors. He must have walked away from the crowd to establish some small measure of privacy. 'It's a taboo subject.'

'I never said that,' I reminded him, and Angie's eyes widened. 'Just not now.' Angie's eyes became, let's say, less entranced.

'*Anyway,*' I went on, if for no reason other than to change the subject quickly, 'I'm more worried about Richard's next witness and about the pictures he showed the jury today than I am about our dear Ms Danforth.'

Stephanie, whose mood had changed from alarmed at the courthouse to downright relaxed here (was she using again?) waved a hand in a gesture that showed her lack of concern. 'You don't have to worry,' she said. 'I can always take the plea deal.'

Angie looked livid, but I had resolved to myself never to address that subject again so I completely ignored the comment. If Steph decided she was going to sell herself out, I could always resign the case, and I would. I had decided she was bluffing, but I couldn't figure out why.

'Who's his next witness?' Angie might have wanted to throttle Stephanie, and I would probably have cheered her on, but she knew how to read the room and had shifted gears. She can do that like a well-tuned Jaguar. I'm more like a 1978 Chevy Nova with a bad clutch.

'I believe he's going to bring on our old pal Lester Schultz.'

Angie made a gagging sound. 'The Woodbridge detective.'

'The same.'

'Surely the detective won't have any evidence other than what the jury has already seen.' Patrick's voice on speakerphone was something of a reminder that he was there.

'Cops have an air of authority for a jury,' I told him. 'Some jurors are afraid of the police and others think they never do anything that isn't perfect. Either way, it's not great for the defense.'

'How will you counter his testimony?' Patrick asked. Stephanie, staring without actually looking at anything, was barely paying attention. She had adopted this laissez-faire attitude toward her own trial and that worried me. Should I broach the subject of her addiction and whether it had reasserted itself?

'The same way I did with Bernice Danforth, probably,' I said. 'Emphasize the fact that he didn't see anything happen and neither did anyone else.'

'But he'll have evidence and stuff,' Angie argued. She interns with Nate Garrigan twice a week and thinks she's Lieutenant Columbo. 'Sand, how well do you trust this Mae Tennyson?'

Well, that was a stumper. 'I trust Mae fine. She's done a very good job with Steph's case. Why do you ask?'

'I think, as an investigator, there are still a lot of things we don't know. Maybe you should let someone else take a crack at it.' Angie is as subtle as a Mel Brooks movie.

'Ang, I am *not* hiring you to investigate anything. Forget it. Mae is doing a good job and she has associates helping her. The only reason we don't have more information is that the prosecutor isn't playing by the rules and nobody except the person who killed Brandon seems to know who killed Brandon.'

'That's two reasons,' Patrick contributed. I never said he was perfect.

'OKaaaaay . . .' Angie said.

'I'm not kidding. Do nothing about this. Patrick, tell her she can't be away from you that long for professional reasons.'

Patrick's line was suddenly very quiet, but I did still hear hammers and saws in the background.

'Don't tell me you just went into a tunnel,' I said.

When Patrick spoke again, he was playing the part of a stern boss. 'Angela, you must not do any investigating that Sandy doesn't ask you to do. As my management executive, you're dedicated to getting me through these rehearsals. Are we in agreement?'

Before she could answer, I looked behind Angie's back. 'Uncross your fingers,' I said.

'You heard her,' Patrick said. He might not be perfect but he is very good.

'Oh, OK!' Angie crossed her arms on her chest like a petulant eight-year-old.

'Better not to investigate,' Stephanie said.

We all stared at her for a moment. Not Patrick, but he would have if he had been there.

'Huh?' Angie said. She is as articulate as she is subtle.

'I mean, we had the plea offer. We know what happened. Let's just forget the investigation.' OK, Stephanie had to be high one way or another. 'I mean, Sandy just took that witness apart and there wasn't any *investigation* that did that.'

I gave Angie a look and she nodded. She was wondering the same thing as I was. 'Hey, Steph,' she said. 'I'm hitting the restroom. Want to join me?'

Stephanie looked at her with disbelief. 'Do people actually do that? Is this the 1960s?'

'Come on. We can talk.'

Stephanie seemed to think Angie was very far away and squinted at her. 'We are talking.'

'Go on, Stephanie,' Patrick said through the phone. 'Angie wants to talk to you privately.'

Without an eyeblink, Steph stood up and followed Angie to the door marked *LADIES*. I realized that I was now alone at the table and not, given that Patrick was in some way still there. 'What do you think?' I asked him.

'I think you're a brill . . . a wonderful lawyer, but you don't have a lot to hold your case together this time.' Patrick was prohibited from saying I was 'brilliant' when we first met, and he remembers. I don't really care if he says that anymore.

He was right. I was ad-libbing, doing the law equivalent of an improv show. The fact that I didn't know how I would approach Schultz as a witness was evidence enough of that. I felt as though I just had to keep working hard enough and something would come to me. But so far all I was doing was making myself tired.

'I know,' I said.

We just sat there not talking to each other for a minute, a long and comfortable silence that we didn't want to conclude by hanging up the phone. It lasted as long as it lasted and then I saw Angie leading Skinny back to the table. Angie caught my eye when Stephanie wasn't looking and shook her head slightly: No, Skinny wasn't using.

That was less disturbing than if she had been, but more puzzling.

They sat down again and Stephanie, her eyes a little more

focused, made a point of looking into my eyes. 'I'm clean, Sandy, and I have been for two years, two months and six days.'

'I'm glad to hear it.' I said that because I was glad to hear it.

'But I'm scared because I'm on trial for murder.'

I smiled at her. 'You'd be crazy if you weren't scared,' I said.

'No. You don't understand. The charges are one thing. I think you can get me acquitted OK, or something else will happen.' She didn't give me time to ask what that something else might be, because that was a stumper. 'But what really scares me is that you want me to testify.'

A lot of clients are more worried about testifying than they are about standing trial, which has always astonished me. Here's the chance to tell your story in your own way and they feel like it's a trap. 'I know it's scary that the prosecution is going to cross-examine you, but if you just tell the truth the way we've discussed, you should be fine,' I told her.

Again, it was clear that I'd made the wrong assumption, something that rates among my strongest talents. Stephanie shook her head. 'I'm not worried about him questioning me,' she said. 'I'm worried about *you*.'

Maybe I was misunderstanding. Or she was. 'I'm on your side,' I reminded her.

'I know, but you are used to prosecuting people and you have that way about you, where you're judging everybody all the time.'

I was about to protest loudly when I noticed Angie studying a spot on the ceiling just over my right shoulder. I changed my response to 'Do I judge people all the time?'

'Perhaps a bit,' Patrick chimed in. That warm moment of silence we'd had was over.

I sat there without an idea of what to say. I almost turned around to see what was so damned fascinating about the spot on the ceiling, but that would have been too obvious. No answer to what had been said occurred to me.

'I mean, I love you,' Stephanie said, which surprised me in itself. 'But you have a way. You just kind of seem to be observing everybody and amusing yourself. Like you're better than us and you think it's funny.'

'I'm . . . I'm . . .' This was not a good way to feel before having to go back to court. I took a breath and a sip of water. I don't drink alcohol during the day when I'm working a trial because I'm a responsible adult. 'I promise you, Stephanie, I'm not judging you and you have nothing to worry about from me when you're testifying.' OK, so I was judging her right at that moment, but it was because I was hurt by what she'd said and how everyone had reacted.

Taylor approached the table before anyone else said something. 'So are you guys ready to order?' she asked.

Patrick's voice came over the speakerphone. 'I'll have the club sandwich.'

THIRTY-NINE

'Detective Schultz, were there any fingerprints found on the knife after it was taken from the defendant's hand?' Richard just couldn't resist being a world-class jerk.

I stood, of course. 'Objection. The fact that Ms Silverstone was holding the knife was made abundantly clear from the photographs Mr Chapman so enjoyed showing the jury,' I said. 'Of course her fingerprints were going to be on it because she had it in her hand. Inferring that they were there because the prosecution alleges she killed Mr Starkey is misleading.'

'Overruled,' Grossman said. I probably would have done the same if I were a judge. Sometimes you object just to create a break in the opponent's rhythm.

'Yes,' Schultz said. This was not his first appearance as a witness.

'Whose fingerprints were found on the bloody knife?' Richard asked.

This time I didn't even stand up. 'Your Honor,' I said.

Grossman nodded and pointed at Richard with the business end of his gavel. 'Restrict your questions to the facts of the case, Mr Chapman. Don't editorialize.'

'Of course, Your Honor.' Of course, my butt. He was going

to editorialize all he wanted. 'Were there anyone else's finger-prints found on the knife handle?'

'No,' said Schultz. The man was a brilliant conversationalist.

'And was there any question the blood on the knife was that of Brandon Starkey?'

I was in an objectionable mood after having been brutalized at lunch (the conversation had not circled back to my alleged judgmental behavior), so I stood again. 'Is the witness an expert on DNA testing?' I asked Grossman.

'If the defense counsel prefers, I can submit the full medical examiner's report in which DNA testing *was* done, but Detective Schultz was also privy to that report and was the lead investigator on the case.' *Until you took it away from the Woodbridge PD!*

'The prosecutor should have already submitted that report,' I told the judge.

'I have,' Richard broke in. 'Now may the witness answer the question?'

I gave him my best innocent look. 'I'm not the judge, Mr Prosecutor.'

'If the two learned attorneys are finished sniping, I will rule that the witness may answer the question as the police officer who was investigating the crime,' the judge said. 'Detective Schultz?'

'According to the medical examiner, the blood on the knife was that of the victim, Brandon Starkey,' he said.

Richard was overcome by an attack of smug. With him, it's a chronic condition. 'Detective, you examined the crime scene. Was there any indication in the Elks kitchen that anyone else had been present at the time of the murder besides the victim and the defendant, Ms Silverstone?'

Schultz examined Richard's face. 'Any indication?' he asked.

'Any physical signs of a third person – something that would have pointed to a murderer other than Ms Silverstone?'

That was a no-brainer. 'Object to the prosecutor character-izing my client as a murderer.'

'I don't believe that's what he was doing, Ms Moss. Be more prudent with your objections.'

'Yes, Your Honor.' I sat down, properly admonished.

All eyes turned to Schultz, who was still looking at Richard with as low-IQ a face as I'd seen in a while. 'What physical signs?' he asked.

Richard did his best not to sigh impatiently and mostly succeeded. 'Were there any footprints in the blood on the floor other than those of the defendant?'

'Oh. It was hard to tell. There was a lot of smearing.' A couple of jurors bit their lower lips.

'No distinct footprints, then.'

Schultz glanced at Richard and remembered his witness training again. 'No.'

'No further questions.' Richard walked back to his table, giving the young assistant a confident smile. I'm sure she was thrilled.

I stood up and walked toward Schultz. 'Detective, you testified that there were no fingerprints other than those of my client on the handle of the knife. Is that correct?'

'Yes.' He was going to be even more terse with me. Prosecutors think defense attorneys are the enemy, and some believe them to be downright evil. I know. I used to be a prosecutor.

'Were there fingerprints anywhere else on the knife?' I asked.

That seemed to take Schultz aback. Sort of. He blinked three times, which was two more times than necessary, and ran his tongue over his upper lip, which was totally unnecessary. 'Anywhere else?' he asked.

It had seemed like a simple enough question. 'Yes. You mentioned the fingerprints taken off the handle of the knife. Were there fingerprints found on the blade or any other part of the knife?' I'd seen the instrument in question. The blade and the handle seemed to be the only two pieces of it, but I'm no chef and maybe it's broken down into more sections than I could see.

'I'd have to consult the ME's report,' Schultz said. He clearly didn't want to answer the question and was looking for an excuse, as if I were his third-grade teacher and he had a sniffle.

'I'm sure the court will be happy to supply a copy to your screen,' I said. 'Is that so, Your Honor?'

Grossman gestured toward the tablet mounted in front of Schultz. 'Can we have that report brought up, please?' he said.

Within seconds, the image of the medical examiner's report on Brandon's autopsy was visible on his screen but not the one the jurors could see. Schultz looked at it as if it might bite him and made a show of 'reading' it, in that he looked at it and his eyes went back and forth. He spent at least a full minute doing that without even trying to swipe it across to get to the next page.

'Detective?' I said. The jury wasn't getting any younger.

Then I noticed that Schultz was spending less time looking at his iPad and more watching Richard, who, to the naked eye, was sitting impassively at his table. But I knew the man, dammit, and he wasn't at all pleased with the way things were going.

I'd read the autopsy report, so I was wondering what in it was causing this level of consternation. I hadn't seen any mention of fingerprints on the blade; I'd been more interested in establishing that no examination of the blade had been done for anything other than identifying the blood as Brandon's. This development was puzzling.

Then Richard almost imperceptibly nodded in Schultz's direction.

'Yes,' he said, sounding relieved and stressed at the same time, which isn't easy to do.

'There *were* fingerprints on the blade of the knife?' I said, both to clarify that was what he meant and to remind the jury of what question was asked back in the previous decade before the detective had started stalling. I also wondered why this information wasn't on the copy of the ME's report that had been sent to my office through Richard's.

'Yes.'

OK, so he was going to make me ask. 'Whose fingerprints were those?'

Schultz looked as though he'd rather be pretty much anywhere else on earth at that moment. A snake pit, a maximum-security prison, Kelly Ripa's house. Anywhere. 'Some were from an unidentified person,' he said.

'Just some? Were there others?'

'Yes.' He *really* didn't want to say.

'Whose fingerprints?'

'They were Mr Chapman's,' Schultz mumbled.

Partly because I was stunned, I made him repeat what he'd said. It gave me a moment to think.

'The county prosecutor?' I pointed at Richard. '*This* Mr Chapman?'

'Yes.'

FORTY

'Wow,' Patrick said.

'I know.'

We were spending a rare quiet evening alone in his apartment in the Village. Angie had accepted the invitation of a Dairy Queen friend to get together and reminisce about the good old days that Angie didn't miss at all and her friend was still inhabiting. So Patrick and I had dined on elegant French takeout (this was New York) and now were sharing a bottle of red wine on the sofa in the living room. There are worse things than being treated well by a New York theater company.

'Why didn't you immediately move to have your ex removed from the case and perhaps slapped in irons?' Patrick has a really interesting impression of the American legal system, and he's not all that far off.

I leaned back and let the sofa swallow me up a little. Relaxation is something you don't appreciate until you've spent a few months on a shuttle between coasts and then tried a homicide case with your family watching your every move. Whoever had designed this sofa should have been awarded a Nobel prize.

'Because I hadn't known his prints were there. It's *not* in the ME's report. So Schultz was speaking strictly from his own knowledge. I questioned him a little about how he knew that and he said it had been included in the incident report. Richard was cringing the whole time and didn't even bother to object. It was late in the day and we weren't going to sort it out in time, so Judge Grossman sent us all home so he could look for a precedent on this situation. And I'll be impressed if he can find one. Jessica's hard at work for me looking through legal records that date back to *Washington v. Cherry Tree.*'

Patrick regarded me a moment. 'That's an American thing, isn't it?' he said.

'Yes, and one you needn't bother yourself with.'

Patrick took a fairly large sip of wine and put the glass back on the table next to his side of the sofa. 'You're tired,' he said. He patted his lap. 'Put your feet up.' I didn't need a second invitation.

'You're tired, too,' I told him, because surely he didn't know he was tired until I pointed it out. 'How are rehearsals going?'

'I think well.' He patted my feet. 'It's been such a long time since I did a play, and then I think I had seven lines. I wasn't exactly a box office draw in those days.'

'What about the role?' He'd told me about some trepidation he'd had going into such an unorthodox comedy. 'Do you feel like you've cracked it yet?'

Patrick winced a little. 'Not quite. But I think I'm starting to get there. Playing a woman without playing a woman is, I should say, a challenge.'

My phone buzzed with a text, which I should have anticipated would be from Richard. *We need to meet.* A man of few, but annoying, words.

I chose not to answer but the phone was persistent in not letting me enjoy Patrick's lap or the couch. When I checked, I moaned because I couldn't ignore a call from Mae Tennyson. 'What's up, Mae?' I was getting right to the point so I could indulge myself with my boyfriend and his rented sofa more.

'I think I found Lucia D'Alessandro.' Mae was getting right to the point because she was Mae.

I sat up, pivoting my feet off Patrick's lap. He looked less surprised than disappointed. 'What do you mean you *think* you found her?' I asked Mae.

'Well, I tracked her to Millville, as you know. The Ohio thing turned out to be wrong, just the county investigator wanting to visit relatives in Cincinnati. She was renting an apartment in Millville as recently as two months ago, but she hadn't been seen there for a few weeks when my operative talked to the property manager.'

'That doesn't sound like you found her,' I pointed out.

'Hang on, I'm getting there. The property manager was pissed because suddenly Lucia wasn't paying her rent. They went in to check and, sure enough, the place was just as she'd left it. One bed, one table, one chair. No clothing, no cosmetics, no sign of a human woman, or a human anybody.'

'No cosmetics?' The very thought was terrifying.

'Get over it. So that led to the landlord, the corporation that owns the place, sending a collection agency after our pal Lucia,' Mae continued. 'They worked harder than the county, apparently, and picked up a trail that led to Colorado, of all places.'

Well, west was definitely a direction to go in from New Jersey. Especially if you didn't have a working passport. 'So did you find her there?' My patience to return to resting on Patrick again was wearing thin.

'Yes. She was listed as deceased.'

Maybe that had been what Richard had wanted to meet with me about. Maybe it was to explain why his fingerprints were on the murder weapon. Maybe it was to explain why he retrieved the spare kitchen key, or to tell me why he had been withholding evidence, all things that could see him fired, disbarred and possibly jailed. Or maybe it was to try to sell me on that bogus plea deal again.

'She died in Colorado. From what?' I asked.

Mae sounded a little hesitant. I got the feeling it wasn't because she was unsure of her information, but more because she didn't care for how she anticipated I'd react. 'I said she was *listed* as deceased. The fact is, they don't have her body.'

I leaned forward and Patrick, seeing the expression on my face, poured me another glass of wine. 'Then how do we know she's dead? How do we know she didn't just move on to Oregon, or whatever is next to Colorado?' (Utah, New Mexico or Arizona, going west. But I was a little agitated at the time.)

'Because she was declared dead by the county coroner in El Paso County,' Mae answered. 'The official cause is listed as heart failure.'

OK, so that was vague. I'm not a cardiologist but it seems

to me that anybody who dies has heart failure. 'Are we in contact with that coroner?' I asked.

'Funny, it's an elected position and he resigned a week later. Went back to his job as a salesman at a Cadillac dealership.'

This case was getting weirder by the moment. 'You got his phone number?' I said.

'I'm way ahead of you.'

'Yeah, I'm getting used to that. So when you called him, what did he say?' I looked at Patrick, who couldn't decide if he was concerned or amused. I could see his point but it still annoyed me a little. This was a strange turn in an already difficult case.

'He referred me to the Denver office of the FBI. And believe it or not, the special agent there didn't feel like talking to me.'

The FBI? When did the feds get involved in this lunacy? 'The death certificate is a matter of public record. Is there any indication that the FBI might be interested in that document?' I asked.

'It's standard. The least possible amount of information is offered. But I can fly out there tomorrow if you think it'll help.' Mae was a good investigator and her team had done fine work, but now I was seeing that this was a case where good investigators doing fine work would probably run into walls.

I needed Angie. She wasn't at all a good investigator – not yet – and she wouldn't do fine work. But she could be as blunt and irritating as anyone I knew when she was on the scent of something. In this case, those might actually be useful attributes.

'No,' I told Mae. 'I don't think anybody has to go to Colorado just yet. But do me a favor and call Jess. Tell her I need a precedent on calling the prosecutor as a witness and I won't have time to do it myself.'

Mae was scribbling on an actual paper; I could hear it through the phone. 'Got it. What are you going to be doing?'

'I've got two stops to make and I don't want to go to either place,' I said.

Mae took a moment. 'Sounds promising,' she said.

FORTY-ONE

Anthony D'Alessandro was a very polite man in his late fifties, almost completely bald and a little on the heavy side, but not obese. He had accepted the fact that I'd need to come to his house in Linden (Lyft was making a fortune from what I was billing Stephanie) and ask him about his daughter, who had been declared dead in Colorado only a few weeks earlier.

'Luch' – he pronounced it 'Looch' – 'was really crazy about that Brandon kid,' he said, after apologizing that he'd have gotten cake if he'd known I would be visiting. 'I guess when he got killed, she just lost the will to live herself.'

'But she'd broken up with him before that happened,' I noted. 'Everything I've heard is that she told Brandon she was leaving him weeks before Stephanie's wedding was scheduled to take place.'

Anthony tilted his head to one side a little and shrugged. 'She doesn't tell me everything; I'm her father,' he said. I felt it was best not to correct the tense of the verbs he was using. 'I knew they stopped seeing each other after he got robbed at the gas station.'

'The night someone stole the receipts and hit him with the gun,' I said. Because maybe Anthony didn't know what 'robbed at the gas station' meant. I can be as insensitive as the next person.

He nodded. 'I don't know if she thought he should have done something else, or if she was just scared that he was working at that place.' He stopped and considered, as if deciding whether he should go on.

'If you know something, you should say so,' I said. 'I'm trying to keep an innocent woman out of jail.' Probably innocent. At least, I was fairly sure she hadn't stabbed a man to death.

Anthony moved his lips around like he was chewing

something, probably his next sentence. 'You know that gas
station is owned by the mob,' he said.

I'd heard that from Mae, but you've heard all the stories and
seen *The Sopranos*. You think all of New Jersey is owned by
the mob. And I'm here to tell you that in all my years living
in the Garden State, I never knew anyone personally who was
connected to organized crime. Everyone claims to *know* someone
who is connected, but when they're pressed on the subject, they
tend to downplay the whole idea and say maybe they just heard
a rumor. Even when I was a county prosecutor, I never
dealt with a mob case, largely because they're handled almost
exclusively by federal agencies.

Like the FBI.

'The gas station where Brandon worked?' I said. That was
just to give myself time to think. Of course I knew which gas
station he meant.

Anthony nodded and his voice fell to just above a whisper.
Maybe he thought Don Corleone was bugging his house. 'From
what I hear, the Russian mob.' OK, so Don Coreloneoff.

This was only just starting to come together in my head. 'Did
they think Brandon was in on the robbery? That he stole from
them?'

'I don't know,' Lucia's dad said. 'But Luce was scared for
sure, and she said she didn't want to be part of whatever this
was, so she broke it off. But that only lasted maybe a week.
She kept sneaking over to Brandon's place to see him and she
thought I didn't know.'

Anthony, it struck me, was exhibiting much less emotion
than I'd have expected from a man who had lost his daughter
so recently. I didn't know how to broach that subject but thought
it might have some relevance, so I said, 'I'm so sorry for your
loss, Anthony.'

I watched his eyes for signs of misting but there was none.
'Thank you,' he said. That was it.

Something was definitely up here. 'Do you know why your
daughter was in Colorado?' I asked.

'I think she just wanted to get as far away as she could,' he
answered. 'She was probably on her way to Los Angeles; she
always wanted to go there. But she didn't call me after she left.

No note, nothing. I was used to her not coming out of her room, especially since Brandon died. Eventually, I had to look in there and she was just gone. She didn't take clothes, she didn't take shoes, nothing. Just gone.' Still no sign of emotion, but some people are just like that. It's how they cope, and he had a lot to cope with.

'You got a call from the FBI out there?' I asked. The jurisdiction on Lucia's death was unusual, to understate it. I thought maybe Anthony could clarify it, even if he didn't know that's what he was doing.

'No,' he said. 'I got a knock on the door from a guy from the US Marshals.'

The US Marshals Service! That made even less sense than the FBI. What would they have to do with Lucia showing up dead somewhere south of Denver? Unless she was herself a fugitive from justice, but I'd found no outstanding warrants on her or Brandon. Anthony was giving me even more to think about, which was the last thing I needed.

'Why were the marshals involved?' I certainly didn't know, so maybe they'd explained it to him.

'I don't know. Isn't that something they do?'

No. It isn't.

'Do you remember the name of the person who came to your door?' Any contact would be helpful, especially since the FBI didn't seem eager to talk to anyone. They rarely are.

'He gave me a business card,' Anthony said, and he walked to a small side table near the front door. He opened a drawer and pulled the card right out; it must have been recently added to whatever Anthony stored in there. He brought it back and handed it to me. 'This was the guy.'

The card read: *William Radisson, United States Marshal for the District of New Jersey.*

That told me a few things, and all of them were disturbing. Radisson's title wasn't Assistant US Marshal. He was *the* US Marshal in New Jersey, appointed by the president and overseeing the rest of the state. And he was coming to Anthony D'Alessandro's house to inform him of the death of his daughter from what every law enforcement agency involved was calling natural causes. Something was definitely wrong.

And on top of all that, I couldn't shake the feeling that William Radisson was my old pal Bill, the enforcer who had come to Patrick's apartment to convince me Stephanie should take Richard's ridiculous plea offer.

I thanked Anthony, once again noted my sympathy for the loss of his daughter and walked outside. But I didn't even make it to my car before I had texted Richard:

Where do you want to meet? Make it public.

The least glamorous place in the world to hold a clandestine meeting after ten p.m. is at a White Castle, but I refused to go there so Richard and I met at a Dunkin' Donuts in Edison near JFK University Medical Center. The only other people in the place were a man and a woman in the uniform of a local ambulance service having a lively discussion about what constituted a date. And by the way, the last thing you want to see parked in front of a Dunkin' Donuts at night is an ambulance.

I was sipping a decaf iced coffee with a shot of coconut because I'm a wild woman while Richard, still in his business suit and having come in from ninety-degree heat, was nursing a hot coffee because he's actually crazy.

'You've been weird about this case from the beginning,' I told him, largely due to my desire to get this all done as quickly as possible and then let Lyft take me back to Patrick. 'At first, I thought it was strictly because you wanted to get back at me, but now I'm thinking there's more to it than that.'

'Yeah, that was just a perk.' Richard thinks he has a mordant wit. He's just mordant.

'I'm not going to chronicle all the stuff you've done, but now your prints are on the murder weapon and I have video of you at the crime scene picking up evidence and putting it in your pocket. I've always thought you were a little nuts, Richard, but I've never even considered the idea that you're stupid as well.' What the hell. He couldn't fire me anymore and I had dumped *him*, so there was little he could do other than trump up charges and put me in jail. I had so little to lose. 'You want to tell me what's going on and why you sent your pal Bill from the US Marshals to where I'm staying in New York?'

That last part was a serious reach, but Richard didn't try to deny it. 'I've been trying over and over to convince you that the plea deal is the way to go,' he said. 'I thought maybe someone who wasn't me would find a more sympathetic ear.'

'"Your client will live longer if you take the plea deal." *That's* what you think is going to find a sympathetic ear?' I was starting to put some pieces together, but I wasn't sure what the puzzle was supposed to look like yet and that's always something of a problem. Pushing Richard's buttons – something I had grown to consider a strong skill set – was my best bet at getting to the truth.

'Obviously, I miscalculated. I shouldn't have sent William.'

'You're damn right.' I didn't use the word I was really thinking. Two words, really.

'I should have sent someone more persuasive.'

There's just no dealing with some people. 'You're a prosecutor, and up until recently, I would have grudgingly said you're a good one,' I told him. 'Tell me straight: Why would any self-respecting defense attorney agree to the plea deal you're offering? I'm so much better off taking my chances at trial and that means my client is likely to do much better even if she's convicted. So answer that question from a defense lawyer's point of view. Why should I think it's a good idea? Dazzle me.'

I sat back and folded my arms across my chest. And that's not because it was cold in the Dunkin' Donuts.

'I've already told you why,' Richard began.

I held up a hand, palm out like a traffic cop. 'No. Don't give me the same spiel. I want the actual truth this time. You know me well enough as an attorney. You knew I was going to tell Stephanie to reject that offer. Why did you even send it to me?'

Richard shook his head in disbelief that he and I had ever been a thing and took a sip of what was now probably a lukewarm coffee at best. I'd given thought to getting a chocolate frosted doughnut, too, but rejected it as a sign of weakness.

'I've already told you there are things going on in this case that I can't discuss,' he said, dropping his voice for fear that the two EMTs deciding whether they were dating or just on a break could hear him. 'When the county prosecutor can't discuss something, it's because that thing shouldn't be discussed. And you're not going to get any more out of me than that.'

Exactly at that moment, my phone buzzed and Angie was on the other end of the line. I didn't care if the amorous ambulance personnel heard me, but I sure wasn't going to let my opposition in a trial catch my end of any conversation, whether it involved the case or not. I excused myself and walked into the restroom, fully aware that this was what Stephanie had done at the Elks Lodge.

'Can it wait, Ang?' I asked. 'I'm sort of in the middle of something.'

'Kiss Patrick for me.' Angie has a mischievous side. It's the one she faces the world with.

'I'm in a Dunkin' Donuts in Edison,' I admonished her.

'Kinky. But this won't wait. I was talking to my friend Katy from Dairy Queen.'

Now? Really? Gossip from the world of soft serve? 'I get that, Angie, but right now—'

'Listen!' Angie doesn't yell much, so when she does, I pay attention. 'Katy had some pull with a few of the credit card companies because she was in charge of dealing with them for the store, OK? So we did a little looking into Lucia D'Alessandro's MasterCard. And we found something interesting.'

Lucia D'Alessandro was dead. Who cared whether she went to K&M for a sweater? 'Angie, Lucia is dead. She was pronounced dead in Colorado three weeks ago.'

'That's going to come as a surprise to MasterCard. She charged a hotel room in Boise, Idaho, day before yesterday.'

OK, that's not unusual. 'Somebody got hold of her card or her card number after she was pronounced dead and used it while they still had a chance,' I told Angie. 'It's a pretty awful thing to do, but it happens a lot. I'm surprised the card wasn't canceled after just a day or two, though.'

'That's because the person using it was the Loochmeister herself,' Angie said. She was giddy with what she felt was a vindication of her investigative skills. 'There's security video of her checking in and I had Stephanie verify it.'

I just sat there a moment. If Lucia was alive, then the FBI, the US Marshals Service and the Middlesex County prosecutor were all mistaken about something that seemed very easy to not be mistaken about.

Or there was another possibility.

'You're a genius, Ang,' I said.

'About time you noticed.'

'I noticed it a long time ago. I just didn't want you to get a swelled head.' Someone tried the doorknob on the restroom. 'Listen, I've got to go but let's meet back at the apartment later.'

Angie sounded interested. 'Something up?'

'No big deal. I think I've got this whole thing figured out.'

I hung up the phone and let the woman from the ambulance into the restroom as I left. I used some sanitizer on my hands because you never know and walked directly to the table where Richard was sitting, looking at his phone.

As I sat down, he blacked out his screen and set the phone, face down, on the table. His coffee, which must have been frigid by now, was maybe one-quarter gone. My iced coffee was mostly ice, which was melting into the bottom of the cup. Maybe I should have used the bathroom while I was in there. Opportunity missed, and all that.

'OK,' I said. 'You're lying to me, and I think I know why.'

FORTY-TWO

Richard had the nerve to look at me blankly and say, 'I don't know what you mean.'

I would have hurled the iced coffee into his face, but there was so little liquid left that it wouldn't have had the desired effect, and besides I could take little sips as it melted. I just looked back at him, trying to emulate the zombified expression he was giving me. I said nothing.

I knew that at some point he wouldn't be able to take the (relative) silence anymore. There was another person at the counter buying doughnut holes (they call them 'Munchkins' and I'll leave it at that) but that only caused a little murmur in the background and made me wonder why the hell someone needed doughnut holes at this time of night. There is no rhyme or reason to the occasional craving for fried dough.

Finally, Richard, as I had expected, couldn't stand that I wasn't answering him. 'Seriously, Sandy,' he said. 'What have I lied to you about?' I considered asking the college student behind the counter if they had any butter so I could test whether it would melt in his mouth, but they probably only had margarine.

'Pretty much everything, the way I figure it,' I told him. 'So how about we start over and you tell me exactly why you're prosecuting a woman you know for a fact couldn't possibly have murdered Brandon Starkey.'

'I've tried to offer—'

'A halfhearted plea deal you knew any competent attorney would turn down flat,' I finished for him. 'So let's just dismiss that as the hollow ploy it was and move on. You *know* Stephanie didn't kill anyone. And yet you brought it all the way to court. Why? Is this about trying to make a run for the state legislature next year?'

'I have no political ambitions.' Richard made it sound as if I'd insulted him, when really he was pissed off because I knew better. 'Anyway, this case isn't about that.'

It was late and I was tired and now I really was regretting not using that restroom. But another interruption would give Richard the chance to run out on me and that was the last thing I needed. I let him hear me take in and let out a deep breath of frustration and irritation. 'Then what *is* it about? And keep in mind that telling the truth will allow us both to leave sooner.'

The words seemed to come from Richard's throat and not his mouth. He was trying so hard not to be heard that I almost couldn't hear him. 'Sometimes things aren't about what they are. They're about what they *look like*. Do you get that, Sandy?'

Yet he didn't want me to think it was about politics. And for some reason I wouldn't have been able to explain even then, I believed him. So my brain started seeing part of the jigsaw puzzle for the first time.

The FBI.

The US Marshals Service.

The Russian mob.

The bloody dress.

The fingerprints on the knife.

The spare key to the Elks Lodge.

The county prosecutor handling the case himself.

How did I not see this before? I sat back on the molded plastic chair, which did my spine absolutely no good at all. 'Richard,' I said.

Still with the deer-in-the-headlights look. 'What?'

'You've got to make the plea deal better. You've got to keep Stephanie out of jail.'

He sat back too, but as if he'd been pushed. 'You know I can't do that. Someone has to pay for Brandon Starkey.'

I shook my head slowly. The puzzle was looking clearer and more complete. 'No. You have to give me a deal she can sign that keeps her completely out of prison or I'm going to do the one thing you absolutely can't afford for me to do.'

Now Richard looked legitimately worried because he knew I had figured him out. 'You can't, Sandy.'

'I'm in this for my client, Richard. Not for any crazy deal you've made with the feds. If you don't put it in writing that Stephanie Silverstone won't go to prison, I'm going to the press with the news that Brandon Starkey is still alive.'

FORTY-THREE

Whenever a guilty person is cornered with the knowledge that you are on to their deception, they always say the same thing. They say you have no proof. And sure enough, that was how Richard started his defense (ironically) when I told him I knew about Brandon Starkey.

I'll spare you the whole conversation. I had him dead to rights and I knew it. He knew it too but had to pretend there was nothing to my assertions. But the band of sweat around his hairline and the slowly draining color from his face just reinforced my certainty. And then, of course, he pulled out the 'no proof' ploy and he was dead in the water.

'There's no other explanation that fits the facts,' I told him. I'd been reading a lot of Sherlock Holmes on this trip because a bound volume of Conan Doyle was part of the collection in Patrick's rented apartment, and aside from the glaring racism and sexism in spots, it had helped me understand the process of observation. 'You made a mistake by letting me know the US Marshals Service was involved. You know full well that they're the agency that oversees the Witness Protection program, and that is the one and only reason they'd be lying about the supposed death of Lucia—'

'No names,' Richard hissed. 'This is a public place because *you* insisted on a public place.'

'Still going to deny it?' I asked, giving him my most innocent look. Which is about sixty percent innocent, if I'm being honest.

'Sandy,' he pleaded (again, legal irony there). 'People's lives are at stake.'

'Yeah, and one of them is my client. So you're going to figure out a way to make her jail time disappear and then in six months you're going to expunge her record entirely, because I took some phone numbers when the media was all over Stephanie after her arrest, and I kept them in my phone.' I picked my phone off the table for emphasis.

'You need to understand the situation,' Richard said.

I pointed at him. 'First time you've been right tonight. I definitely do.'

'It's a matter of great importance and nothing can appear to be the least bit out of the ordinary,' he said, choosing his words carefully so no critical information could be divulged to the kid behind the counter (the two EMTs had left, holding hands). 'It's been a cooperative effort between my office, the FBI and the US Marshals Service.'

'That would be *among* your office, the bureau and the marshals,' I said. 'The word *between* assumes only two parties.'

He kept looking around as if waiting for the gathered crowd of no one to charge our table. 'Can we take this outside?' he asked. 'Maybe talk in my car?'

I could feel my forehead wrinkle, something I prefer not to picture whenever possible. 'If you think there's any chance I would ever get into your car, Richard, you are even more delusional than I already think you are.'

'All right, your car,' he said. 'You have a rental?'

'I took a Lyft. If you're desperate to discuss this matter in the parking lot of a Dunkin' Donuts, I'm happy to oblige, but I'm not allowing myself into any enclosed space with you if I don't have at least two bodyguards, or Angie, which would be the same thing.'

We dickered back and forth on that for enough time that the Dunkin' attendant was looking at us with a you've-been-using-that-table-long-enough expression and agreed to walk across the street to a convenience store that had a bench in front of it. (First, I used the bathroom.) We did not discuss the matter on the way there because Richard must have thought there were spies in the crosswalks. I'd seen him in a lot of moods, but paranoid was a new experience.

'You don't know anything,' he said in a 'confidential' tone once we had parked ourselves on the bench. There was no one within earshot but there were people coming and going from the convenience store every few minutes. Not one of them seemed even remotely interested in us or what we might be saying.

'Fine,' I said. 'Here's what I *think* and how I came to that conclusion. Brandon must have seen or heard something involving a branch of the Russian mob when he was robbed in the gas station however many months ago.'

'Five months.' Richard couldn't resist mansplaining.

I decided, as ever, that the best course of action was to ignore him and keep going. 'He was approached, I assume by some FBI agents, about testifying in maybe a RICO matter, an organized crime case. I have no idea if he resisted the feds or not, but at some point, he was convinced the best way to get out of Dodge alive was to cooperate. How am I doing so far?'

'You're completely wrong,' he lied.

'Good. Once Brandon—'

'For the sake of safety, can we call him Bobby?' Richard asked.

I regarded him for a moment. *'Bobby?'*

'What do you prefer?'

'Fine, *Bobby*. So *Bobby* started telling what he knew and it was a doozy. The feds liked it but they had a problem. Somebody in the organization must have known he was spilling the beans and was going to come and, um, correct the situation. Yes?'

He sniffed. 'Again, I have no idea what you're talking about.'

'You want me to go on?'

Richard winced a little but said, 'Yes.'

'So you and your friends in the government decided the best thing to do was make sure all of Bobby's old bosses thought he was dead. And a nice public death, preferably a violent one, would be best because then they could think that someone was trying to help them out. So you set up this fake stabbing at the rehearsal party. Did' – hell, if he could change people's names so could I – '*Patricia* know ahead of time that you were setting her up to be the patsy in your little melodrama?'

'No one is being framed here, Sandy.'

I had to laugh even though it wasn't funny. The blatant display of nerve was enough to knock down a charging rhinoceros. 'Oh, someone is being framed here. My client is being framed here. As evidence, I offer the fact that she's currently on trial for homicide despite the fact that nobody's dead, and you are offering her a deal that might, if all the pieces fall the wrong way, only keep her in jail for twenty years. How is that *not* being framed, Richard?'

His head kept swiveling to see what mob informant was coming in for a Diet Mountain Dew at eleven p.m. There was no one within earshot. 'Can you *please* keep your voice down!' he pretty much shouted. Then, perhaps realizing that even Alanis Morissette would have at last found something genuinely ironic in what he'd just done, he dropped his voice down to a hiss. 'If you'd just gone along with the deal, like your *client*, who has known the whole time that you should, we could have knocked down the sentence to maybe six months or something after she was in jail. So don't you see, that's exactly what you should do now.'

'If you're so sure this plan is foolproof, why didn't you make her confess right away? Why wait for me to throw a monkey wrench into the works?'

'She couldn't look like she *wanted* to go to jail.' So now she'd end up being convicted of murder and having her record expunged? Great deal for Skinny.

I promise you with full sincerity that what I said next was not in any way predicated on the completely justifiable urge I had to see Richard suffer and possibly be disbarred. 'I'm not going to do that,' I told him.

His eyes looked like the headlights on the green Nissan Sentra going by and stopping at the red light in front of us. 'Are you out of your mind?' he seethed. (If you've never heard someone you know seethe, it's not lovely and I don't recommend it.) 'I'm telling you she'll be out of prison by spring.'

'And I'm telling *you* that you can do that without Steph doing any time. My client has a history of drug addiction and you know that. She's deathly afraid of spending time behind bars. I'm here to protect her rights, her sanity and maybe her life, and besides, we're going back into that courtroom tomorrow just in time for you to explain to Grossman why you withheld evidence and how your fingerprints got on to a bloody knife. I'm willing to bet the judge isn't in on your little miniseries here, right?'

Richard sat back on the bench, which was when he found out there was no back to the thing. He had the agility not to fall backward on to the concrete but not to avoid banging his head on the thick glass window of the convenience store. His stunned expression was almost worth being outside on a minor highway at night with a man I had once dated and now really couldn't stand.

Almost.

Without acknowledging his slapstick escapade, I added, 'By the way, how *did* your fingerprints get on the knife, and what were you doing picking up the spare key next to the dumpster? That's pretty hands-on for a prosecutor.'

He just kept shaking his head. This was not how the evening had played out in his head before he'd texted me that we needed to meet.

'You know, I was in love with you back then,' he said finally.

'You're so full of crap you could become the northeast distributor of manure,' I said. 'Answer the question, Mr Prosecutor. The knife? The key?'

Richard seemed to gather himself. He sat up again from the reclining position he'd had against the store window. He adjusted his jacket to remove any wrinkles. He took a larger-than-usual breath and let it out. I knew this attitude. He was deciding. If the decision was that he was going to go back to court and let me twist in the wind, this would be when I'd find out.

'The knife was just sloppy,' he said with regret in his voice. 'With all the blood we'd put on the handle and all the prints I'd gotten your cousin to provide, I just didn't wipe off the blade well enough because I thought it would look like it had been wiped off and the report would show that. I figured the prints on the handle would be enough.'

I'm no math whiz but I can add two and two together. 'So you were the person who came in through the back door. That's why you knew where the key was. Why'd you bring it to a police station, of all places?'

'There were things that needed to be done that I couldn't be seen doing. Like setting the scene for when the "body" would be found. The key was going to be another piece of evidence. We were going to allege that your cousin had an accomplice and that she'd provided a key.' He actually sounded sad now. 'But her performance coming out of the kitchen was so convincing that we ended up not needing the key. Everyone saw her with the blood and the knife.'

'Why her? Why'd you have to use Stephanie as the patsy who was going to get all the press and have her life ruined forever? Was it because you were mad at me?' I asked.

Richard blew some air out of the corner of his mouth in a sarcastic laugh. 'Oh, get over yourself, Sandy. Not everything's about you.'

'You just told me a minute ago you used to love me,' I pointed out.

'And it didn't work, did it?' Oh yes, now I remembered why I despised Richard. 'Your cousin was the best choice because it was going to be her wedding dinner, a well-attended event, and she was willing once Bobby and his girlfriend explained it to her. I had to do a *little* persuading, but not much.'

'So it's clear now that you'll offer a deal that exonerates Stephanie and keeps her out of jail and you can just say the county detectives are still looking for the killer, right?'

He was silent.

'*Right?*'

Richard stood up. Again with the wrinkle thing on his suit,

like he was about to face inspection. 'I don't think so, Sandy. The plan is working. It'll have to go to a conclusion.'

I was about to leap up when we both realized that the green Sentra hadn't gone ahead when the light had turned green. Instead, it had pulled into the parking lot and a man had got out of the driver's seat.

A man who was deliberately concealing his right hand, which looked to be holding something heavy, in his pocket.

'Uh-oh,' Richard said.

FORTY-FOUR

The man walked toward us casually, as if he were just going into the convenience store for an ill-advised pack of Marlboros and we were in the way. Except that Richard and I had moved away from the door and the guy from the car was walking toward us and not the entrance.

'Get behind me,' Richard said.

I considered him, at five foot nine and thin as a rail, and snorted. 'Why?' I said.

My ex-boyfriend and ex-boss (they're both the same person) turned to look at me with an expression of exasperation. '*Why?*'

This wasn't the time for a discussion. I reached into *my* pocket for the can of mace I carry with me whenever I might be anywhere near, you know, men. But like our assumed assailant, I kept my hand in my pocket. If he turned out to be a Jehovah's Witness out on night patrol, I didn't want to feel foolish. Any more foolish than I already felt, anyway.

The guy, who I decided was named Lester (I'd been right about Bill, keep in mind), stopped a few feet away from us as Richard and I stood side by side about fifteen feet from the bench where we'd been sitting. I put my left hand on my phone for the expressed purpose of dialing 911 if it became necessary.

Lester looked me in the eye, then Richard, and then looked

me in the eye again. 'You Sandy Moss?' he said, and what really chilled my blood was his accent, which was Russian.

(I feel it's only fair to note here that I have no general quarrel with the Russian people, but that in this case, the involvement of a Russian mob of organized criminals, scary enough to put two people into the Witness Security program, was enough to get me more than a little agitated.)

Richard, macho idiot that he is, felt the need to step in. 'Who's asking?'

Lester (because I don't know the Russian equivalent) curled his lip in Richard's direction. 'I not talk to you,' he said.

'Well, you'd better damn well—'

I decided, against my better instincts, to save Richard from himself before Lester shot him through his jacket pocket. It was eighty-six degrees at eleven at night. He needed a jacket? I took a step to my left, away from Richard, and said, 'I'm Sandra Moss. What can I do for you?'

'You know where kid is?' Lester's grasp of English was quite good, but he hadn't reached the advanced class of ESL yet.

If he was asking about Brandon, he knew Brandon was still alive and that was bad. Richard's eyes betrayed his panic. Despite being an excellent courtroom attorney, he has absolutely no poker face. I won the payment on my moving van from him in an office poker game.

On the other hand, if Lester was asking about Lucia, that might be worse. That would mean they knew *she* was alive and were hoping to track her to Brandon. Any way you looked at it, that was not the question I wanted to hear.

'Kid? What kid?' What the hell. It was worth a try.

Lester was luckily not looking at Richard's face, which practically screamed, 'I KNOW WHERE THE KID IS!' at the top of its lungs. He was regarding me and finding me, if I was reading him right, not formidable. I felt it was necessary to change his opinion.

He directed his sneer at me. 'Come on. You know. Kid is missing.'

That opened up all sorts of new and unpleasant possibilities. 'You're going to have to be more specific,' I said. 'If it's the person I think you mean, I can't say where he is.' *Your Honor, the witness is being unresponsive.* So many courtroom objections sound like a young child telling on their sibling.

Lester took what I can only describe as a terrifying step toward me. 'Don't play stupid. You know what I mean.'

The fact, if we're being totally accurate, is that I *didn't* know what he meant specifically, but I had no intention of answering no matter what that turned out to be. 'No, I don't,' I said. 'Tell me the name of the person you're looking for, and if I know them, maybe I can help you.'

Lester's voice lowered to a hiss delivered through clenched and jagged teeth. 'Tell me and maybe I won't kill you,' he said.

What a lot of people might not understand is that while I was petrified by what he said, I was mostly pissed off. You don't threaten a Jersey girl and expect her to cower and collapse into the role of compliant servant. That ain't gonna happen.

'Tell me who you mean and I might not kick you in a place you really don't want to be kicked,' I told him. 'Or you can just get the hell out of my way and go back to the sewer you crawled out of.'

Lester started to pull the hand out of his pocket, and I was planning where to dive in a strip-mall parking lot. There was broken glass on the pavement and something that fell into the 'mud' category elsewhere. I'd have to dive straight ahead into Lester or straight back into the wall, neither a terrific option.

But there was no time for any of that. Richard decided again to be my hero in shining armor, something I'd never once asked him to be, and stepped in front of me. 'Back off,' he attempted to say.

Lester, however, had other ideas. The hand he pulled out of his jacket pocket did not hold a firearm but was decorated with some actual brass knuckles, the like of which I hadn't seen since my prosecution days. He was going to try to hit me, but Richard's ridiculous attempt at heroics changed Lester's trajectory and he caught Richard in the right side of the head. It caused a wound, but not a bad one. Richard, no doubt astonished, dropped to the concrete, probably with a concussion from the brass knuckles or hitting his head on the pavement.

It might have occurred to you by now that I am not a nice person all of the time. If it hasn't, consider my choice in the next second. I saw an opportunity, noted that Lester was not brandishing a weapon that would be lethal from a distance, turned and ran, leaving on the concrete a man I had once known intimately and who, despite his obvious faults, was not totally an evil person. I hoped the police would come soon and send an ambulance for him, but I couldn't guarantee it.

On the plus side, I managed not to get my face caved in by a set of brass knuckles. So there was that.

There's a state of mind one discovers when running for (in this case) her life. You're not aware of anything except what's in front of you, what you are running toward and whether or not you can still breathe. That's about it. So I really didn't have an accurate bead on Lester for at least ten seconds after I took off like Usain Bolt if he'd broken both his legs. I did have my hand on my phone, and as soon as my arms started pumping, it came out of my pocket and toward my face. The only thing I could think of doing was pushing the button that made it call Patrick.

'Sandy!' He sounded like it was a pleasant surprise that I was calling well after eleven on a night he knew that I was going to confront my ex-boss and courtroom adversary. Patrick assumes everything is just fine until he finds out otherwise definitively. He assumes this because it has been true in his life for so long that he forgets it's not that way for everybody.

'Call the police!' My voice was coming out in gulps. Lester was behind me, and he was Usain Bolt with at least one working leg. He was closing on me. I was heading directly for the sidewalk, where, even at this hour, I'd been seen by passing cars looking like a woman being pursued by a mad killer.

Patrick took a second. 'What?' he asked.

'Call the cops! Tell them I'm on . . .' (Gulp, gulp.) 'Route 27 in Edison and I need help right now! There's a man chasing me with brass knuckles!'

'What? Knuckles?' Patrick was having a hard time keeping up and so was I, because Lester was closer. If I could get back to the Dunkin' Donuts, which was open all night, I might be able to find refuge. I headed for the crosswalk because even when being hotly pursued, I wasn't crazy enough to try to cross a highway in New Jersey without the green light in my favor.

'Patrick!' I wasn't going to win this race and needed professional assistance as soon as possible. 'Call the police! Now! Call nine-one-one!'

'Why can't you call them?' It wasn't, I'd like to be clear, that my boyfriend didn't *want* to get the cops to save my life. It was more that he was genuinely curious as to why I hadn't thought to do that myself.

'I don't have them on speed dial!' I shouted and disconnected the call. Lester was behind me enough that I could bolt out on to the highway if the light would turn green.

But it didn't. And I couldn't. And he caught up with me.

From this distance (which admittedly wasn't very far because as you might have surmised I don't run too well), I could see Richard sitting up on the pavement outside the convenience store. So he was alive, and I was glad about that, but not a lot. I couldn't see what he was doing.

What I *could* see was Lester's face, grim as ever, standing only a few feet from me. But he didn't raise his metal-enhanced hand to deal me a debilitating blow. He just looked at me.

'Where is kid?' he insisted again.

I bent over to catch my breath and try to clear my head. Breath took precedence over brain, and I just gulped back air, which is what you're not supposed to do. You can take that up with my lungs when you meet them.

At this point, I was less terrified of Lester and more flat-out annoyed with him. 'Look,' I said when I could push air back out through my throat. 'I don't know what kid you're talking about. You don't have to believe me if you don't want to, but that's the fact. So unless you can check with Duolingo to tell me what you really mean, I can't help you. And the truth of the matter is, I probably can't help you even if I *do* know who you're talking about, because I have no knowledge of anyone you might be associated with. But first you tell me how you found me here. Were you following me or him?' I pointed vaguely in the direction of Richard, who appeared to still be sitting down in front of the convenience store bench and not doing anything useful. Which was his overall practice in life.

'KID!' Lester appeared to be – no, *was* – crying. What? He reached into his jacket pocket again and I braced myself, but this time he pulled out an iPhone, fiddled with it for a few moments and then turned the screen toward me.

It bore a photograph of a small boy, perhaps eight years old. He was smiling an angelic smile and, if one were to look at it carefully, bore at least a passing resemblance to Lester. I stared at it.

'Kid,' Lester said. 'Please.'

'Lester,' I said, 'I'm sorry but I've never seen that boy before in my life.'

My assailant looked confused. 'Who is Lester?'

I shook my head. 'Don't worry about that. Is this your son?'

'*Da.*' I knew what he meant, and he understood that I did. 'Where is boy?'

I shrugged. 'Honestly. I have no idea at all. What happened to him?'

His face froze. It was clear to me that he was fighting tears and doing so just barely successfully. 'Took him,' he said. He struggled around his mouth again, his lips moving, then tightening to hold in the pain. 'They. Took him.'

'Mobsters?' I asked, but he looked at me blankly. 'Criminals?' Quietly. '*Da.*'

'Why?'

'Because . . . because they can't kill me.'

In the distance, I heard police sirens; my darling Patrick had done as I'd asked. That buzzing of my phone in my pocket was probably him trying desperately to find out if I was all right. But now the cops would be here in seconds. Even Richard, who had been standing in front of the convenience store, was gone. I looked at Lester.

'You like doughnuts?' I asked.

FORTY-FIVE

This time I ordered the chocolate frosted. What the hell. Lester, whose name turned out to be Alexei (meaning I was one-for-two in guessing names this time out), sat slouched over the table, no doubt concerned that there were windows everywhere. The police cruisers that had parked in the lot across the street still had their lights flashing, but the cops who had gotten out were walking aimlessly in front of the stores, no doubt trying to find the crazy lady who had made the TV actor call them frantically.

I had texted Patrick to let him know I was OK after noting that he'd tried calling four times and texted seven. If he'd had a car 'brought round,' he'd probably have been driving up and down Lincoln Parkway in Edison shouting my name, but now he knew I was out of danger and had promised to stay put until I could get back.

Richard had not shown up back at 'our' Dunkin' Donuts, but I did notice that his car was no longer in the parking lot, so the whole façade of chivalry he was trying to project had hit the ground about the same time as he had. Predictable, but in this case, I was better off without his protection. Actually, in pretty much every case.

'So there are gangsters holding your son somewhere to keep you quiet?' I said to him. Alexei was drinking an iced tea but had not ordered a pastry. He didn't look as though he wanted the tea, either.

He nodded. 'They know I don't talk to cops while they have him.' Slowly, he shook his head. 'Is killing me.'

I had to be careful how I asked my questions. Alexei wouldn't give away the secrets that were holding him and his son hostage. 'Why do you know things they're so worried about?' After all, if I was now having a casual dessert with an assassin, it would be valuable to know.

He raised his head a bit, forgetting he was trying not to be seen. 'I don't tell you,' he said.

'I don't need to know what you're hiding, but I do need to know how you got it,' I answered. 'Don't tell me anything that will get you in more trouble.'

Alexei's English really wasn't bad at all. He was better at understanding what I said than at responding, which is not unusual in someone learning a second (or, as I was soon to discover, fourth) language. 'I'm in all the trouble,' he said. 'Can't get in no more.'

'How long has your son been gone?' Maybe I could get him into a more open frame of mind that way.

'Six days. They took him . . . at . . . before your trial.'

So there was a connection! I was barely able to see the instruction manual for putting this do-it-yourself bookshelf together. 'What does the trial have to do with you?' I asked. As if I didn't know the Russian mob was involved. I'm so cagey.

'Boy who died, from the wedding,' he said.

'Brandon Starkey.'

'*Da*. They was gonna kill him and then he died. They are . . . what's the word?'

I didn't want to say it, but it was going to speed the process along. 'Suspicious?'

Alexei nodded. 'They think too easy, he's dead. But I tell them no, he's dead.'

'How do you know these people?' I asked.

'From back in Bulgaria. I was a kid with them. They come here, I come here. They get in mob but I don't. I'm just too scared for me and my family.'

I put up my hands, palms out. 'I completely understand that. But I don't get how you knowing them got your son kidnapped. Were you going to testify at the trial?'

'*Nyet*. No. I'm scared to go to cops, but was going to go to you. I almost talk to you that day at restaurant but too many people.'

Restaurant? 'At Catherine Lombardi? You were there?'

Alexei nodded. 'Too many people.' My mother, my sister, Angie and Patrick. Too many people. He had no idea. 'But before trial, I decide I talk to you. Couldn't find office.'

Of course he couldn't. 'I don't really have an office here,' I told him. 'See, I live in Los—' Why was I telling him this?

'Don't matter,' Alexei said. 'I'm stupid.' I was about to contradict him, but he went on immediately. 'I tell friend I'm gonna talk to you. He tells boss and they take my son.'

'Some friend,' I said.

'*Da*.'

Before I could respond, two Edison police officers, in uniform, walked in and, for once, they were not here for coffee and doughnuts. They surveyed the room and, since we were the only two people present who didn't work there, focused on Alexei and me. Alexei looked like he wanted to crawl under the table and, believe me, no sane person would want to be there. I felt like it was my fault he was at risk, even though he had been trying to hit me with a pair of brass knuckles maybe a half hour before.

'Something we can do for you, officers?' I asked. Best to keep Alexei silent as much as possible, I thought.

There was a Caucasian cop and an Asian cop. The Asian one spoke first. 'We had a report of an incident between a man and a woman,' she said. 'The woman told a friend she was being chased by a man who wanted to kill her. Do you know anything about that?'

I did my best to look surprised, but as Patrick will tell you, I'm no actor. 'No,' I said. 'I didn't see anything like that, but we just got here a few moments ago.' Some of that was true.

Then the other cop took up the questioning, staring at Alexei. 'We also got a call from the county prosecutor saying a man had assaulted him across the street.' He pointed toward the convenience store.

I shrugged. 'Like I said, we just got here.'

The first cop made a point of looking at Alexei. 'Sir?' he said.

Alexei sucked in his lips like he was trying to find an American accent and coming up short. 'Yes?' Not bad. He hadn't said *da*.

'Were you across the street before you came here?' Maybe Richard had provided a description of the man who'd hit him.

'No,' Alexei said. 'I drove here.' Luckily, we'd moved his car from the strip-mall parking lot to the one outside Dunkin' Donuts. The first solidly right decision I'd made today.

The two cops looked at each other for an extended moment. Then they both seemed to give up the pursuit; their shoulders fell a bit and the taller one tugged on the brim of his cap. 'Thank you both,' he said, and they left, nodding at the counter clerk, who was buried in his phone and didn't notice. Cops in a doughnut shop. Might as well be one of the fixtures.

'Alexei,' I said after they had crossed the street and driven off in their cruiser, lights no longer flashing. 'You want to give me a ride home? Maybe we can figure something out.'

FORTY-SIX

'Your Honor, the prosecution and the defense have reached a plea agreement in this case.'

Stephanie, as ever to my right, looked unusually calm, but in a moment Judge Grossman would ask her to rise (they never ask you to stand up, just to rise, giving one the impression that the court has some power of levitation that was left out of the state criminal code) and she'd be asked if she agreed to this plea of her own accord. I was only hoping she would not state for the record that she'd asked her attorney – that's me – to sign off on the damn thing at least three times before.

This moment had taken a great deal of explanation and some serious negotiations (for example, Richard had been coerced into not filing assault charges against Alexei) in order to accomplish a great deal, from my point of view and that of my family, many of whom were in attendance today.

Patrick was luckily on an off day from rehearsal (the only one he'd have for three weeks) so he too was there. Angie, as to be expected, was sitting beside him wearing her proudest grin. She loves it when I win, even if I do so by having my client plead guilty.

Alexei hadn't known about the whole plot, but when confronted with him and (on the phone) Anthony D'Alessandro, who actually *did* know his daughter hadn't died in Colorado, Richard had filled in the rest. We'd met in the least likely place for such a summit: Patrick's rental. Angie had needed to put on pajamas for the meeting. Angie sleeps without such encumbrances but did not want to distract the assemblage. She's nothing if not generous.

Stephanie had been called but it was well after midnight and she wanted to sleep before court in the morning. Then I told her (from Alexei's car) that I knew Brandon was alive, and she actually beat us to Patrick's apartment. You don't have to worry about traffic at that time of night.

'The bottom line was that our Mr Starkey had seen things that could get him killed, including the gas station holdup, which was possibly the worst-advised robbery in history,' Richard began. 'The thief's name was . . . not important.'

'Odd name,' Patrick said from his chair in one corner, softly enough that I could hear him but Richard could not.

'He didn't realize he was stumbling into a front business, a money launderer, for a group of Bulgarian mob bosses,' Richard continued. 'But by the time the thief discovered he had about seventeen times as much cash as he should have, he'd already been tortured and pummeled to death. And Brandon Starkey saw it all happen. All he'd done was take a job for the night shift at a gas station and now he was witness to a crime that could put a lot of scary people in jail for a very long time. They made it clear they were not going to let him testify, but he managed to get word to a friend who had an uncle who was a cop, and that cop called my office.' With Richard, it always had to be about how his office was the competent law enforcement agency and nobody else knew what they were doing. It's a way to get through life. I suppose.

'So Brandon wanted to testify,' I said. I wanted it to be Brandon's decision. Now that I knew he wasn't dead, I didn't have to think badly of him for my client to come out ahead. But more on that in a moment.

'*Wanted* is a complicated word.' Richard needed to make it about his brilliant tactics of persuasion again. 'He knew that he stood a better chance of staying alive if he talked to me.'

'I want to stay alive, too,' Alexei said. 'My son, to stay alive.'

'In a minute,' Richard told him. Alexei rolled his eyes and pointed his palms toward the ceiling in a gesture of exasperation, which I thought was pretty effective, truth be told. Richard, either unfeeling or unseeing (choose your lack of sense), looked at me. 'I realized almost immediately that the only avenue out for this guy was Witness Protection, so I called a friend at the FBI.'

'The Marshals Service runs Witness Protection,' I pointed out. I knew he knew that. I just wanted to annoy him.

'But my FBI friend knew a guy,' Richard said with a testy tone. 'He set things up and I suggested that we make it look like

Brandon was dead so his former employers would be off his trail.'

'Also my former employers,' Alexei noted. Alexei was not going to be forgotten in this morass.

Richard, of course, ignored him. 'Somebody at one of the meetings suggested that we make it a murder, so it would get press attention. We just needed to create a scenario where Brandon was killed in public.'

'This is the part I never understood,' Patrick said. 'I was at that party. I saw people going into the kitchen and coming out. One of your witnesses' – he was smart enough not to mention Delia's name – 'said she saw Stephanie and this Brandon shagging on a table in the kitchen. What was going on?'

'Shagging?' Stephanie asked.

Patrick looked embarrassed. 'Being . . . intimate.'

'Oh, no. I was rubbing the front of my dress up against his suit after we spilled the blood all over it, so it'd look like I stabbed him. We were never . . . *shagging*.' Skinny looked mortified.

'So you never dated Brandon?' Patrick asked.

'Nah. It was supposed to be motive or something, right?' She looked at Richard, who didn't even have the integrity to look embarrassed, or to answer her.

'Why was everybody in the kitchen if they didn't know about the whole plan?' Angie wanted to know.

'We were supposed to be celebrating,' Stephanie said. 'I called them all in there so they'd know Brandon and I were both in the room, and we shared a toast.' She looked at Richard. 'That's what I was supposed to do, wasn't it?'

Richard nodded. 'You were perfect,' he said. A perfect patsy. (No reference to Patrick's late wife intended.)

'How did you get the blood to match in the ME's report?' I asked Richard. 'They said it was definitely his.'

Richard puffed himself up, so excited to show off how clever he was. 'We had him donate a pint of blood the week before,' he said. 'Then we confiscated it. The whole thing was very well planned.'

'Uh-huh,' I said, indicating that it was maybe not too well planned. 'You left the back door open, and Michael wandered in and then out once he got offended that everybody was drinking champagne except him.' I looked at Skinny. 'Champagne?'

'It was supposed to be before a wedding,' she said. 'Sarah and Stephen were there. I had to pretend I couldn't wait to be married. They didn't know what was going to happen.'

'Did Michael?' Angie asked.

Skinny puffed out her lips and blew out some air. 'Michael,' she said. 'I was gonna break it off with Michael until *he* showed up and said the rehearsal party was all about saving Brandon's life, and Lucia's.' She gestured toward Richard. 'Michael. He was seeing three other girls while we were engaged, can you believe it?'

Patrick stifled a smile and Angie saw him do it. Loyal. That's what they kept telling me about Michael. He was loyal.

'You see,' Richard said, annoyed that the spotlight had shifted off him, 'we needed a venue that could be public without being *very* public. Witnesses but not an arena full of people.'

'So you chose my cousin's wedding?' I said.

'She volunteered,' Richard protested. 'The invitations' – except mine – 'were already out and Brandon was going. We engineered a fake breakup with his girlfriend to keep the focus on him and not Lucia.'

'Volunteered,' Stephanie said. She didn't sound as if she agreed.

'Stephanie?' I said.

My cousin and my ex-boyfriend exchanged a look that was not convivial. 'Tell her,' Skinny said.

So Richard complied, but he avoided eye contact with me or Stephanie. He stared mostly at Patrick, because he knew Angie could be . . . a little impulsive when angry.

'Once we decided the wedding was the proper venue because it would be public enough to have our suspect be as visible as possible,' Richard began, 'Stephanie here became the most logical choice.'

I looked at Skinny. 'Why did you go along with this?' But she just kept looking at Richard, forcing him to answer the questions she didn't want to address.

'We were vetting possible suspects and noticed Stephanie's history,' Richard said. His tone was the same as the time I'd seen him lecture the police academy – detached and arrogant. Old dog, new tricks and all that. 'And once we did, we found an outstanding warrant for trafficking in a controlled substance.'

That took a moment to sink in for everybody but Angie. 'Skinny, you were *dealing*?' she demanded.

Stephanie suddenly found her shoes to be remarkably interesting, and they were just a pair of Skechers. 'A little,' she said quietly. 'It was years ago, before I got clean.'

I turned and faced Richard, forcing him to look me in the face. 'So you blackmailed her to get her to confess to a fake murder.'

'The trafficking charges have been expunged,' he said, as if that excused everything.

'So it's just the murder charges that remain on her record,' I countered. I looked at Skinny. 'If I'd have known when he offered you this demented gig, I would have told you not to do it.'

'That's why I didn't ask,' she mumbled.

'So you could make Steph do time for something that neither she or anybody else did?' That was Angie.

Richard, despite being the most irritating person in the room, looked annoyed. 'The plan was never to have her serve a whole sentence,' he said. 'She would have been paroled at the earliest possible date, after a second plea agreement was signed once she was in jail. That wouldn't have been easily spotted by the people after Starkey and D'Alessandro.' In short, the Bulgarian mob.

'You said at the beginning that I'd never spend a night in jail,' Skinny said, a new anger in her voice. 'Then you arrested me and sent me to jail for at least two nights.' She looked at me. 'That's why I wanted you to be my lawyer.' Of course. Because Richard, being Richard, had immediately double-crossed my cousin.

'It was only a couple of nights,' he said. I've rarely heard a worse defense. 'You were going to be driven off to prison and end up in a safe house for six months.'

Skinny's mouth dropped open. Clearly, she'd never heard that part before, either.

'But you never told *me*, and I was never going to sign off

on that plea deal,' I reminded him. 'I'm still not putting my name on something that'll muddy my reputation like that. It's a matter of public record. My next client will be able to see it. So what are you going to do to fix that, Richard?'

Patrick smiled proudly at me out of Richard's gaze. Angie actually laughed.

Richard looked considerably less amused. 'You make my life difficult, Moss,' he said. He hadn't called me by my last name since the first year I worked in his office. He knew I didn't care for it. 'OK. What can you live with that won't send up a red flag to the judge, who could easily impose his own sentence, and won't alert our Eastern European friends that maybe they're not as safe as they think?'

'How about you drop the charges and say the county is still looking for the real killer?' I suggested. 'It keeps Brandon dead in everyone's eyes and gets Stephanie off the hook. I can live with that.'

'I can't,' he said. Flat. Matter-of-fact. Completely expected. 'I have a reputation, too. To say that I took a woman to trial for murder, who was seen covered in the victim's blood and holding the murder weapon, and I've suddenly decided she's not guilty? I'd be out of office by Tuesday.'

I pictured that first night at the Woodbridge police station when Stephanie had suddenly realized what she'd agreed to and what it would mean for her, and her begging me to keep her out of jail because she hadn't done anything wrong and was terrified. 'My client can't go to jail,' I told Richard. 'You reneged on that original deal until I got involved. Now you can work that out however you want, but that's the bottom line. She didn't commit any crime and she's not going to be locked up. You have one hour to present me with a workable proposal or we'll go to court and I will spill your guts.' I would have stood up and left the room, but it was Patrick's living room and that would have just been silly.

'All right!' Richard knew me and he knew my tone. There would be no further negotiation. 'Here's the deal: Your client has a documented history of drug abuse and rehab treatments. So you plead guilty due to mental illness, we agree to send her back to rehab. She spends ninety days there. By the time she gets out, a lot of arrests will have been made and nobody will be looking for her anymore. Her record will be quietly expunged a month after she gets out when nobody's looking anymore. Brandon testifies on Zoom from a secure location not far from his girlfriend Lucia and everybody's happy. How's that?'

I looked over at Patrick, who was staring in awe at me, and then at Angie, who was thinking and then nodded in my direction. 'I think I can sell that to my client,' I told Richard. 'But I want it in writing at least two hours before the court reconvenes tomorrow.'

Richard tapped the face of his wristwatch. 'Today,' he said. 'I'll draft it and get it to you as soon as possible.' He stood up. 'We could have avoided so much of this.' He shook his head. 'See you in the morning.'

Alexei stood up, brass knuckles back on his right hand. 'No tomorrow,' he said. 'What about Alexei? I tell you what I know and they have my son.'

Richard snorted a bit. 'No, they don't,' he said. 'Your son was picked up by New Jersey state troopers an hour ago at an apartment complex in South Orange, based on what you told us. He's perfectly fine.'

Alexei's face changed. His eyes got damp and he pulled in his cheeks, his head shaking a bit. 'Thank you,' he said. He took Richard's hand and kissed it, which looked funny with the brass knuckles. 'Thank you.'

'My client wants some form of protection,' I told Richard, pointing at Alexei. 'He's put himself and his child on the line to do what's right.'

Richard considered it and then blew his lips out like he was about to play the trumpet. 'Alexei,' he said. 'I'd like you to meet a friend of mine at the US Marshals Service.'

They were barely out the door before Patrick gave me the first hug.

FORTY-SEVEN

'This is the plea?' Judge Grossman said. 'Not guilty due to insanity?'

'That's the terminology, but we're referring to mental illness and drug addiction,' Richard told him. 'We believe the defendant is a danger to herself or others and in very serious need of treatment rather than incarceration, as she clearly doesn't even remember committing the crime. We see no benefit to a prison sentence.'

Grossman looked at me, standing by the defense table. 'Ms Moss?' he said.

'The defense concurs with the prosecution on the plea and the sentence,' I said. I wasn't going to publicly declare my cousin insane when I knew she wasn't. Stephanie wasn't even using drugs anymore, as a number of tests had proven. But she didn't mind at all going back to rehab and then having a clean record, with the conviction expunged. That would be handled quietly as well, and the judge needn't be informed of the elaborate machinations necessary to come to this fairly ridiculous conclusion.

My Aunt Fern, however, was not the least bit pleased with me for causing the family such shame. Her face looked like all of Grant Wood's *American Gothic*. She had briefly conversed with her daughter and then not spoken to me at all.

Mom, on the other hand, had suggested rather delicately (for her) that she thought it odd I had 'steered' Stephanie toward this outcome, but acknowledged that it was 'certainly better than spending the rest of her life in jail,' because most laypeople don't know the difference between jail and prison. I'll explain it to you some other time.

'I would think you would,' Grossman told me. He looked back down at his tablet screen again. 'Three months in rehab.'

I held my breath. Was the judge going to throw all our hard work out the window? Was he that convinced Skinny had knifed

Brandon Starkey again and again? Would I have to make Brandon materialize, perhaps on FaceTime in the judge's chambers, just to convince Grossman this was a good thing? I became aware of my breathing, and it wasn't light and carefree.

But after shaking his head for a few seconds, the judge took off his readers and looked Richard in the eye. 'If that's what the prosecution thinks is best,' he said.

'I do.' Richard was either rehearsing wedding vows to be exchanged with someone he hadn't met yet or trying as hard as possible to sound like a man who had been beaten in negotiations with a superior attorney. I like to think it was the latter.

'Very well, then.' Grossman banged his gavel on the bench. 'So be it ordered. The defendant will be escorted to the state rehabilitation facility immediately. Bailiff, please inform the jury' – who had been waiting in the room they would have used for deliberation – 'that they are dismissed, and offer the court's sincere appreciation for their time and their hard work.' The jury had sat there and listened, which can indeed be hard work, but they weren't exactly mining salt. Which was weird because I'd always thought salt came from the ocean.

The bailiff agreed, Grossman declared the business of the court completed and we all got up and left the courtroom.

Stephanie, actually looking grateful, hugged me and whispered into my ear, 'I might not come back after rehab. Thank you for what you did. I'm sorry I couldn't tell you.'

'I understand,' I told her, 'but the next time you're asked to pretend to murder someone and take the rap for it, call me first, OK, Skinny?'

'You bet.' She didn't even glance at Michael, who was at this point leaning against the door frame at the back of the courtroom, waiting for the moment he could leave without looking like the lowlife he was and always would be. Steph had 'broken up with him' that morning (after he'd done the same at the time of her arrest but had stuck around to offer what he considered to be 'support') and nobody except their caterer seemed at all upset about it.

Stephanie led the two guards assigned to her out of the room, ready to begin what she thought of as her new life. Sometimes you just can't figure people or events. Steph actually turned and waved when she hit the door. 'Don't call me Skinny,' she said and left.

Patrick put an arm around me as I walked, and I leaned into him a little bit because he had, after all we'd been through together, become a major source of stability and support for me. And that seemed unexpectedly weird.

We passed Jessica Berliner, who had been stunned by the turn of events I couldn't explain to her but somehow understood, and Mae Tennyson. I thanked both of them, and we shook hands very professionally. Jess smiled at me and said, 'Someday you'll explain?' I shrugged. Mae slipped a piece of paper into my hand as I walked by. When someone does that, you don't read it right away in front of everyone, so I stuck it into my pocket.

Luckily, I had a pocket.

Richard walked over to me with a confident, purposeful gait that I knew was a lie – but then, what about Richard wasn't a lie? 'You did as well as anyone could do, Sandy,' he said, eyeing Patrick and coming up short in everyone's mind but his own. That was his form of congratulations for beating him to a bloody pulp, if not in court. (I like to think I would have won the jury as well, but there's no way I'll ever know.)

'Richard, have you met Patrick McNabb?' Patrick did not remove his left hand from my waist while extending his right to Richard, who took it as if it were something that might go off.

(Of course, Richard had met Patrick the night before at Patrick's rental, but we were pretending that hadn't happened.)

'Nice to meet you, Pat,' Richard said, using the name Patrick least likes to be addressed by because, well, he's Richard and can't help it even when he doesn't know he's being Richard. 'That's a special girl you've got there.' For those wondering, he meant me.

'She's an extraordinary woman,' Patrick said, agreeing and upping the stakes, 'and I don't have her so much as she lets me stay around.'

They let each other's hands go. Richard nodded in my direction and was about to leave when I held up a hand. 'Just one last question, Mr Prosecutor,' I said.

'Yes, Counselor?'

'Did you choose Stephanie to be the patsy here just because she was my cousin and you wanted your revenge?' I did not break eye contact; I wanted to see his expression as he answered.

'She volunteered,' he said.

'Answer the question.'

Richard's face almost clenched because he wanted his annoyance to come across as the mock variety when it was not. 'I chose your cousin because she was available and she was willing,' he said.

'Wow,' I said. 'That sounds really familiar.'

As he slunk away, I swear I heard Richard say, 'I should have sent her to prison.' It wasn't clear which one of us he meant.

Patrick smiled at me because he almost always does. 'I'm very grateful to that man,' he said. 'If there were no Richard, you and I never would have met.'

We turned and walked toward my mother and Aunt Fern at the back of the room, talking to Angie. Aunt Fern sniffed and walked out of the room. So it was going to be like that.

'Aunt Fern feels you could have gotten Stephanie acquitted without exposing her addiction problem and taking her away for three months,' Mom said.

I had the presence of mind not to point out that Skinny *hadn't* been acquitted and gave her a sour look. 'Aunt Fern—' I began.

Mom cut me off. 'Your Aunt Fern has always had a stick up her ass,' she said. 'I think you did a wonderful job.'

I stood there and gaped at her. 'That's the nicest thing you've ever said to me,' I said.

'Oh, it is not.' Go argue with her.

We walked out into the hallway to head for the exit and then the parking lot. But I didn't expect to find my sister Delia standing right outside the courtroom door, looking – and this was a first in my experience – a little downtrodden.

Mom, naturally, rushed to her side. 'What are you doing here?' she asked. 'I thought you had to work.'

'I didn't have anything scheduled for today,' Delia said, but her gaze was never directed at our mother. She was looking straight at me. 'I'm taking this week off. I'm leaving Mark.'

I took a step back instinctively, waiting for the shrapnel of my mother exploding to dissipate.

'It's about time,' my mother said. 'But you'll need a good family law attorney.' They both looked at me.

'I'll give you some phone numbers,' I said.

They both started to laugh.

On the way to my car, I pulled Mae's note out of my pocket.

It read, 'Brandon Starkey's alive, isn't he?'

I never answered. I figured Mae knew why.

FORTY-EIGHT

The opening-night crowd was on its feet, applauding in a way I can't describe other than rapturously. The cast was spread out across the stage, arms around each other's shoulders, taking bow after bow.

Finally, Josie Bartlet, the leading lady, let go of Patrick's shoulder and pretty much shoved him to the skirt of the stage on his own. Patrick looked back at her, embarrassed, so naturally that I almost forgot having seen them do this in rehearsal.

If anything, the applause got louder, and Patrick took four more bows before the curtain finally dropped. Angie and I headed immediately toward the backstage entrance, and I had only a minute to sift through my feelings at this moment.

The Scottish Play was going to be a hit. Patrick had managed huge laughs even on the corniest of jokes, as when a real Scottish terrier walked out on the stage and Patrick was given the line, 'Out, out, damned Spot,' at which point the dog hightailed it (literally) to the wings. But the rest of the material was better and the cast had performed it beautifully.

Especially Patrick.

I'll be honest. Of course, I was thrilled for Patrick. This was exactly what he'd wanted and he'd conquered it completely. From here, he could have a distinguished stage career to go along with his successful television career and his . . . well, maybe he'd start getting offered better movie scripts.

But a huge hit show on Broadway meant he'd be in New York for an extended period of time, maybe as long as a year. And I'd be in Los Angeles, probably living in the house we'd bought together, wondering why I had left New Jersey after Stephanie's trial.

I'd been away now for a month and flown in only the night before. I'd gotten used to Patrick not being nearby and that was more upsetting than the fact that he wasn't there. Now I was walking backstage to find him in his moment of glory, and I didn't know how to react in a way that was happy for Patrick without being a real stick-in-the-mud about myself.

But even though I'd had months to rehearse for this amateur performance, I had not prepared myself adequately. I had no clue what I was going to say.

Angie, in the meantime, was positively gleeful, no doubt certain that Patrick's success was largely due to her efficiency in handling his business. Maybe she was right, but he'd managed to deliver a terrific comic performance and that was all Patrick.

It was cramped backstage, which is not at all unusual in any theater, but especially the Broadway houses that present straight plays (non-musicals) and were generally built more than a hundred years ago, when presumably people fit into tight spaces more easily. Cast members, family, friends, producers (there are dozens) and stage personnel were all milling around, giddy with a post-performance high and hugging each other a lot.

But the pandemonium all faded into the margins for me when I saw Patrick. He was smiling his actor smile, the one that is meant for those who don't know him well. He hugged a couple of his castmates and, glass in hand, toasted the director, a lovely round woman named Claudia whom I'd met twice before, briefly. Then Patrick turned and I caught his eye.

Then the real smile came on to his face and we made a beeline for each other. Patrick captured me in a bear hug and held on.

'You were wonderful,' I said with the amount of breath he was allowing me.

'I loved it,' he said. 'And I never want to do it again.'

I'd been back in LA for three months, almost the entire length of Patrick's New York run, and had been back East only twice during that time. I was counting the hours – not the days – until he would return. So I wasn't ready for Holly Wentworth when she came to my office.

Things had been pretty normal professionally since Skinny's trial. She was almost ready to get out of rehab, her record would be expunged in days, and she had, as promised, decided not to return to her old life. She texted me that she was moving to Oregon because her college roommate was there and said the people were very polite. We in Jersey don't necessarily see that as a plus, but it was what Stephanie needed.

Patrick's reviews had been ecstatic, and those for the play were remarkably good. A Broadway run had indeed been arranged, but Patrick had informed the production that his contract on *Torn* required him back in California, which was true. But because the reception to the play had been so positive and the move to Broadway was so prestigious, the company had not been stuck too long for a new not-so-Lady Macbeth. They were currently negotiating with Matt Damon.

Holly strode into my office with that same look on her face, which was odd. There had been no mention of the thing she would only tell me if she could murder me afterward since I'd returned, and my work had been entirely focused on Southern California, which I felt should have made the firm happy. So the tense stare from Holly's eyes was disconcerting.

'Everything OK?' I asked.

She took a deep breath and let it out. Then Holly broke into a very broad smile.

'I have been authorized,' she said, 'to offer you the opportunity of becoming a partner in this firm.'

And she didn't even kill me afterward.

AUTHOR'S NOTES

I t was just time to bring Sandy back to New Jersey for a bit, and to introduce the Nation of Jersey to Patrick. He surprised me by mostly being amused. He's known Angie long enough, I guess.

I mention the same people for every book and they all absolutely deserve it. Thank you to Rachel Slatter and everyone at Severn House for continuing to believe in Sandy and her entourage. Next time I'm asking for a travel budget so I can get the Los Angeles street names right (that's another reason this book is set in New Jersey). You've been nothing but gracious and supportive and everything an author could ask for, so thank you.

Of course thank you to Josh Getzler, agent *extraordinaire*, who keeps me from having to confront the demons that surround me when I'm not writing. Josh is an agent but also a friend and if I ever have to vent about stuff in my life or, more seriously, about baseball, I know who I can call.

To readers and booksellers (even that one), you keep the stories coming. You're the reason they happen. To librarians, who are among my favorite people (especially one in Cape May County, NJ), don't despair of the people who would ban books for not agreeing with their personal issues. You're the front line in the war for all expression, and you do amazing work. If there's anything an author can do to help, please don't hesitate.

These are scary times, but then all times are scary times. We don't know what's coming, and we're barely dealing with what has just passed. If you can read a book and chuckle a time or two, maybe it's worth it all.

If you didn't chuckle at all, do me a favor and don't email. I am blissful in my ignorance.

To the incomparable Jessica, Josh and Eve, you are my reasons.

E.J. Copperman
Deepest New Jersey
May, 2023

Milton Keynes UK
Ingram Content Group UK Ltd.
UKHW011959040724
445002UK00006B/366